BURNOUT

A CHARLIE COBB THRILLER

ROB ASPINALL

Copyright © 2017 by Rob Aspinall

All rights reserved.

No part of this book may be reproduced in any form or by any electronic or mechanical means, including information storage and retrieval systems, without written permission from the author, except for the use of brief quotations in a book review.

MEET CHARLIE COBB

He's known to the criminal underworld as Breaker. The legendary fixer the mob sends in to sort out the scumbags who've stepped out of line.

When he knocks on your door, you'd better be ready to pay up, shape up or get up and run. Only now he's burned his mob bridges. And made some powerful enemies in the process.

Traveling from place to place, he walks the straight and narrow. Yet while the line between good and bad may be narrow, the path to redemption is anything but straight. Because Charlie doesn't have to go looking for trouble. Trouble comes looking for him.

When he sees injustice—rules being broken—he can't help but get involved. And when Charlie's in town, you'd better hope you're on the right side of wrong.

PROLOGUE

Careful what you do with your dreams. Some towns'll take 'em and twist 'em into full-blown nightmares.

Nowhere'll do that better than the L.A. And here lies another dreamer. Chewed up on Sunset and spat out on a hillside. An arm hanging limp out of a smashed window. The pale moon turning the blood an oily-black. It runs steady down the arm. It comes from the back of the head and over the left shoulder. But a blunt trauma is the least of a dead man's problems.

The car is like the body trapped behind the wheel. Mangled, squished, upside down.

Steam eases out of a broken radiator. I straighten up, almost slipping down the steep hill. It sits way above the bright city lights.

Some of 'em twinkle. Some of 'em don't.

I hear the faint cry of sirens in the far-off distance. Could be for anything. If they're coming for this poor bastard, they're bloody fast.

I check my pockets for my phone. May as well call it in. But shit, I left it in the black Ford SUV I'm driving.

I look up the hill to the missing section of barrier. The car must have come off at speed on the bend, caught some serious airtime before tumbling to a stop.

I decide to head back up the hill. I start walking, but get a sense of something.

Ever feel like you're being watched? Well I glance up beyond the SUV, where the road curls tight in a hairpin. It rises steep, to a higher level up the hill.

A stranger stands and watches. Nothing but a shadow with the orange dot of a lit cigarette. The shadow takes the cigarette from its mouth and flicks it into the bushes. It climbs into a car. An engine roars and a headlight powers on full-beam.

I start up the hill again. Walking. Running. The gradient sapping the life out of my legs. Or maybe it's the shock. The scene of the crash. The sight of the body.

And I don't shock easy.

I make it up to the SUV. The stranger swings back down the hill and around the bend. Driving a dark-grey saloon on fat tyres with just the one working headlight beam. The car roars past and down the hill into the distance. This is all my fault. And the stranger's gotta be involved. I've gotta catch 'em before they get away.

I jump behind the wheel and drive.

1

 FEW WEEKS EARLIER...

Now this is what I'm talking about. Sat in a red Camaro convertible. A cool breeze in my hair. A windscreen full of palm trees and a spotless blue sky. The car sparkling clean and "Cherry Cherry", a Neil Diamond classic on the radio. I squeeze the wheel between my hands, smell the leather and relax into the luxury seats.

Welcome to L.A.

"Charlie! You're supposed to clean the damn car, not fill it with your fat fuckin ass."

I snap out of a smile. "Yes, boss," I say, grabbing my cloth and bottle of cleaning spray off my lap. I push the driver door open and climb out of the Camaro. I hurry under the ceiling fan and past the freestanding poster featuring California palm trees and a bright yellow headline about a million dollar prize draw.

Grant is stumpy, podgy and sweats his way through a pink, short-sleeved shirt. He checks his gold watch strapped tight to a hairy wrist. "You done in here?" he says.

"Yep, just finished."

"Good, then I've got a lot full of cars need a wash and a wax."

"Right on it," I say,

I walk across the showroom. The place smells nice at first. You know, that new car smell? But after a couple of weeks, it starts to get right up your nose.

A bit like Grant.

He runs the place. Pays a pittance, but it's cash in hand so I'm not complaining. I open the door and step out into the forecourt. Rakesh was a rocket scientist back in India. Or was he a computer genius? Either way, he's already hosing down the first in a row of twenty cars on the lot. I grab a bucket and sponge and go to work on the next one along.

"What did you used to do again?" I ask Rakesh, a slip of a guy swamped in baggy white overalls.

"A Digital CPU Design Engineer."

"Say again?"

"Computers and shit," he says.

"Ah yeah, I knew that," I say, slapping the sponge on the windscreen of the car—or *windshield* as Grant keeps reminding me. I've gotta remember the terms, he says. "You're not in 'la-de-dah' London now," he said to me, not realising that's the swankier part of England and I'm from the northern part.

As I soap up the car, Rakesh turns off the hose. "What did *you* used to do?" he asks me with a big smile. Always a smile. Even in the heat, the smog, with only a few bucks in his pocket and four lanes of traffic rumbling by.

Not what either of us were sold on those TV ads Schwarzenegger used to put out.

I try and think of a good occupation. Nothing springs to mind except . . . "Rubbish, I mean, garbage, trash, whatever it's called over here."

"Collection or processing?" Rakesh asks.

"Sometimes I'd pick it up. Other times I'd drop it off," I say, thinking about the last guy I tipped over a fourteen-story ledge. His name was Burke and he'd knocked over a bar he really shouldn't.

"This job any better?" Rakesh asks, helping me sponge down the second car.

"It's cleaner," I say, thinking about the mess Burke made on the pavement.

2

L.A. is a sprawling, pulsing, humming mass of a city. A good place to be if you wanna be another face in the crowd, where no one pays attention and most people are sat behind the glass of a tinted car window.

But the traffic is unbelievable. There's always a smoking auto wreck in the distance and a five-minute nip to the shops can turn into a four-hour crawl in a heartbeat.

That's why I use the Metro system. Either the orange and grey buses or the silver subway trains. Today I'm riding the bus towards Hollywood, straight to my second job.

If you were with me in Arizona, you're probably asking yourself where the leftover change went from the bank raid. Well, it went right into my daughter's university fund. She'd go absolutely apeshit if she knew it was blood money. She still thinks me and her mum get a grant from the government. And so long as she doesn't ask, I'm not gonna tell her. I buried a lot of bodies and did a lot of unpleasant things to get that money.

But that's all in the past. Now it's hard, honest labour. I'd even pay tax if the companies I'm working for weren't cooking the books and avoiding the minimum wage. Speaking of labour, my bus arrives at the stop a block away from my night job.

It's a short walk under a pink sky and through a side door as the neon sign above *Infinity* glows into life.

In the locker room, I sit and eat a pastrami sandwich I bought on my way out. I read a free newspaper I find on a bench before checking my watch. Eight p.m. Time for my shift.

I open my locker and pull out my stab vest. I fix the velcro straps and pull a fluorescent orange band up over the top of my right arm. The other guys on the team come in and we grunt at each other. Some big units among 'em. I'm six-five and one of the smaller guys. Then there's Candice. Mess with her and she'll take that mess and beat you to death with it.

I'm only a week into the job. An outsider. They don't trust easy in here. And why should they? Most of 'em have got a sideline going on, either dealing on the door, in the club itself or out in the side streets.

Well they don't need to worry about me. I'm here to do my shift, keep my head down and preserve the peace. And I don't intend on getting to know anyone too well.

Infinity's a good gig, after all. When I turned up for the security firm trial, I thought I'd get a rundown bar or a seedy downtown nightclub. Somewhere the boozers and brawlers went to pickle their livers and punch, stab and shoot each other for a good time.

I certainly didn't expect the hottest VIP spot in town. Guess they must have been impressed by the way I took three of their senior instructors down. Or maybe it's 'cause I'm a polite bastard who can string a few words together, which is useful when you're spiriting the glitterati inside, away from the paparazzi.

And after a few hours of a Friday, the place starts to fill up with 'em. I stand in a dark corner of the main room, out of sight of the rich and famous and not so famous, but just damn rich, bloody beautiful or well connected. The club is decked out in leather and marble. There's a sunken dance floor in the middle and the clear glass bottom of a swimming pool above, with a couple of water dancers in skimpy bikinis.

The shimmer of the pool is part of the lighting scheme —a pale-blue glow with matching neon strips along the two-sided bar to my far right. People queue either side, while the really important people sit in roped-off booths ordering table-service champagne.

It's quiet on the radio. Usually is. No trouble on the door and not much to do but usher the odd drunk guy or girl out of the club. So I play spot the famous person. I reckon I've seen four or five tonight. Most of the crowd are stunning young things tanned from the California sun. And half of 'em look like high school kids.

Christ, I'm getting old.

As I'm stifling a yawn and feeling all of my four and a bit decades, Ty speaks in my ear. "Joshua Speed, in the house. Charlie, you're on the rope."

I move through the club, over to the VIP booths against the far wall. They're big, semi-circular areas with oversized white leather sofas. There's a reserved sign on the centre table and a purple rope in front. I stand by the rope and watch out for Hollywood's highest paid actor. It's pretty tough to miss the guy. He's in his late-twenties but looks more like twenty-one. The same black-haired, blue-eyed, square-jawed heartthrob we're all used to seeing on the big screen. What was that latest piece of shit he was in? Some superhero franchise thing.

Nonsense. Absolute bloody nonsense.

Gem, Speed's personal hostess for the night, leads him, two male friends and his two minders to the booth. They look like brothers with their matching black suits and shaved heads. They give me the eyeballs. I wonder why they need me to guard the rope in the first place. Must be beneath 'em. Not in the contract.

I unhook the rope and pull it aside. I don't look Speed or his entourage in the eye. We're trained not to do it. They get enough people staring and snapping cameras at 'em as it is. Instead, I stand by the rope and guard the booth.

People walk by and steal glances in Speed's direction as the champagne flows.

As the night wears on, Speed and his pals are getting pretty loud. Climbing up on tables. Pouring champagne into each other's gobs. Spilling the stuff over the floor and sofas. The minders sit back on their arses, letting Speed do what he wants. They hit me with a stare that says *turn around*.

I look across at Ty. He's the team leader. Six-eight, black and bald and carved out of granite. He's guarding his own booth of VIPs. One's a supermodel I recognise from one of those big billboards you see on the sides of buildings. I nod my head towards Speed and his entourage. Ty waves a subtle hand, down by his side—*let it go*. So I do, scanning the club for any signs of trouble.

"Shit," Ty says in my ear. "Carlos is in tonight."

"Who's that?" I ask.

"Far side of the room. White suit, black shirt."

I look across the club, over the dance floor to the far side. Carlos is a Latino guy with cornrows hair and a sharp black goatee. He walks with a human bulldozer in tow—another

Latino with a shaved head and a white short-sleeve shirt that's too big for him.

And that's saying something.

"Who's Carlos?" I ask Ty.

"You don't wanna know," Ty says. "And don't go askin'."

"None of my business anyway," I say.

Gem returns to the booth with more champagne, tall with light-brown hair and a gold dress that goes well with her figure. I open the rope and let her in. She smiles and enters the booth. Pours the party some more bubbles and gets a slap on her toned arse for her trouble.

Speed is taking serious liberties if you ask me.

Gem smiles through it.

I feel like giving the little shit a clip round the ear. Movie star or no movie star. But I turn away. Eyes to the front. Tracking Carlos as he moves around the club. He reminds me of those coyotes I saw during my time in Arizona. Skulking around. Head bowed. Eyes roaming from left to right. His black shirt open wide at the collar. Disco light bouncing off his platinum-plated teeth. Carlos moves around to my left, fixes his gaze on Speed's party and taps his giant friend on the arm. He points towards the booth. The two of 'em come my way.

Meanwhile. Speed is shouting over to the supermodel in Ty's booth. She's playing it cool. Speed takes a swig from a giant bottle of champers as Gem leaves the booth with a couple of empties. He freezes mid-drink. His face drops and drains. He lowers the bottle. I track his stare over to Carlos, closing in.

Speed shrinks into the leather sofa, as if trying to hide. The minders look worried. So does Ty.

Carlos stops in front of the booth. He's not that big a guy, but broad-shouldered. A mean glint in his eye. He looks me up and down, then past me, towards Speed.

"Can I help you, sir?" I ask.

Carlos smiles. It's not genuine. "No, but you can help yourself."

"Let him in, Charlie," Ty says.

I look across at him. "Serious?"

Ty raises both eyebrows. I look around at Speed. He and his party have quietened down. Speed's minders are on the edge of their seats, either side of the kid. Whoever this Carlos clown is, I guess the kid's well protected.

I unhook the rope and let Carlos in. "Good doggy," he says as he brushes past me.

Carlos' supersize friend barks low like a dog at me, his face in mine.

I ignore it. Like I said, not my business. But I keep a close eye on events. Carlos stands in front of the kid. He looks at Speed's bodyguards. The pair of 'em stand up and shuffle out of the way, onto other sofas.

Carlos and his friend take a seat either side of Speed.

Speed puts on a smile, but it's a nervous one as Carlos talks in his ear. Speed talks back, shoulders shrugging, hands out as if trying to reason with the man. Carlos puts an arm around Speed's shoulders. I can't hear shit over the booming dance music, but he's making a point with a tattooed finger. Speed argues some more. Carlos lets go and stands in frustration. He taps a diamond-encrusted Rolex.

What's he saying? Time's almost up? I dunno, but Carlos and his pal clear out of the booth. I close the rope off behind them. They drift over to the bar without a look or a word in my direction.

I glance over my shoulder at Speed. He shrugs to his friends. Puts on another smile and reaches for a champagne glass. His hand shakes. He gets up and heads to the toilets with a minder and his mates in tow.

Not long after, he comes back. Red nostrils and pupils like saucers. The swagger back in his stride. He beckons the supermodel over. She's a six-foot brunette. She wafts past me into the booth. I try not to gawp. Instead I watch Carlos take a seat in the far corner of the club. He catches my eye. I look away. Don't want any trouble.

I unhook the rope again as Speed and the girl head down onto the dance floor, hand in hand. They're getting close. The music thumping. The swimming pool dancers spinning in the water.

I check my watch and roll my neck out. Hours left on the shift and this stab vest is pulling my shoulders forward, killing my posture.

Luckily, Gem comes over with a bottle of chilled water for both me and Ty. But Ty's elsewhere, turfing a drunk guy out of the club.

As I'm chugging the water down, I catch sight of Speed and the supermodel playing tonsil tennis. Speed is five-ten tops and she towers over him in her heels.

They break off and Speed leads her by the hand, up the dance floor steps. They're heading for the stairs up to the roof terrace. His minders are up on their feet, too, shadowing close behind.

Carlos nods to his friend and they rise from their seats. They follow on through the door that leads to the stairs up to the terrace. I look around and see Speed's entourage. One's on his phone. The other's copping a face full of a girl.

Sod this.

"Ty, this is Charlie. I'm heading up to the roof," I say into the microphone plugged into my right ear.

"I'm heading back in now," Ty says. "What's happening?"

"It's that Carlos guy," I say crossing the club, pushing my way through a throng of bodies. "I'm checking it out."

Ty tells me to stay put. Too late for that, pal, I'm already through the door and striding up the transparent staircase up to the roof. I head through a set of glass doors with chunky chrome handles.

The night is still. The stars out. Speed and the supermodel have their ankles in the water, laughing and flirting on the far right of the pool. The minders stand to the left of the pool, giving them space. Carlos and friend are a little ahead of me, passing by Speed's minders.

The minders don't do shit about it.

I stay by the doors, in the shadows, seeing how it plays.

"What's the water like?" Carlos says.

Speed looks up and sees Carlos and his giant friend approaching slow around the pool.

"Josh?" the supermodel says.

Speed puffs his chest out, toughened up by the bubbly and coke. "Listen Carlos, I told you . . . I'm not gonna give you ten percent of my fucking earnings."

"You fucking owe me," Carlos says.

"For what?"

"Management services," Carlos says, as he rounds the far end of the pool. "You just fired your last agent, right?"

"Yeah, how do you know?"

"Forget about how I know," Carlos says. "I'm your new one."

"Oh yeah? Since when?" Speed says, getting to his feet.

"Since a month ago. You earned seventy million last year, correct?"

"I might have done," Speed says.

"Then a month, that's, uh—" Carlos struggles with the maths.

"Five-hundred and eighty three grand," his fat friend says.

"There," Carlos says, squaring up to Speed. "But I'm a nice guy. Let's call it an even five."

"Are you out of your fucking mind?" Speed says.

"Please, watch your language," Carlos says. "There's a lady present."

As the supermodel pulls her feet out of the water, Speed looks across the pool at his minders. "Are you gonna get rid of this asshole, or what?"

Speed's minders are silent. They stay put.

"So where's the first payment?" Carlos says, stepping into Speed's face.

"What are you talking about?" Speed says. "I don't carry around that kind of cash."

"Then you can get it tonight," Carlos says.

"Tonight? What are you—?"

"Bank transfer. I give you my account details," Carlos says.

Speed shakes his head, disbelieving.

"What, you need an invoice or something?" Carlos says.

"You're not getting shit," Speed says, only to take a punch from Carlos in the gut. He drops to one knee, coughing, wheezing. His minders do nothing.

The supermodel backtracks away slow on the balls of her feet, taking her shoes with her. Carlos drags the kid up to his feet by the collars of his shirt and snarls something quiet I can't hear from this distance. The supermodel pushes past me, back into the club, walking on shaken legs that go on forever.

"What's going on, Charlie?" Ty says in my ear.

"You'd better get up here," I say, keeping my voice low. "I could use some backup."

"For Carlos?" Ty says. "Don't do it Charlie, you don't know who you're—"

I pull out my earpiece and step out of the shadows. I walk along the opposite side of the pool to Carlos and Speed, past his minders. "There a problem here, gentlemen?" I ask.

Carlos pauses, Speed still in his grip. "No, no problem," he says. "Now run along little doggy before you get hurt."

"Looks like there's a problem to me," I say.

"Don't do it, buddy," one of the kid's minders says under his breath.

I ignore 'em and keep walking. One slow step after another along the poolside.

"Maybe we can all take it easy," I say. "Come to some sort of arrangement."

Carlos lets go of the kid and fixes his attention on me. His rather large friend cracks his knuckles. They clack like stones hitting a rock floor.

Carlos seems amused by me. "Okay, Kofi Anan. What do you fucking suggest?"

I round the deep end of the pool and square off in front of Carlos. "Look, your business is your business. But I can't have it happening on club grounds." I hold up my hands to make peace. "You know how it is."

Carlos snorts. "What are you, British?"

"British, yeah."

"British, I see," Carlos says, slapping his friend on the arm. "That explains it, Mike. He doesn't know who he's talking to." Carlos thumbs his nose and leans towards me. "I'm gonna give you a pass on this one. Get the fuck out of here."

"I appreciate that," I say, "but I'm still gonna have to ask you gentlemen to leave."

"You got some big-ass cojones, Britishman." Carlos turns to his friend. "Hey Mike, get rid of this piece of shit."

Mike steps forward, ready to do some damage. He throws out a gorilla-sized hand. I grab it by the ends of his fingers and pull 'em apart at the index and middle.

There's a nasty crack. He screams. I push his hand all the way back. A snap at the wrist. Doesn't matter how much meat you've got on 'em. Bones are bones. Mike screams again. He cradles his hand. I boot him hard on the side of the kneecap. He's down to a kneel. The next boot puts him in the pool.

As he falls in, the water makes its way politely out.

I turn to Carlos. His hand inside his suit jacket. He pulls a gold-plated piece. I catch his trigger hand and rip the gun away. I remove the clip fast and toss it in the pool. I open his jacket and slide the pistol back in his shoulder holster.

It all happens before he can react. I jam a thumb in a pressure point on the left side of his neck. "Seeing as you're so very important, you can use the secret entrance," I say, leading him away from the pool.

Mike pulls himself out of the water and rolls onto the tiles behind us.

"You too, Tiny Tim," I say to Mike. "Let's go."

We take the fire exit, down a very un-exclusive staircase and out into a deserted road down the side of the club. I push Carlos away into the road. Mike limps after him. A dripping mess, still whimpering over his broken fingers and fractured wrist.

Carlos turns to me. Speaks through gritted teeth. "Pick out a nice plot," he says. "You're a fuckin dead man."

I watch Carlos and Mike disappear into the night. I step inside the fire exit door and head back into the club.

3

The nightclub is closing. The last of the clientele leaving for the hills. I take off my stab vest and close my locker.

Ty catches up with me. He shakes his head. "You're a maniac. You know who that was?"

I shrug.

"That was Carlos Campuzano."

I shrug some more.

Ty removes his vest and slides it inside his locker. "From Tijuana. They call him Rata Loca . . . Crazy Rat. He's a fucking hood, man. Runs his own operation out of the Paicoma.

"Then what's he doing here?" I say.

"Trying to move up in the world, I dunno . . . I tried to tell you."

"Don't worry about it," I say, slapping Ty on the back on my way out.

"You're a dead man now, Charlie. You know that?"

"So everyone keeps saying."

"You would have lost your job, too," Ty says. "The boss wanted you fired tonight."

"A human sacrifice?" I say.

"He doesn't want that kind of heat on him," Ty says.

"Then why am I still standing here?" I ask.

"Joshua Speed, that's why."

"At least someone appreciates me," I say, pushing my way out of the door. "See you tomorrow, Ty."

"If you're still breathing," Ty yells after me.

The house lights are on as I come out of the club. I check my watch. Three-thirty. The last bus is in ten minutes. I trudge down the road and wait at the stop.

I look up and down the street both ways. Multiple lanes empty of traffic. Signals turning red to green with no one around to care.

I see a car roll out of an underground car park a block up the road to my right. It's a red Ferrari. The V12 roars out onto the street. It speeds up and then slows down fast.

I tense up, bracing myself for a drive-by.

The Crazy Rat, coming to get me.

The Ferrari stops tight to the kerb. The engine hums, the exhaust crackles. The driver's window whirs down. I bend over and see a flash of white teeth. It's Joshua Speed.

"Hey man," he says.

"Alright?" I say.

"What you waiting for?" he says.

"The bus. What does it look like?"

"Bus? Come on man, get in. I'll give you a ride."

"No thanks," I say, looking at the cocaine in his eyes.

"What, I'm too good for you?" he says, laughing at his own joke.

"Something like that," I say.

"Come on, man. Don't be a douche. I owe you one."

I stay where I am and look up the road for my bus.

"The bus'll take you an age. I'll have you home in five."

The offer is tempting. I feel like I'm about ready to drop, my body aching all over. "Alright," I say.

I round the back of the Ferrari and climb inside. Sweet Jesus what a car.

Speed asks me where I live. I explain the route.

"Yeah, I know where that is," Speed says, revving the engine.

The Ferrari takes off like a rocket. I hold on for dear life.

"You ever been in a car like this?" Speed asks.

"Yeah, I used to own one," I say.

"A Ferrari?"

"No, a red one," I say, pulling my belt on as Speed lives up to his name. "Volvo estate," I say.

Speed laughs. We blast through a green turning red, my head snapping back against the seat. I look across at the kid. I reckon there's more Charlie in him than there is in me.

"Where are your minders?" I ask.

"Those assholes? I fired them."

"Don't blame you," I say.

"Hey, um, what do I call you?" Speed asks, pulling past a yellow Prius cab.

"Call me Charlie."

"I wanted to say thanks, Charlie. For saving my ass back there."

"Just doing my job."

"No you weren't," Speed says.

I watch the speed dial on the dash. Thinking I shoulda followed my first instinct and taken the bus.

Speed brakes hard and turns sharp into a right-hand turn.

He glances across at me and laughs. "Don't worry. I do some of my own stunt driving."

"Not drunk and drugged up, you don't."

"Don't I?" Speed says, grinning his head off and hanging a left.

"So how did you get mixed up with a character like Carlos?"

"I don't know, man. He just started following me around. Making threats. Asking for money. Tonight's the first time it got real."

Speed heads downtown, where the traffic thickens up, even at this hour of the morning. He slows for a red in the nick of time, the tyres smoking. A train of young girls totter across the road in the headlights of the Ferrari. Speed revs the V12 engine. One of the girls flashes her bra.

"You'd better get yourself some better minders from now on," I say.

"Tell me about it, man," Speed says. "Those guys suck . . . Hey, what about you?" Speed smokes the wheels again and leaves the rest of the traffic for dead.

"Let me worry about me," I say, almost pulling the grip off the door as Speed drives us to our doom.

"No, I mean how about you working for me?" Speed says. "My personal bodyguard."

The offer takes me by surprise. "I, um . . . I don't think it's such a good idea."

"Then you must really like working in that club," Speed says. "Earning a measly few bucks for pulling on that stab vest every night."

"It's not so bad," I say.

"How about two-hundred?" Speed says.

"Two hundred dollars a day?"

Wow, that's good money. Now I've gotta think about it.

Speed laughs at me. "No you dick, two hundred grand," Speed says. "Six-month rolling contract."

Two-hundred bloody grand? Is he serious?

The last thing I want is any attention. And the kid draws it like a super magnet. But two-hundred big ones . . . That's Cassie's college fund paid for. Maybe even a pile of bricks somewhere out in the suburbs.

"That's a very generous offer," I say.

"Cheaper than paying off that prick, Carlos," Speed says.

The more I think about the two-hundred grand, the more sense the arrangement seems to make. And Speed could bloody well use my help.

As I chew it over, the Ferrari screeches to a stop outside the complex I'm renting in. A world away from the Hollywood hills.

Speed eyes the rundown condos. "You telling me you don't need the money?"

I sigh, tired and defeated. Can't keep working these eighteen-hour days.

"Okay, pal," I say. "But I want three-hundred. And half upfront."

"Deal," Speed says with a spaced-out smile.

"Now get out of here before you get car-jacked," I say, getting out of the Ferrari.

I shut the door behind me.

"See you tomorrow," Speed yells through his window.

"What time?" I say.

He's gone without an answer. The V12 roaring and taillights shrinking as the low-slung car takes a hard right around a corner.

4

I wake up. Sit up. My head in a fog. Eyelids stuck together. I grapple on the bedside table for the alarm clock. It's ringing like a bastard. I forgot to reset the damn thing. I knock it off the table. Roll out of bed and onto the cracked brown tiles. Just gotta stop the thing ringing. On my hands and knees, I scrabble around on the cold, hard floor. I feel the shape of the vibrating clock. Pick it up. Hurl it against the far wall of the tiny studio room of the condo. It hits the wall and stops.

Thank Christ for that.

I open my eyes—my eyelids snap apart and I blink, rubbing away hard rocks of sleep.

Is it seven already? Shit, I feel like I only just got my head down.

I stagger to my feet in my boxers and t-shirt. Wander over to the window. Throw open the curtains. The California sun burns the film off my retinas. It's a shock to the system. But the fastest way to wake up.

I yawn and look around the small, basic studio. A sofa bed, a boxy TV with a wire coat hanger for an aerial, a two-ring electric stove, yellowing fridge and single, pale-blue counter top that looks like it's been self-harming. Oh, and a porcelain sink I use for washing my hands, my face and the dishes.

The toilet is in its own little cubicle where my knees wedge up against either wall.

Three-hundred grand.

Was last night a dream?

I scratch my crotch and try and remember. But there's a knock on the door.

It gives me a jolt. No one ever knocks on that thing.

I pad over to the door and peer through the spy-hole. There's a bendy figure in black. I unlock the door and pull it wide open.

The figure in black is a chauffeur in full suit and cap. An average-built guy with sandy hair and a broad smile.

"Morning," he says. "Charlie, isn't it?"

"Who wants to know?"

"Mr Speed sent me to pick you up."

"How did you know which condo—"

"I asked the supervisor. Ready for your first day?"

So I didn't dream it.

"Yeah, um, I guess," I say. "Just give me a minute—"

"Take twenty," he says. "I'll be in the car." He motions to a gleaming black Mercedes saloon parked by the kerb. "And pack a bag," he says, as I close the door. "A big one."

5

The chauffeur's name is Bradley. He takes us up through Beverly Hills, past joggers out early enjoying the sunshine. The roads are caramel-smooth, with wide, spotless pavements and precision-cut grass verges.

Evenly spaced palm trees stand tall against the blue sky. The radio plays low—sports breakfast chatter. I look out of the window as the Mercedes cruises in near silence. Most of the mansions sit behind high stone walls and solid steel gates. Not a cig butt, crisp packet or a strung-out beggar in sight.

Bradley steers us higher into the hills, where the roads wind tighter and steeper and the views grow more and more spectacular over the city. Bradley tells me the higher you are up the hill, the bigger your fame and wealth. And we're climbing pretty damn high.

At one point, we pass by a small bus unloading with tourists. They take pictures of each other next to a set of gates. The closest they'll get to the movie star who lives inside.

I reckon we're three-quarters up the hill when Bradley pulls up in front of a solid white automatic gate. The walls are high and crawling with vines, the palm trees behind 'em rising even higher. Only a sliver of white roof peeps out between the trees.

Bradley makes a call. Tells someone or other we've arrived.

The gate slides open and we roll on through, into a big courtyard with a knee-high circular fountain in the middle. The water is a shimmering dark-blue. It spits a trio of small frothing jets into the air every few seconds. The house itself is glass and white stone, four levels high and built at all kinds of weird angles. There's a huge garage building directly across it with two white doors.

As I climb out with a holdall stuffed full of clothes and belongings, a door opens on the ground level and a woman steps out. She beckons me in.

Bradley tips his hat. I tip him ten dollars and shake his hand. He climbs back in the Mercedes and spins it around the fountain on the way out.

I walk to the door. The woman is in her forties—short and plain with brown hair tied back. She's dressed in a grey trouser suit with iPad and iPhone in hand.

She looks tired.

"I'm Christine," she says. "Assistant to Mr Speed."

"I'm Charlie," I say offering to shake her hand.

"This way, please," she says, leaving me hanging and waving me on. "Mr Speed will be with us shortly," she says, leading me across a white limestone floor to a pair of grey designer chairs by a giant wall of glass.

I flop into one, dropping my bag on the floor.

"Now," she says, resting her tablet and phone on a glass coffee table between us. "A few things before we get started."

"Started with what?" I ask.

"The master bedroom and bathroom are out of bounds, unless expressly permitted and instructed by Mr Speed."

"Of course," I say.

"You're to drive within no more than twenty metres of Mr Speed's car. He doesn't like to feel suffocated."

"But that's what bodyguards do, isn't it?" I say. I let out a laugh. Christine is a stern woman. Impatient, too. She makes me nervous. I stifle the laugh and sit up in my chair. "Yes, ma'am."

Christine slaps her thighs. "Okay, did you bring your resume?"

"My what?"

Christine rolls her eyes. "Your past work experience?"

"Yeah, about that—"

I'm scrabbling around, thinking of what to say when a plain white door opens to our left. Into the hallway walks Joshua Speed in pastel-pink shorts and a pale blue tee with a bib of sweat and a black gym towel round his neck. He's a little out of breath, but he's bright as a button. And this was the guy on champagne and coke last night?

"Hey Charlie, my man!" he says, striding over.

Christine tenses up even more. If she was wound any tighter, she'd be a spring. "I was just asking your new recruit for his qualifications."

"It's okay Christine," Speed says. "The job's already his."

Christine is fuming. "But we have a vetting procedure, remember?"

"Trust me, he's qualified," Speed says.

"Why do I bother?" Christine mutters to herself as she scoops up her tablet and phone.

Speed walks off down the hallway. "Come on, I'll show you around," he yells over his shoulder.

"Yes, Mr Speed," I say.

"Call me Josh!" he yells back.

I shrug at Christine. She leaves in a huff.

I leave my bag where I dropped it and jog after Speed—hell, let's call him Josh from now on.

I catch up to Josh as he leads us along the hallway into the biggest kitchen I've ever seen. The swankiest, too. You know the kind. Those shiny white German cupboards without handles and appliances that can think for themselves.

Josh takes the towel from around his neck and dumps it on a central island.

"You been working out, already?" I ask.

"Six every morning," he says pulling open a tall cupboard door and revealing one half of a fridge-freezer the size of a wardrobe. "Four if we're shooting."

He tosses me a spring water in a green glass bottle. He takes a gulp on one of his own as I look at the label. Organic. Swiss. I try it. Bloody hell, I had no idea water could taste this good.

Josh ditches his bottle on a black marble top and takes a big plastic box from the fridge. He tears off the lid, grabs a cooked chicken breast and pops it in a large blender. He does the same with a handful of cooked broccoli and pours the rest of the mineral water in on top.

What the hell is the guy doing?

He turns on the blender and gives it a few seconds. The thing revs up like it's about to take off.

Josh detaches the blender cup and removes the top. He stops and turns. "Chicken smoothie?"

"You blend your chicken?"

"Uh-huh," Josh says, taking a sip that gives him a thin white moustache. "Cuts out the chewing," he says with a smile, walking and talking with the smoothie in hand. "Worst thing about clean bulking for a role. Every two hours you've gotta chew a plate full of chicken and broccoli. Got a company that cooks the meals, but I still haven't found anyone to chew all this shit down for me."

I follow in tow as he gives me the grand tour.

"Christine is a professional hard-ass, so don't take it personally." Josh says. "Bucky might bust your balls, but he does that to all of us."

"Who's Bucky?" I ask.

"You'll meet him later," he says, swigging on some more pulverised chicken. "This is—I guess you could call it the living area," he says, as we walk into a room the size of most apartments.

It's open-plan, all glass walls, full of designer furniture and views over the hills and city. Oh yeah, and there's a flat waterfall running over a slab of granite on the far wall.

Off into another hallway and we pass by a row of three giant movie posters. On all three posters, Josh strikes a superhero pose in skin-tight black rubber while the world burns behind him. A glowing orange ring logo in the centre of his chest.

Nightburner. That's the name of the film I couldn't remember. The one about the guy who punishes criminal scum and leaves 'em tied up or dead for the cops, circled in a ring of fire.

There's Nightburner One, Two and Three. Each one worse than the last.

Josh catches me looking at the posters. "You a fan?" he asks me.

"Nah," I say.

"Really?" he says. "Why not?"

"'Cause they're shite."

Josh pauses a moment. I think he's gonna cry. Or fire me. Me and my big trap. But the lad bursts out laughing. He wags a finger at me. "Now that's what we need more of around here . . . Come on, I'll show you the rest of the house."

I don't know what he wants more of, but I follow him up the stairs anyway. There are seven bedrooms, all posh and massive. Josh is on the top floor. Kind of a penthouse deal, tucked away behind double doors. We don't go in there—he leads me out onto the sun deck instead.

What a bloody place. And what a bloody view. You can see right across the city from here, totally unobscured.

And the view is framed by the sun deck, set around a large infinity pool that appears to drop right off the edge. White leather sun loungers lie in a neat and tidy line in front of the pool. There's a big chrome barbecue at the far end and a folding glass wall that opens up into another giant living area.

Yep, we've got folding walls.

"So, what do you think to the place?" Josh asks me.

"How much does a place like this cost?" I ask, looking around.

"Oh, say about thirteen million."

I let out a whistle.

"A lot of that goes on the land," Josh says. "Had the old mansion that used to stand here demolished and this one built in its place. It's a Frank Lester."

I nod along like I know who the hell he's talking about.

"Leo's the next house up there," he says, pointing up the hill to another luxury pile swamped by trees.

"Leo?"

"Di Caprio," he says.

"Ah, Leo, of course," I say, casting another eye over the infinity pool.

"I coulda gone higher up there," Josh says, "but you've gotta wait 'til one of the old guard goes bust or bites it." Josh stares at the top of the hill through narrowed eyes. "Come on fuckers, die already."

Josh snaps himself out of it. Finishes his drink. "So you okay with one of the guest bedrooms?" he asks, polishing off his chicken smoothie.

"Uh, I guess so."

"Check 'em out again and take your pick. The rest of the staff commute in."

The rest of the bloody staff. I can see this is gonna take some getting used to. I walk around in a daze the next couple of hours, gawping at the opulence of the place. The stairs are lit from underneath. I get lost at least twice. And my room? I pick the best one, obviously. Overlooking a valley down the side of the hill. The ocean in the far distance and the city in between.

The room is decorated in classy shades of beige. It comes with a king size bed, a sofa and a flatscreen TV on the opposite wall. There's an ensuite with a wet room, a walk-in wardrobe I could live in and a glass wall that slides open onto a private balcony. There are more cushions on the bed than I know what to do with, plus a giant painting on the inside wall. Looks like someone chucked red paint at the canvas. Something I could do in three seconds. I wouldn't pay five quid for it, but it probably cost a million.

6

There isn't much time to talk tactics, itineraries and movements. It's a Saturday. So Josh's first and only agenda for the day is a pool party. The place is crawling with the rich and the beautiful. I could swear I just saw a guy from Star Wars.

I try and stay close to Josh, yet give him enough room to play party host. Most of the guests are stripped down to their bikinis and swim shorts.

I try and look anywhere but the young, tanned flesh of the models and actresses roaming the house and lying out in the sun by the pool. I feel over-dressed in my customary black jeans and t-shirt. And out of shape compared to all the six packs and chiselled muscles on show.

So I try and stay as invisible as I can, sipping on water while everyone else nails the cocktails prepared by a barman out by the pool.

I stick out like a sore thumb. Feel like an intruder.

It's funny. I'm here in VIP land. The kind of party most people would kill to get into. Yet all I wanna do is leave.

I try and think of the money. Focus on the job. Keep

checking on the bank of CCTV screens Josh has hidden behind another splash of modern art on the wall in the main entrance. I've got the hang of the remote, now. I push a button and the painting slides up, revealing a flatscreen full of black and white squares—different cameras around the home. I check the front gates. The side gate. The courtyard. Half expecting Carlos and his crew to show up.

But we're okay. A camera on the outer wall shows a gaggle of paparazzi snapping celebs on the street as they enter via a hired-in pair of doormen, but nothing more.

I relax and return the painting over the screen.

"So you're the new bodyguard..."

I turn and see a guy holding a Scotch on the rocks. A baggy white shirt and cream linen pants. A smouldering cigar caught between two hairy knuckles of the hand holding the glass.

"How did you guess?" I say.

"Just a stab in the dark," the man says, scratching his greying, cultivated beard and looking me up and down.

The guy is six-foot. Broad. Most of the breadth from fifty-odd years of living.

"Wyndall Buck," he says, extending a hand. "I work for the studio Josh is contracted to."

"Ah, you make those Nightburner films."

"For our sins," he says. "I heard you stepped in last night. I'd like to thank you for that. If only our own security were so dedicated."

"It's nothing," I say.

"Still, if there's anything you need, you let me know."

"You the big cheese or something?" I ask.

"Hah! No, I . . . how do you put it? Resolve issues."

"You're a fixer?"

He nods. Puffs on his cigar. "Something like that." Buck

removes the cigar from his mouth and blows out a cloud of rich, earthy tobacco. "Now about young Josh . . ."

"Seems like a nice kid," I say. "When he's not off his tits. Not like the media'd have you believe."

"Hah, don't let him fool ya," Buck says. "Today's one of his good days. But it doesn't take much, believe me."

"Sounds ominous," I say.

"The trouble with these movie stars," Buck says, checking over a shoulder. "Their pockets are very well lined. And their asses are very well kissed. Even the best of 'em start to believe their own hype, you get what I'm saying?"

"Sure," I say.

"They're a lot like psychopaths," Buck says. "They know how to act all nice. But they'll turn on you in a heartbeat. Spit the dummy. Go off the rails . . ."

"Psychopaths, huh?" I say. "Then I'm on familiar turf."

"All I'm saying is, keep your wits about you. And don't be surprised by anything that kid does. Those gossip columns aren't all gossip."

"Who's this you're talking to, Wyndall?" a voice full of gravel says.

Buck looks over his shoulder. A guy coming through the front door. Sixties, maybe seventies. A roly-poly figure dressed like Buck and cooked to within an inch of his life by the sun.

The man slaps Buck on the shoulder with a hand dressed in fat gold rings.

"This is Josh's new bodyguard," Buck says.

"Thought we had Mr Speed set up with our own security?" the older man says, eyeballing Buck.

"We did," Buck says. "But you know Josh. He's got his own ideas. And . . . Sorry, I didn't catch your name," he says to me.

"Charlie," I say.

"Seems Charlie here helped our star attraction out of a bind."

"Well thank you Charlie," the older guy says, puffing on his own cigar, grey curly hair retreating as the years advance.

I wave the thanks away again.

"Charlie, this is Art Solomon, Founder and Chairman of Solomon Pictures," says Buck.

"Alright?" I say, shaking his hand.

Solomon nods and tries to give me the power squeeze. I let him try, in case he's tied into the money that's coming my way. I also accompany them up to the sun deck, where music pumps out of a set of hidden speakers and Josh's Hollywood pals drink cocktails in the pool.

Josh himself strolls over to greet Solomon and Buck, dressed in a pair of neon-blue swimming shorts and matching flip flops. Josh is in ridiculous shape, with abs and muscles popping and shining in the sun. I notice he has a mojito in hand. I wonder which number he's on.

I'd check his eyes, but they're tucked away behind a pair of designer Wayfarers.

"Arty, Wynnie! You showed the fuck up," Josh says, wearing a beaming smile.

"Yeah, yeah," Solomon says, eyes roaming over the bikini-clad girls.

I step out of the conversation as the three men talk business for a while. Something to do with screenplays and choice of directors. Josh seems to have a say. Probably a big one, seeing as he's the cheekbones and baby blues that bring in all the fat, sizzling bacon. But I don't make it my business, preferring to keep my beak out of affairs.

Instead, I wander around the pool area. I keep an eye on

Josh, of course, but I'm not here to wipe the lad's arse or catch the crumbs out of his mouth. I take a seat inside the house where the glass wall folds in. I perch on the end of a cream leather bench as a pair of young women do lines of coke on a glass coffee table behind me.

To kill the time, I play spot the star again. I reckon that could be Tom Cruise over there. And is that the girl out of Harry Potter?

"Hey, you wanna party with us?"

I turn to see one of the girls offering me a line on the table. She's a redhead in a dark-green bikini, rubbing her nose.

"I'll stick to my water, thanks, I'm working."

"Working on what? A screenplay?" she says.

"Not exactly," I say.

"Haven't I seen you on TV?" the redhead's blonde friend asks—freckled and pale with twigs for limbs. Maybe another supermodel.

"Yeah, didn't I see you in Law and Order?" the redhead says.

"I was on the six o'clock news once," I say.

"Oh yeah? What did you do?" the redhead asks.

"Seven years with good behaviour."

The pair of 'em look at each other. Neither have a clue what I'm on about, so they go back to powdering their noses.

After a few hours of star gazing and a gourmet burger cooked by an award-winning chef, the night draws in and I see Buck and Josh arguing at the far end of the pool.

Josh is drunk. They both are.

Meanwhile, Solomon's busy in a hot tub getting handsy with a nubile blonde. She squirms away and climbs out of the tub. He's not happy and yells something after her.

I drift over to Josh and Buck and attempt to play peacemaker.

As I approach, they're still talking industry turkey.

"Go-a-fucking-head," Josh says. "Cut the franchise by two. A contract's a contract. The deal was six."

"Yeah, well that was before you broke the franchise with your little scandal."

"No, you and your executives broke the fucking franchise," Josh says. "Fucking up the script and replacing Chris as director."

I enter the fray with care. "What's the problem, gents?"

"This doesn't concern you, Charlie," Buck says.

"Hey, he works for me," Josh says, as if I'm not there.

"Yeah and you work for me," Buck says.

"No, you work for the studio, who I work *with*," Josh says, talking loud. The kinda loud you notice when you're the only sober one in the room.

"You're under contract," Buck says. "And I've told you before to quit the dope. You're supposed to be training for a damn movie."

"I'm training just fine," Josh says, flexing a bicep. "Check it out, motherfucker."

"Straighten yourself out," Buck says.

"Hey," I say. "Calm down. The pair of you."

Josh's got his shades off now. I can see he's been at the powder. "You telling *me* what to do, Charlie? You wanna get fired, you piece of shit?"

"You haven't paid me anything yet," I say. "So be my guest."

Josh stares at me. "Fuck you, asshole." He turns his back on me to continue his slanging match with Buck. "You shelve five and six, and I'll sue you for the shit out of your ass."

"Try it," Buck says. "You think you're the first little prick we've counter-sued? We've got more lawyers than you've got pubes."

I look around the sun deck. People are starting to point and stare. The pair of 'em are causing a scene. Getting in each other's faces. I drag Josh away by the arm, for his own sake.

He tries to wriggle free. "Get the fuck off me."

"The more you say out here, the deeper you dig," I say. "Let your lawyer do the talking. Take it from someone who knows."

"You been to court?" Josh asks.

"I've been a lot further than court, pal. And I learned the bloody hard way, believe me. You don't say anything to anyone. Not without your lawyer."

"Maybe you're right," Josh says. "The fat fucker gets under my skin is all."

I lead Josh into a dark corner. "Take a deep breath."

Josh does as I say. It takes him a few big ones to calm down. "Revenge should be served cold, that what you're saying, Charlie?"

"That's exactly what I'm saying."

The truth is, I'm saying whatever he needs to hear right now. From today's display, I'm guessing one half of my job is to protect the lad from other people. The other is to protect him from himself. I let go of his arm and he relaxes out of the argument.

"You don't know what it's like, Charlie. They've got people spying on me. Spreading shit in the media. Anything to keep me on a leash."

Josh has got that paranoia in his eyes. I've seen it happen a hundred times. You give a young guy wheelbarrows full of cash and more power than they can handle. You introduce 'em to an unlimited supply of drink, drugs, women and hangers-on. Sooner or later they develop a habit. Then they get a complex.

They think the whole world's against 'em. That everyone wants a piece of their own personal kingdom.

Usually, I've seen it happen with the sons, nephews and star protégés of mob bosses. More often than not, they end up with a bullet in the head and their body parts ground into homemade dog meat.

Sometimes, I've been the one grinding the meat.

I try to lighten the mood. "Never mind all that. It's Saturday night. What are you doing talking business? A lad of your age. You should be partying with all these lovely young women."

Josh slaps me on the arm. "You know what, big guy? You're right!"

And with that, Josh returns to the party, dive-bombing into the pool. He swims over to a rather attractive brunette, a waiter handing him a glass of champagne. I settle back down on my leather bench and catch Solomon and Buck looking over at me from the shallow end. They're talking about me, I can tell. And it's not long before they mosey over, cigars and tumblers in hand. I rise off the bench and step out onto the sun deck to meet them, the sky now black, the stars out above and the pool lit up a pale-blue.

"We were just talking about you," Buck says. "You handled the kid well back there."

I don't say anything. Don't wanna make any enemies this early into the job.

"How much is Josh paying you?" Solomon asks.

"Three-hundred," I say.

Solomon chews on his cigar and blows out a plume of smoke. "What if we matched it?"

"What are we talking about?" I say.

"Working for us," Buck says.

"Thanks," I say, "But I feel like I owe the kid."

"Josh fires people like a circus fires guys out of cannons," Solomon says.

"Join the security team we outsource to," Buck says. "They'll give you healthcare, holidays, company car and your own apartment."

"I dunno," I say, looking over at Josh, dancing by the pool with a pair of fellow movie mates.

"When the kid fires you, which he will," Buck says, "we'll put you straight on another star. Lower maintenance. Good work. Part of a team."

I shake my head. "Your boy needs my help. Your other minders bottled it and meanwhile he's being threatened by this Carlos guy."

"So are seven or eight other actors," Solomon says. "Nice people. Clean living people with families."

"And you could do with some protection yourself," Buck says. "Way I heard it, Carlos is gunning for you, too."

"How would you know?" I say.

"I know everything that goes on in this town," Buck says. "It's what Art pays me for."

"Well thanks for the offer," I say, "but I reckon I'm just as safe on my own."

Solomon grunts. "Alright, dammit. Just name your price. You want four-hundred? You got it."

Four hundred? Benefits? Holidays? Nice people? Shit it's tempting.

"Of course, you'd have to fall in line with company policy," Buck says. "Follow orders. Work under a team supervisor."

I look over at Josh again. Off his tits. He tries a canapé off a silver tray offered by a male waiter in black shirt and pants. He spits it out, knocks the tray from the waiter's grip and pushes him into the deep end of the pool. Josh and his pals burst into laughter.

"You think you can take another six months of that?" Buck says, hooking a thumb towards Josh.

I let out a sigh. "Believe it or not, I've worked for worse . . . Sorry gents. It's a generous offer, but I'll have to pass. My word's my word, you know what I mean?"

Solomon and Buck look at each other, disappointed.

Solomon shakes his head and then my hand. "Respect to you, sir," he says.

Buck shakes my hand, too.

As the pair of 'em leave the party, I head over to the pool. The waiter is Middle-Eastern. Looks as if he can't swim. He thrashes around in the water, trying not to drown. Josh mocks him from the side of the pool, flapping his arms and laughing like a hyena. Everyone else stands around with drinks in hands, doing nothing.

I drop to my knees by the water's edge. I reach out an arm, grab the waiter by the collar and haul him out of the pool.

7

Monday morning. Six a.m. We're on set for filming. A cop film Josh is doing between Nightburner movies. He was quite happy to rabbit on about it last night at another of those mansion parties. But this morning, he barely says a word. Two days straight of drink and drugs'll do that to you. He sits in his chair as a woman touches up his makeup. I stand nearby as we wait for the film crew to set up a stunt.

Josh groans, sipping on the Starbucks I got him. Black. No sugar. Not 'cause he doesn't like sugar. Sugar is banned, he tells me. Direct orders from his personal trainer.

"Ugh, I don't remember shit from this weekend," he says to the curly blonde makeup artist. "I didn't do anything bad, did I Charlie?" he says over his shoulder.

"Like what?" I ask.

"Like, uh..."

"Throw any waiters in the pool?" I say. "No, of course not."

Josh misses the joke. "Oh good," he says, taking another sip. "When I've had a drink, I can get a little... You know..."

"I know," I say, watching the film crews at work.

It's not as glamorous as I thought it'd be. In fact, it's pretty boring. There's a lot of standing around. Note to self, get yourself a fold-up camping chair to sit on next time.

The sound stage is huge, like a vast warehouse with a roof full of lights, gantries and a crazy amount of equipment and activity around the set that stands in the middle. The director wanders over as Josh stands out of the makeup chair. The director has a mess of long grey hair and a 'granddad-bod' as my daughter would say, which shows itself under a thin maroon sweater. He wears glasses and shuffles around the place with a piece of paper in his hand and a set of headphones around his neck. He talks with a schooled English accent. But one that's been living on this side of the pond for a long time. Josh tells me his name is Christopher Lipton.

"Right Josh, you okay with the scene?" Lipton asks.

"Remind me again," Josh says.

Lipton points across the set to a stage built from brick and concrete eight feet off the floor. Part of a mockup of a New York rooftop, complete with skylights and ventilation pipes. "It's really simple," Lipton says. "We'll pick it up where you're on the ledge of the building with Klaus."

"Who the fuck is Klaus?" Josh asks.

"The bloody stuntman?" Lipton says in disbelief. *"He's playing Marcus? The bloody bank robber?"*

"Oh yeah," Josh says.

"Now, you exchange blows," Lipton says. "You struggle. Marcus thinks he has you, but he loses his footing. He grabs your tie but you pull a flick-knife from your pocket and cut the tie."

"Okay, I got it," says Josh, stroking his chin. "But what's my motivation here?"

Me and Lipton say it in chorus. *"You don't wanna die."*

"Oh yeah," Josh says, handing his coffee off to Christine, who lurks close by. He claps his hands. "Cool, let's do this!"

Josh jogs over to a rusty ladder attached to the side of the building wall. He climbs the ladder and joins a bigger guy on the roof close to the ledge. Josh is dressed like a plain-clothes detective in a white shirt, black tie and a grey suit. 'Marcus' is dressed in a charcoal suit and tie, too, except he wears a ski mask and black leather gloves.

Lipton calls for quiet on set. Everyone settles down and Lipton calls action.

"Fuck you, bitch," an actor says from the side of the stage. I'm guessing he's the real Marcus—the guy the stuntman is filling in for.

Josh and Marcus exchange blows. Missing by an inch on purpose. It's weird seeing 'em fight like this, without the music or the fast action cuts you see on the screen. It all seems like a load of dressing up and pretending.

Josh throws a fake punch. Marcus snaps his head back, but he returns with another air shot. They wrestle. Marcus steps back onto the ledge and leans backwards. He grabs Josh's tie. Josh whips out a flick-knife and motions to cut the tie. It snaps in half, as if designed that way. Marcus falls backwards eight feet to a green crash mat on the floor, hands outstretched as if plummeting to his doom.

The actor at the side of the set lets out a wail.

Marcus hits the crash mat with a heavy thud and lies there silent.

Josh stands on the rooftop. He looks over the edge and says, "No, fuck you . . . *Bitch*."

Josh pauses, sweating and breathing heavy. He doubles over and throws up on the set. There's a collective groan.

"And cut!" Lipton yells through a loudhailer.

Josh straightens up and wipes his mouth. He smiles a boyish smile at Lipton. "How was that, Chris?"

"Fantastic, Josh, fantastic. Let's do another take. But this time, try it without the puking."

8

Another day, another chicken and broccoli smoothie. And a home workout session with celebrity trainer, Gunnar Toft. He's around my age and ripped. A pocket rocket of a guy who Josh tells me can bench three-hundred pounds.

I'm not even sure what that is, but his eyes bulge and his neck veins pulse when he talks. In fact, the guy doesn't so much talk as bark. I'm told by Josh not to mention anything about his drinking the other night. And especially not the lines of coke.

Josh steps off a weighing scale and gets a high-five from Gunnar.

"Good job," Toft says in a local accent. "You've lost two pounds of fat and gained an extra pound of muscle since last week."

I swear the kid must have alien DNA. He's one of those guys who looks good no matter what you throw at him.

And he's surprisingly strong, too. The workout starts with hand-stand push-ups. Moves onto pull-ups, squats and overhead presses. Toft tells him it's cardio time. A run in the early morning sun.

"My bodyguard has to come," Josh says.

"This guy?" Toft says, looking me up and down. "I'm not insured for heart attacks."

I take it as an insult. And an invitation to prove the bastard wrong. "I'll get changed," I say.

But ten minutes in and I'm regretting it big time. Hell, make that five minutes. Josh and his trainer set a fast pace. They chat as they run. I slog on, falling further and further behind, barely able to breathe and enough sweat pouring off me to flood the valley.

Josh spins around and runs backwards. "Come on, Charlie, you can do it!"

At first I thought the kid was being cautious. Looking out for his own safety. But now I get it. That dimpled fucking grin and the twinkle in his eye. He made me run up here on purpose to punish me.

What he doesn't realise is I'm a stubborn shit. And I've got a job to do. To protect his skinny little arse. So I push on faster, lungs burning to ash as we hit the steepest part of the hill.

We make it to the top and spin around.

Thank Christ for that. A nice leisurely walk back from here.

"Now a downhill run," Toft says, slapping the muscles above the knees. "Good for the teardrops."

We run down the hill, my legs jelly-weak and struggling to control my own momentum.

But I make it back alive, into Josh's basement gym. It's big and plush, as you'd expect. Mirrors along either wall and the full range of equipment. Music and air con pump in from the ceiling and huge flatscreen TVs play MTV videos that match with the tunes.

"We'll finish off with some light sparring," Toft says.

I feel like I'm gonna be sick, but there's no let up now. I'm part of the workout. This had better not be a regular thing. Five a.m. film shoots I can handle. Two-hour workouts before the sun's even all the way up? No bloody chance.

While I'm bent over double, trying not to die, Toft tips out a bag full of gloves and pads. I slip the pads on while Josh belts the crap out of 'em. The kid couldn't punch his way out of a paper bag. But I pretend as if he's packing some serious power—make him look better in front of Toft.

"Come on, Charlie," Josh says, tossing me the gloves. "Show us what you're made of."

While Josh takes a breather and a drink, I tap away at the pads, knackered and not really interested.

"Is that all you've got?" Toft says, clipping me on the side of the head with the pad.

"Alright, leave it out," I say.

"You're supposed to duck," Toft says. "Now come on. Let's see those size fourteens move."

I put up my hands and try and wake my feet up into some kind of rhythm. I hit the pads a couple of times, holding back a good sixty percent.

"Better get yourself a new bodyguard," Toft says to Josh. "This one hits like an anorexic girl."

Toft laughs at his own joke. He comes at me with the pads. Swiping left and right. I duck under one. Sidestep another. Throw a straight right at half-power. It misses the pads and lands plum on Toft's chin.

I might have missed by accident. I might not. But it knocks the bugger flat on his back.

"Holy shit, you KO'd Gunnar!" Josh says, spitting out his water.

"You were supposed to duck," I say to an unconscious Toft.

9

My induction to the Hollywood life continues. During the day, Josh likes me to ferry him around, ushering him in and out of a Ford SUV with dark, tinted windows. There's always a scrum of journos, bloggers and gossip show presenters to deal with. It's a flashbulb frenzy. And as well as shoving the paparazzi out of the way as I push Josh in and out of film studios, restaurants, hotels and whatever else, I have to take my own precautions, always wearing shades and keeping my head down. Not letting anyone get a clear snap of my ugly mug. Josh is not the only one trying to keep a low profile, after all.

It gets to Thursday and we're in a hotel from ten in the morning until four in the afternoon—a gruelling, non-stop blitz of interviews for the young lad. I stand outside the luxury suite, my back aching and stomach rumbling.

Today is all about damage limitation. Turns out Josh has been told by the studio to charm his way out of a media storm that landed after he broke up a co-star's marriage in a 'three-day coke-fuelled romp'. Don't ask me to remember their names, but they were some kinda darling Hollywood couple and the celebrity bloggers and keyboard warriors went bloody nuts.

"Bucky says it's damaging the Nightburner franchise," Josh tells me. "What's damaging the fucking franchise is the lame-ass scripts."

I can do nothing but listen and shrug when he talks business. It's all a nonsense over nothing to me, and I haven't got a clue what he's on about half the time. Ninety percent of this job is babysitting. But I try and stay focused on the other ten percent. Keeping the media scrum away. And keeping a keen eye out for the likes of Carlos.

No sign of him yet. Josh comes out of the room with Christine, who doubles as his press agent.

Christine is on one after the latest interview, "You didn't have to insult the woman," she says to Josh.

"She didn't have to ask the stupid fucking question," Josh says, bickering the whole way down the corridor with Christine.

So much for damage limitation. We head back to the mansion with Christine on her phone. Complaining about another Twitter storm. It's not long until Buck is on speaker in the SUV, too, tearing a strip off the kid. I close my ears and watch my mirrors. I could swear there's a car tailing us —a white Range Rover. But I can't be sure. So I take a detour on the way back.

"What are you doing, this isn't the way," Christine says, taking a breath from the three-way debate going on in the car.

"Testing something out," I say. "You do your job. I'll do mine."

Christine takes it on the chin. Goes back to her argument. I throw a couple of consecutive lefts, then a sharp right, heading back towards Beverly Hills. Nothing they can't follow, but not a natural route for any other car to take. I look in my mirrors again. The Range Rover is gone. Nothing to worry about.

* * *

I CHECK MY WATCH. Eleven already. Two hours since Josh started getting ready. His stylist and fashion advisor called in at the last minute to blow-dry his hair and coordinate the perfect outfit. I sit out by the pool on a sun lounger, under the night sky. I call Cassie up on an iPad Josh is letting me use. It ought to be seven in England right now and Cassie's an early riser.

Sure enough, she's up—and home for the holidays, by the looks of it.

"Hey Dad," she says, sitting at the ex's kitchen table, eating cereal in a set of light-pink pyjamas, her blonde hair a fashionable mess.

"Hi Cass. You not at uni, then?"

"Nah, holidays."

"Another bloody holiday. Christ, what am I paying for?" I stand up off the sun lounger and stretch my legs.

"Mum's here. You wanna speak to her?"

Not really. But before I can say anything, Cass spins her laptop around to face Mandy, fully dressed in jeans and a white vest top, dirty blonde hair tied up in a ponytail.

"Say hi, Mum," Cassie says, off-camera.

Mandy looks up from a red compact. Always messing with her makeup or hair.

We exchange nods.

The webcam spins back around to Cassie.

"So what are you two up to?" I ask.

"Going shopping," Cassie says. "How about you?"

"Oh, just working."

"Working where?" Cassie says. *"Is that a pool?"*

"Yeah, one of those infinity ones," I say.

"Where the hell are you?" Cassie says.

"LA. The Hollywood hills."

Suddenly, Mandy's interested. Her face looms large on the iPad screen. "Did you say Hollywood?"

"Been working here a week," I say.

"What doing?" Mandy asks.

"Security work."

"Who for?" Cassie asks.

"Oh, no one. It's no big deal. Anyway—"

"They must be someone important," Mandy says. "Look at that place. Wow, look at the view behind you!"

The last thing I wanna do is tell Cassie it's Joshua Speed. I still remember the posters she used to have of him on her bedroom wall. Though I'm sure she's grown out of that by now.

"Anyway, what are you going shopping for?" I ask, trying to change the subject.

But suddenly, Josh appears over my shoulder, hair styled perfect, in a grey tailored suit, crisp white shirt and his customary thin black tie.

"Oh my God, is that..." Cassie says, spoon dropping in the cereal bowl, eyes like saucers. She starts to tremble. Hands to her mouth. *"Oh my God!"* She says, wiping the milk off her chin.

"Oh my God, it is!" Mandy says, pulling her hair out of the ponytail and straightening it out around her shoulders.

Bollocks.

"Hey Charlie, who are these two lovely ladies? You didn't tell me you had two beautiful daughters."

Mandy falls for it hook, line and sinker. She and Cassie fight over the compact, arranging themselves as fast as they can.

But that's the last I see of 'em. Josh snatches the iPad off me and walks off round the pool with it. "Hi, I'm Josh."

"I've seen all your films," I hear Cassie say.

"Me too," Mandy says, bullshitting for all she's worth.

"You have such a cool place," Cassie says.

"Ah, it's nothin'," Josh says. "Hey, you wanna see the view from up here?" Josh angles the iPad screen out over the hills, towards the city.

"Wow, it's amazing," Cass says.

"And Leo Di Caprio lives just up there," he says, showing them the next house up.

"Wo-o-o-w," the pair of 'em say in return.

Josh flips the screen back to his pearly-toothed mug. "I can't believe Charlie didn't tell me about you guys. You'll have to come over and stay. We can hang out. I can show you the sights. Take you to a few clubs . . ."

"That's it." I grab the iPad off the bastard and walk away with it into a corner.

"I can't believe I'm on here talking to Josh Speed," Cassie says.

"Can't believe he's employing *you*," Mandy says to me.

"Well if we can all settle down a bit, maybe we can have a normal conversation—" I say.

"Sorry Dad," Cassie says. "I've gotta tell everyone I've ever known, ever."

"Me too," Mandy says.

The call cuts off.

"We ready?" Josh says.

I follow him back into the house and glare at him.
"What?" he says.
"My daughter's out of bounds, understand?"
"Just chatting, buddy. Take it easy."
I keep glaring.
"Okay," Josh says. *"Jeez."*

10

Josh insists on driving his Ferrari to the club. And he drives like a loon, forgetting the whole point of hiring me and leaving me for dust. I run a couple of reds to keep up as we head down into the city. But by the time I catch up, there's a white Range Rover between us. It could be a different one, but seems like a coincidence.

We pull up at a set of lights, not far from the club. Josh in front, then the Range Rover. And me.

I pull up alongside the Range Rover. Try and get a look inside, but the windows are tinted black.

The lights turn to green. Josh pulls away in the Ferrari. The Range Rover guns it after him, as though trying to keep up. But I'm quicker out of the blocks, anticipating the lights. I power forward in the SUV and pull in ahead of the Range Rover.

Further down the road, there's another set of lights. Josh blasts through 'em. I slow down as I approach, as if I'm gonna stop for the upcoming red.

With cars either side, there's no room for the Range Rover to get out and around me. A second before the lights turn red, I plant my foot on the accelerator and squeeze through just in time.

If it was the same Range Rover and it was following Josh, it's now stuck on a red, with traffic cutting across its path. I see Josh ahead. He pulls into an underground car park. I follow him in, but wait at the top of the ramp. I see the Range Rover pass by in my rear view mirror. I roll down the ramp and park.

We walk down a back street and in through the side door to the club, Ty stepping aside as we enter. Josh is flying solo tonight. No entourage. He's 'in the mood', he tells me, just minutes after chatting up my daughter.

Well I'm in the mood to wring the little bastard's neck. But I sit with my arms folded in the VIP booth. Ty guards the rope. I check my watch.

"Don't worry, this won't take long," Josh says.

And he's right. It takes him all of two minutes before a pair of champagne flies in tiny dresses are buzzing around the booth. Josh waves 'em in. A blonde and brunette.

Ty turns to me. "Gotta take a leak. You okay watching the rope?"

"I think I remember how it works," I say. "Take your time."

So I sit there and wait while Josh entertains the two girls. Ty heads off to take a piss and the club swells full with bodies. The dance floor is packed, the lighting low and the music thumping loud.

I yawn and stretch on one of the leather sofas. When I open my eyes, there's a guy on the other side of the rope. He's six-two and well dressed, with a slick black side-parting and a bulky gym body under a navy short-sleeved shirt. He's also angry as hell.

"Hey, fucker, that's my girlfriend!"

He's talking about the brunette. The look on her face says it all. Caught red-handed. But she stays tight to Josh.

"Fuck you asshole," is Josh's measured response.

"Stop embarrassing yourself, Chad," yells the brunette.

This really lights a fuse under Chad. He hops over the rope and makes a beeline for the girl. I let it go a moment. Let 'em have it out. If I was still a bouncer here, I would have blocked the guy off, but I'm not. My only problem with it is if he touches Josh.

Chad grabs his girlfriend by the wrist. "Come on, we're leaving."

His girlfriend resists. Chad pulls harder. Josh puts both hands around her waist and all of a sudden we've got a situation. Especially as Josh stands up to square off against the guy.

Chad towers over Josh. "Oh yeah bitch, what you gonna do?"

I'm up and out of my seat before either of these two can swing, but Chad makes a grab again for his girlfriend, getting rough.

"Okay, that's enough," I say, an arm across Chad's chest. "Let's calm down and talk this out."

Chad doesn't like that idea. He steps away from me. "Get the fuck off me."

I hold out both hands, letting him know I come in peace.

"Hey, dickwod," Josh says to Chad, putting an arm around his girlfriend. "I'm gonna take your girl home with me and show her what a movie star fuck's like."

The girl seems open to the suggestion. Chad lunges forward. I catch him and hold him off. He's doing his nut. All the four letter words he can spit out. Josh taunts him by grinding into the brunette.

Chad's girlfriend isn't helping, either. Almost like she's enjoying the two of 'em fighting over her.

"You're nothing without your fucking gorilla here, you motherfucker," Chad says.

"Come on, that wasn't nice," I say.

"Take this bitch outside and beat the shit out of him, Charlie," Josh says.

I turn around and look at Josh.

"I'm not kidding," he says. *"Do it."*

"No one's getting beaten up," I say, grappling with a raging Chad.

"Hey, you work for me, dumbass. That's an order. I *order* you to fuck this bitch up."

Chad tries to lunge again, his shirt all messed up in my grip.

As I hold him off with one hand, I turn and clip Josh around the side of the head.

"What the fuck—?" he says.

I push him backwards. He drops to the sofa with Chad's girl.

"Sit there, shut up and don't bloody move," I say. "I'll be back in a minute."

I turn to Chad. He's tearing up. Bottom lip flapping like a fish in a bucket.

I talk in his ear. "Whatever you do, don't let her see you cry. Hold it together."

He nods and sucks up the tears before they can make a break for it.

Josh mouths off again. I glare at the fucker. He shuts up and grabs his drink. Mutters through his glass but stays put. I glare at Chad's girlfriend, too. She avoids eye contact and sips a cocktail.

Next, I march Chad out of the VIP area. He still resists some, but I think he realises it's a waste of energy.

"That's my fucking girlfriend," he says, as I push him through the crowds, a hand on the back of his shirt and another with a tight grip on his arm.

"I know, pal, I know," I say. "But I've gotta get you outta here."

As we move through the club, Ty passes me on the way back. "Everything cool?

I nod. "Keep an eye on the little shithead, will you?"

Ty gives me the thumbs up and heads back to the VIP area.

I push Chad out of the club. We stand to one side of the glitzy entrance—a short line of people waiting to be let in.

Chad is wobbling again, alcohol and emotions getting the best of him. "She's the fucking love of my life, man."

"I know, pal. But do you really want to love a girl like that?"

"I can't help it. I'm never gonna find another like her."

"Are you kidding?" I say. "Look at you. You're a bloody GQ model."

Chad shrugs, unconvinced.

"How old are you?" I ask him.

"Twenty-two," he says.

"Twenty-two? You could be out with a different woman every night."

"You think so?"

"I know so. When I was your age, I was . . ." Actually, I was cutting up bodies and kicking people's teeth in . . . "Just spare a thought for us old guys, eh? In a few weeks you'll have a new girl on your arm and you'll wonder what all the fuss was about."

"Yeah, I guess," Chad says, pulling himself together and

looking along the line of beautiful women waiting outside the club.

"Do yourself a favour," I say. "Go home, chill out and forget about that silly cow inside. Speed'll probably collapse when he gets home anyway. Can't take his booze."

"He will?" Chad says.

"Like bloody clockwork. I'll be running your girlfriend home by midnight."

Chad seems to buy the lie. He gives me some kind of young person's handshake. Then one of those shoulder-to-shoulder man hugs. "Thanks, buddy. I appreciate it."

The poor bastard wanders off. As I watch him hail a cab, I notice two guys being waved in by the bouncers. One is smaller, average build with a skin head, thick stubble and narrow eyes. The other is chunky, with the faintest whiff of a moustache.

Both are dressed in blue jeans and thin, dark, baggy jackets.

And both are Latino, with what look to me like gang tattoos on their hands and necks.

The pair of 'em skip the line. And no padding down. The bouncers are supposed to search everyone except solid-gold VIPs. Yet they let 'em swan right in.

They're nowhere near the dress code, the pair of 'em wearing trainers. And neither are they mates with the men on the door. There's no high-fives, fist bumps, words or twenty-dollar bills exchanged. I turn and re-enter the club behind them. But the place is heaving, disorienting. Strobe lighting and boom-boom music pounding. The air is thick with sweat, perfume, aftershave and booze. The two guys slip out of view ahead. I have to back up as Ty runs a pissed-up guy out of the place.

I grab Ty by the arm. "Josh okay?"

"I don't know," he says. "He wasn't there."

"Where is he?" I ask.

Ty shrugs and hauls the drunk out of the club. I push through the crowds, polite but forceful. With the dance floor rammed, people are resorting to dancing all over the club. I push through and look around for Josh. The sofas are empty. I look across the dance floor. Josh is with the two girls, talking in the brunette's ear, ignoring requests for selfies from other club-goers.

Now they're heading to the toilets in a far, dark corner of the club. No midnight swimming this time around. I decide to stay where I am and keep an eye on the door that leads to the toilets. I'll track him on his way out of there. Give him some space and reconnect when he's done.

But those two guys. They're walking towards that door. They only just got in and they're heading for the toilets? Could be doing a line. But this isn't right. The way they're moving. Two young guys—they don't even look at the girls in the club. I weigh up my routes. The most direct is across the dance floor.

I walk down the steps and push through the crowds. I accidentally knock a woman off balance. I grab her before she falls. Her boyfriend takes it personally. Thinks I'm making a move. Makes a move of his own, a hand on the lapel of my jacket. I grip his shoulder and squeeze.

Pressure points are wonderful things, if you're on the right end of the pressure.

He cries in agony and backs off holding his shoulder. I keep going, reading and sidestepping the movements of dancing bodies.

I make it across the floor. I head up the stairs and over to the door. A group of women pile out. I let 'em through and step into the dark corridor lit a low red. It dog-legs at the end to the left, into a wider area with three doors. Cloakroom to the right, disabled to the left and unisex toilets dead ahead.

The two guys are outside. Both take a nickel-plated sidearm from inside their jackets. They screw silencers onto the ends.

I duck back around the corner before they see me. There's a gun in the SUV and one at Josh's place. But right now, I'm unarmed. Part of the deal in public places.

I peer around the corner. One gunman nods at the other. They're going in.

11

As the men with guns step into the toilets, I come out around the corner. Dance music pulses through the dark walls. Red transitions into ultraviolet blue as I enter the toilets. It's a huge, square room. There are mirrors and marble sinks all the way round. The cubicles are solid oak, arranged in the centre of the room. Two rows of eight, back to back.

I can hear Josh from here. Him and the girls. Laughing, yelling, having a bloody three-way? Either way, the two gunmen are lining up to kick the cubicle door in. Without thinking I race forward and tackle the bigger one to the floor. He lets off a muffled round into the ceiling. We roll and wrestle for the gun. The other guy tries to shoot me. I kick the gun from his hand. It slides across the cool, white tiles. It's kicked under one of the basins by a pissed-up woman in red, blind to everything as she staggers out.

I angle the pistol at the smaller gunman and shoot him in the arm. It's only a flesh wound, but it gives me time to elbow his mate in the face.

I think I've got his weapon, but I lose it under a cubicle

door.

Before I can kick the door in and get it, the bigger guy is up on his feet. He pushes my face into a different door and my arm up my back. I hear Josh on the other side. Yep, definitely getting his end away with one of those girls.

Why is someone else always having a better time than me? I dunno. And no time to ponder the bigger questions in life. The burning issue is the smaller guy pulling a blade from a trouser pocket.

So I do the only thing I can do—nut the bigger one with the back of my skull. He groans and backs off.

As the smaller one lunges with the blade, I spin-punch him in the throat.

He spits blood.

I grab his wrist and plunge the blade into the bigger guy's guts. It sticks in there good. The guy cries out. I boot the smaller one in the chest. He slides on his back across the tiles.

A cubicle flushes and a young woman in a tiny blue dress steps out. She holds the bigger guy's gun in a limp grip by the butt. "Uh, is this yours?" she asks.

I snatch it off her. Push her back in the cubicle, shut the door and whirl around to take aim at Josh's would-be assassins.

But damn. They're already on their way out of the door. One holding his throat and the other with the knife in his guts. He leaves a trail of blood on the tiles.

On the other side of the cubicle, the action reaches a crescendo.

I slip the weapon in the back of my waistband and pull my jacket over the top. I usher the woman in the blue dress out of the cubicle and tell her it's alright. She walks out of the toilets on wobbly legs.

I rinse the blood off my hands in one of the sinks. I realise there's a towel guy stood to my right, frozen stiff and staring wide-eyed. He's a slip of a young guy with a thin goatee. Middle-Eastern in the usual all-black uniform. He stands flat against one of the sinks, towels gripped tight to his chest as if they stop bullets. He hands me a towel. His hand shakes.

I nod and thank him. Dry my hands off on the towel. Pure Egyptian cotton. Nothing but the best at Infinity.

As I'm drying my hands, there's a flush from inside Josh's cubicle.

Like they're fooling anyone.

The door opens and Josh struts out. The brunette arranging herself and the blonde wiping powder off the end of her nose. They stroll up to the sinks as if nothing happened.

"Charlie," Josh says with a million-dollar smile—all forgiven. "How you doing, man?"

"Not as good as some people," I say tossing the towel in a laundry bin under the sinks.

While Josh checks his hair in the mirror, the girls top up their lipstick.

"Your fly's down," I say.

"Oh shit," Josh says, zipping up.

"How about we take this party home?" I say, nodding towards the girls. "Hell of a lot more comfortable than a cubicle."

"Great idea," Josh says. He leans into me and lowers his voice. "Plus, we're running low on, um—"

"Say no more. Follow me."

Josh corrals the girls away from the sinks.

"What's all this blood on the floor?" the brunette says.

"Guy had a nosebleed," I say.

"One hell of a nosebleed," the blonde says.

I open the door slow and peep out.

Josh laughs. "What are you expecting, a bullet to the head?"

"Just doing my job," I say.

"You need to chill out," Josh says, following me out. "You're getting paranoid."

I lead us into the cloakroom where there's a secret side exit out into a back alley. I hurry the three of 'em up as far as the underground car park.

"You okay to drive?" I ask Josh.

"Course, I'm wired, bro," he says, jumping in his car.

"Yeah, that's what I'm afraid of," I say.

"Just try and keep up," Josh says, as both girls squeeze into the passenger seat of the Ferrari.

I follow behind in the SUV. On the way home, I get a chance to process the bathroom encounter. Those guys had to be Carlos' men. Had to be. But why go after Josh instead of me?

Maybe Josh was the easy target. The first on the list. A way for Carlos to swing his dick without going head to head with me.

Buck had told me at the party there were others being rinsed and squeezed for cash. It could've been a warning to every other celebrity in this town. The biggest earning A-lister takes a bullet? That's one hell of a warning.

Josh shows off on the way home. Slowing down, then speeding up to make the Ferrari's engine crackle and roar and pin those girls back in their shared bucket seat.

I cruise behind, giving the lad some space. I see a white Range Rover again, a few cars back and a lane over. I remember the plate this time. It's the same one. And it's *definitely* following us.

12

Josh evens out his pace as we drive up into the hills. I stay tight to his tail, acting as a blocker. One eye permanently glued to the rear view mirror.

We wind our way up the tight roads. The Ferrari corners like it's on rails. I still think the kid's gonna get himself killed one of these days, driving high as a kite like that. But for now, Carlos and his crew are the bigger danger. I'm convinced it's them, the beam of the Range Rover's headlights no more than a hairpin bend away.

We roll in through Josh's mansion gates. The garage is open across from the house. We pull around the fountain in a circle and ease into the garage alongside each other.

I'm straight out of the SUV, opening the passenger door of the Ferrari and pulling the girls out. They piss and moan about being manhandled. Tough shit. I push 'em out of the garage and grab Josh by the arm.

I hurry 'em along to the house. I double-back and check the driveway. The gate is closed. No one got in. I return to the house and shove the three of 'em away from the front door. I snatch the key fob to the Ferrari out of Josh's hand.

"What's up, Charlie?" Josh says.

"Nothing," I say. "Gonna give you some privacy. Drive around. Take a look over the hills. Don't mind if I have a go in the 458, do you?"

"Go ahead," Josh says, as the girls walk and gawp around the house.

"Have fun," I say, pulling the door closed and locking it behind him the good old fashioned way. I see Josh through the glass. He shrugs and grabs a girl in either arm, steering 'em towards the stairs.

I jog over to the Ferrari, climb inside and slide the seat right back. I start the engine and back it out of the garage. The security gate slides open to one side and I drive out fast, headlights on full-beam. The white Range Rover is parked up over the road just twenty feet down. I blast past, driving like Josh. But as I pull around a bend heading down the hill, I tap the brakes.

Sure enough, the Range Rover appears in the distance.

I keep driving.

The Range Rover keeps following.

Into the city we go, hill roads giving way to multi-lane highways. We hit a stop sign. I let the Range Rover close the gap. Then I pull to the right onto the main streets. I cruise along, the Range Rover no longer keeping its distance.

That's a good sign. They think I'm Josh.

I run through my options. I know the perfect place. Down by Grant's Auto Deals, where only a week ago, I was cleaning cars. So I step on the accelerator and burn away from the Range Rover. The engine fires, the speed of this thing—*wow*. Even better with your hands on the wheel. I dab the brakes and pull off the street to the left. The Ferrari slows like it hit a wall and hugs the life out of the turn.

Grant's dealership is to the right of the street, the showroom lit up bright for the night and cars I polished gleaming inside.

To the opposite side is an underpass. Dark. Deserted. Ideal.

I pull up fast. Leave the engine running and the headlights on. I press play on the stereo. Dance music pumps out loud. I turn it up and climb out of the car and shut the door. Retreat into the shadows and sidestep along

Like usual, it's a warm night.

Petrol fumes fill the underpass. The muffled thud of the music and the hum of the V12 reverberate off the concrete walls.

I pull the gun from the nightclub fight from the waist of my trousers. I wait under cover of darkness.

The Range Rover rolls to a stop under a streetlight. It turns left into the underpass. The driver kills the headlights. It comes to a stop a few metres back, brakes creaking.

I stand against the wall of the underpass, between Ferrari and Range Rover, feeling the weight of the gun in my hand.

Feels like six bullets in the clip. I'll err on the side of four.

The rear doors to the Range Rover open. They close. Two figures walk past me towards the Ferrari.

One looks like the bigger guy from the earlier fight. The other I don't recognise, but cut from the same mean cloth.

They're close to the car now, pistols drawn from their jackets. Holding them close, barrels pointed at the floor. They split up and flank the Ferrari from either side. They nod at each other and pull the doors open.

They aim, ready to fire.

But pause.

Take a closer look inside the car. Straighten up. Look at each other confused.

I come out of the shadows. The two men see me and react, raising their weapons. I shoot the one on the left first. A flash of fire and he's down, a bullet to the sternum. The next one, no time to be accurate. I pull the trigger. Get him in the neck. He drops, letting off a round.

The bullet sparks off the underpass walls. The gunshots echo and I turn to take care of what's left. But the headlights on the Range Rover come on full-beam. They dazzle and blind.

The Range Rover lurches off the spot and pulls into the road. It comes straight at me at speed. I fire at the windscreen, driver-side, diving out of the way against the wall.

The Range Rover veers to the right and slams into the far wall of the underpass. I'm up and over in no time. Gun in front of me. Spots in my eyes.

Carlos is in the front passenger seat. His huge friend Mike lies dead against the wheel.

Carlos draws a pistol, but not in time. I point my weapon at him. It's empty, but he doesn't know that.

13

I turn off the music in the Ferrari. The headlights, too. I reverse it out and park it up on Grant's forecourt, slipping it between a pair of secondhand Buick saloons. I lock it up and jog back under the underpass. Me and Carlos go for a nice little drive in the Range Rover.

He's in the boot now, tied up with a handful of oily cloths I found in there.

One around the ankles, one binding the wrists and the other used as a gag.

There's another little place I know. I remember picking it out while riding the bus between jobs. A boarded-up warehouse I found myself thinking would be perfect for a business meeting.

Old instincts. Hard to let go of. And here we are. Inside the warehouse.

I drag Carlos out of the boot of the Range Rover and across the warehouse floor by the collar of his black silk shirt. It's buttoned low, revealing a fat gold chain over his hairy chest.

It must have been fate that I spotted this place. Serendipity. Whatever.

There's an old, rusting winch with a hook on the end of a thick metal chain.

Carlos shouts at me through the cloth in his mouth. Or at least he tries to. It all comes out in a muffle. I attach the cloth tie around his ankles to the end of the hook. The winch works on a pulley system. I yank the chain towards the floor and the hook travels upwards.

I pull on the chain hard. Carlos slides backwards across the floor and into the air, suspended upside down. I keep pulling on the chain until he's swinging back and forth—his head a few feet off the floor. He moans and groans through his cloth gag.

Is it okay to admit that I miss this? Probably not, but I do.

I pull out my gun. The muffled shouts grow louder. His eyes bulge and splinter into thin red veins in the corners.

"Don't worry," I say, ejecting the clip. "It's empty." I toss the clip away and tuck the gun back in my waistband. "So, Carlos. What am I gonna do with you?" I say, looking around the warehouse. "Hm, let's see, what have we got?"

The warehouse is semi-abandoned. Like someone left in a hurry and couldn't be arsed shifting the last dregs of random crap. I wander over to a corner that's full of junk. There are some old tins of orange paint and an empty coffee can. I bring a tin of paint over, along with the can. "Pretty sure this has got lead in it," I say. "You like the taste of paint?"

Carlos shakes his head.

"No, me neither. Still . . ." I take out a quarter and prising open the top. The smell knocks my head off. "Christ that's nasty. Okay Carlos . . ."

I pour the paint into the coffee can and pull the rag away from his mouth. A swarm of fuck yous escape from his mouth. I lift his head up by the collar so it's as if he's lying down. I hold the can over his mouth. He shakes his head and squeezes his lips together.

I pause with the can. "Ah, this isn't gonna work."

I let go of Carlos. He swings away. I put down the can and walk back to the pile of junk, where I also notice a couple of tools lying around. I pick 'em up and hold one in each hand.

"We've got a file and a Stanley knife," I yell back at Carlos. "Which do you want?"

"You're fucking crazy!" he shouts.

"That's what they say." I ip dip, dog shit it between the two. "Oh, I can't decide," I say, carrying 'em back over to Carlos.

I squat down so we can talk on the same level. "You choose."

"You're name's Charlie, right?" Carlos says.

"Over here, yeah. Back home, most people call me Breaker."

Carlos swallows. Which is hard when you're hanging upside down, believe me. "How much will it take, Charlie? Ten grand? Twenty?"

"You know how much the kid is paying me?" I say.

"Alright, forty. That's all I've got."

"You don't understand, Carlos. I'm not here to negotiate."

I grab hold of his head and bring the knife to his throat.

"You've no fucking idea!" he screams. "You think you can pull this shit in my town? I'm protected, motherfucker!"

"Not *that* well protected," I say, bringing the edge of the blade to the skin.

"Wait-wait-wait!" Carlos yells. "What do you want? You must want something."

"Nothing springs to mind," I say.

"Bullshit. Everyone wants something. What do *you* want?"

"I want you to leave Josh Speed alone. For good."

"Okay, okay, you've got it," Carlos says.

"And I want you to say sorry."

"Huh?"

"I want you to say sorry, Charlie."

"Okay, Charlie," Carlos says. "I'm sorry."

"And I want you to leave all the other movie stars alone."

"Hey, come on, that's none of your fucking—"

I raise my eyebrows.

"Fine," Carlos says. "I'll back off."

I get the impression he's lying, but in this game, there are no guarantees someone'll do what you want 'em to.

Carlos squirms like a worm on the end of the hook, his head blood-red and veins bulging. I'll have to let him down soon.

"Can you cut me loose now?" he says.

"Not just yet," I say. "I like to finish every business meeting with a song."

"A what—?" Carlos says.

"You know, a sing-song. I think I'm in the mood for some Britney Spears. "Hit Me Baby One More Time". Whenever you're ready."

"Go fuck yourself—"

I bring the blade back to his skin and cut a tiny bit into it. Carlos starts singing. Knows all the words. His voice is strained and breaking. He can't sing for shit. But to be fair to the bloke, he gives it a go. I let him get halfway through. I laugh and drop the knife. He stops singing and sighs in relief.

I step forward and belt him hard in the guts. He swings like a punchbag.

He coughs and fights for breath. "I thought you said . . . I thought we were done negotiating."

"We are," I say. "But that was business. This is pleasure."

I step forward and drive another fist in his ribs.

Okay, so I'm *still* not the nicest guy in the world.

14

I park the Ferrari in the garage and lock it up for the night. I walk across the courtyard, hoping Josh and those two girls have burnt off the cocaine and champagne and collapsed together in bed. I could really do with a quiet night's sleep.

I roll my neck and shoulders out, searching my pockets for my key to the house.

But a bang and a flash stop me dead in my tracks. I look up. Another flash of gunfire coming from the top floor of the mansion. I fumble the key into the lock. I run through the hall, bound up the stairs.

Have I been suckered? Did Carlos have another assassin ready to take out the kid?

Whatever the answer, there's no time to go for the weapon I've got stashed under my bed.

I head straight for the top floor. I hit the landing and hear screaming.

Josh and the girls.

Desperation in their voices.

As I sprint to the end of the hallway, there's another

gunshot. More screams from behind the double doors to the master bedroom.

Light breaks out where the door meets the frame. I skid to a stop on the polished floor. Try the handles. The doors are locked. I hang back a few feet and then charge the door on the left with a shoulder.

The door busts wide open. I expect to see one or more of Carlos' men. But there's only Josh and the two girls.

The girls cling onto each other on a vast, black satin-sheeted bed. They're naked, shaking, with white powder round their nipples.

Josh is on the far side of the room. A pistol in hand. He's naked with a raging hard-on, waving the piece all over the place, screaming at the girls. *"You fucking bitches!"* he screams.

He turns his attention to me. Waves the gun in my direction. I hold up my hands. Try and move out of range.

"What's going on?" I yell.

"One of these bitches made a fucking sex tape," Josh says, waving the gun at them.

They shriek and cower, backs pressed against the white leather headrest of the bed. Pillows caught underneath their arses and legs kicking out on the sheets.

"Just put the gun down, Josh," I say, advancing as slow as a man can go into the room.

He ignores my request. "Which one of you filmed it?" he says, aiming the gun from girl to girl. "Which one of you was it?"

"We didn't do anything!" the brunette says.

"You're fucking psycho!" yells the blonde one.

"Shut the fuck up," Josh says. "You're fucking dead!"

"Josh," I say, taking another couple of soft steps over the thick cream carpet. "Come on, pal . . ."

"Did you upload it already?" Josh says, snatching the brunette's phone from her hand. "Did you upload it, huh?" Josh fiddles with the phone. "Fuck, it's locked," he says, frantic. "What's the fucking code, bitch?"

The brunette shakes her head. Shocked into silence.

"What's the fucking code?" Josh screams. He fires the weapon. A giant glass vase explodes off a chest of drawers to the right of me. I duck and cover as I'm peppered with tiny shards.

The girls shriek some more. The blonde starts to cry and begs him to stop. I keep moving forward, trying to stay under Josh's radar. Trying to get close enough.

But that trigger finger isn't just itchy. It's got fleas.

He goes crazy, tossing the phone to the floor and trying to stomp it to bits.

But he's doing it on a luxury cream carpet that's at least an inch thick.

"Why won't it break, damn it?" he says, tears in his eyes and sweat pouring off his forehead.

The girls look at me as I cross the foot of the bed. I put out a hand to let 'em know it's okay. It's not okay, but I'm trying to calm things down. Put some low energy into the room.

"Hey Josh, why don't we sit down and talk about this?" I say. "The girls aren't going anywhere. I'm sure we can work something out."

"Work something out?" Josh says, pacing up and down in front of the windows—one window open and the drapes flapping in the hillside breeze.

"Karen didn't film anything," the blonde says.

"I didn't," Karen, the brunette, says. "You're imagining things."

Josh strides back towards the girls. I move fast and get in

between, my back to the bed. "Alright girls," I say. "Let me do the talking."

"I'm not imagining things, Charlie," Josh says.

"I know you're not, Josh, but you've gotta give me the gun."

"They filmed it," Josh says. "When I had my back turned. I saw 'em in the mirror, across from the bed."

"Don't give me the details," I say. "Just give me the gun."

"They're parasites, all of them," Josh says. "Sucking and chewing and gnawing on my soul."

"I know, Josh," I say.

"No you don't," he says. "You don't know what it's like around here. Everyone wants a fucking piece." As Josh spits out the words, his eyes dart from left to right. They fix on me. "Everyone except you, Charlie." He waves the barrel of the gun at me. "You don't seem to want anything." Josh cocks his head, and the gun. "What's your play?"

"My play?"

Josh takes a step towards me. "Don't act dumb, asshole. What's your play? Who do you really work for? Buck? Solomon? You seemed pretty tight with them at the party the other day." Josh breaks into laughter. Like a maniac. He taps the side of his head with the barrel of the gun. "That's it, isn't it? You're an inside man." His attention darts around the upper corners of the room. "Spies and cameras and little fucking drone worms with fibre optic cameras everywhere."

"Josh, look at me," I say.

He does. Re-targets the gun at me, too.

"I work for you, remember? Now give me the gun and I'll make all this go away."

"What do you mean?" Josh says.

"The girls," I say.

Josh pauses, weapon trained on my chest. His face relaxes. "What are you saying?"

"I'll make 'em disappear."

"I'm not paying these bitches off, Charlie."

"No, I mean, *disappear*."

The girls whimper behind me.

"My job is to protect you," I say. "Whatever that takes."

"But, how would you—"

"It's better that you don't know," I say. "Now give me the gun and let me do it."

Josh waivers a moment, but he steps forward and hands over the piece.

I bring it down to my side, barrel pointed to the carpet. "Go and wait outside."

Josh points towards the sliding window. "What, out there?"

"Around the corner," I say. "This won't take long."

"You're really gonna do it," Josh says. "But, I dunno, Charlie, I mean—"

"I'm not asking," I say, pointing the gun at him. "Outside."

Josh walks gingerly out onto the balcony. He disappears around the corner. I turn towards the girls. They lie there frozen in terror. Too afraid to move, to run. I stand over 'em with the gun.

15

I eject the clip from Josh's piece, open a bedside drawer and slide the gun and clip inside. I turn my attention back to the girls.

"What are you gonna do with us?" the blonde one asks, wide-eyed and shivering.

"I dunno yet," I say. "I'm not gonna kill you. But I need you to tell me honestly. Did you make a film?"

They shake their heads.

"I took a selfie, that's all," Karen says.

"Just you in the shot?" I ask.

Karen nods.

"Show me," I say.

I pick up Karen's phone and hand it over. It's still intact from Josh's failed stomping. She unlocks the screen and scrolls through to a picture. "Here," she says, offering it to me.

I grab it off her. There's a photo of her duck-facing into camera, only her head and shoulders visible. A hand pushing her hair up the side of her cheek. All very tasteful and no Josh in shot. I scroll through her other photos.

"And for the record," Karen says. "Chad tried to cheat on me with my roommate."

I hand back the phone. "I don't give a shit, love . . . Now stay here while I talk to Josh. And put some bloody clothes on."

I step out onto the balcony. Josh is nowhere to be seen. The balcony leads around the back of the house to the sun deck. As I come around the corner, I see the pool lit up a pale-blue. And Josh's naked body floating limp in the water, arms out and head under the surface.

I break into a run, hurdle over a sun lounger and dive into the water.

I swim into the middle of the pool and pull the kid up and out.

He gasps.

I drag him towards the side of the pool. He fights me all the way. Puts his face back under. I stop and pull it out by a handful of sopping wet hair.

"What are you doing?" I say.

"Fuck off, man, I'm trying to kill myself."

Josh sticks his head under again.

And again, I pull his head out. He gasps, coughs and spits out a mouthful of water.

"No you're not," I say.

"Yes I am," he says, trying it again.

In the end, I grab him by the neck and push him to the edge of the pool. He thrashes around, swings at me. Strong little bugger. But I lift by the armpits and push him up onto the edge of the pool.

His body slaps wet on the stone floor. As he catches his breath, he starts to blub. I haul myself out of the pool, a few kilos heavier thanks to the water cascading off my suit.

I sit on the edge and push the water off my face. "You prat. Why are you trying to kill yourself?"

Josh lies in a foetal position, staring at the floor. "I used to be a good person. I used to live on a farm. Milk fucking cows. Now look at me. I'm a fucking monster. I deserve to die."

"No you don't," I say.

"I'm a murderer, Charlie. Those girls are dead 'cause of me."

"Yeah, well, they're not dead, are they?"

"They're not?" Josh says, looking up at me.

"Of course not, you pillock. I just said that so you'd give me the gun."

"How do I know you're not lying?" Josh says.

"Come on, I'll show you."

I get to my feet and pull Josh up onto his.

I grab a white towel off a nearby sun lounger and throw it at Josh. I point at his hard-on. "Cover that thing up, will you? It's freaking me out."

Josh wraps it around his waist. In spite of everything, his chap is still hard and pokes through the towel.

"It won't go down," he says, staring at it. "I mashed up some coke and Viagra."

"Yeah, 'cause Viagra's exactly what you need," I say, leading the way.

We step back into the bedroom, wet footprints on the carpet. The girls are busy pulling on their dresses, still shaken by the experience.

"See," I say. "Alive and quivering."

"Thank God," Josh says, swaying on the spot. "I feel funny," he says.

His eyes roll.

His body goes limp.

He drifts to one side and flops onto the carpet.

I drop to my knees, roll him into the emergency position and insert my fingers into his throat so he doesn't swallow his tongue.

"Josh?" I say, slapping him on the face. "Come on, Josh." I check his pulse. His breath. Still alive. Still breathing. But his heart is galloping like a Grand National winner.

I pull my phone out of my jacket pocket. Thank Christ I bought the waterproof one. I open my wallet and thumb out Buck's business card. It's close to falling apart into mush, but I can still read the number.

I call him up. He answers eventually, sleepy. "Who is this?"

"It's Charlie. I think Josh might have OD'd."

"I'm on my way," Buck says.

16

The bedroom is a mess. Glass peppering the carpet. Girls on the edge of the bed and Josh on the floor, with his head on a folded-up towel.

Buck and the doc were round in a heartbeat. I was gonna call an ambulance. Buck said not to bother.

"It's not my first wake-up call," he says, as the doc gives Josh a dose of smelling salts. "And it probably won't be the last."

Buck sighs, resigned to his fate.

Josh comes around. Looks at the doctor, at Buck, the girls, the bedroom and me. "Fuck, what did I do?"

Me and Buck pull him to his feet. We sit him in an armchair by the bed. I pour him a glass of water from a jug Christine brought up. Josh takes a sip, still fragile.

The doctor is in his sixties. A trim, tanned man with a white wisp of hair. He removes the stethoscope from his neck and tucks it away in his black leather bag. He's dressed in grey joggers and a sweater. Running trainers on his feet and sleep in his eyes. "It's nothing too serious," he says. "Probably caused by a lack of oxygen. Had he been breathing heavily before he collapsed, or had his airways been restricted in any way?"

"He was taking a dip,' I say. "Swallowed a little pool water."

The doctor looks me up and down. My suit still soaking wet.

"That's probably it, then," he says, unconvinced. "I'd suggest you get him in a car and drive him straight to Serenity Valley."

"No, no rehab," Josh murmurs, quiet and woozy.

"Driving him there will be quicker than a private ambulance," the doctor continues. "They'll give him some fluids and something to absorb the drugs. I'll check on him in the morning." The doctor looks across at the girls, perched on the end of the bed looking tired and drawn. "Anyone else in need of attention?"

"They're fine," Buck says, ushering the doctor out of the bedroom. "Christine's out in the hall. She'll take care of the bill."

The doctor slips out through the door.

Buck stands square of the girls. "Okay, cell phones."

Karen looks up at him. "What for?"

"You know what for," Buck says.

"I already checked," I say.

"How thoroughly?" Buck asks, taking Karen's phone off her. He's not scrolling long before he comes across something. He shakes his head. "Here," he says, angling the screen my way. There's a grainy, shaky video of Josh and the blonde girl, Lucy. They're going at it, doggy-style. It's no more than twenty seconds long, but you can clearly make out Josh's face.

I glance over at Josh. He's still too groggy to care.

"Shit," Buck says under his breath. "Please don't let it be viral."

I watch over Buck's shoulder as he checks the girl's social media accounts. There's no sign of the video.

As me and Buck breathe a sigh of relief, he pockets the phone.

"Hey," Karen says, groggy herself. "Give it back."

"You'll get it back when I'm ready to give back," Buck says. He turns and talks quiet to me. "I think we're in the clear. But I'll have a guy I know check through her accounts. Make sure she didn't post and then delete. Gotta cover our asses, you know?"

I nod. "Sure."

Buck reaches inside his pocket and pulls out a large wad of hundred dollar bills folded in a gold money clip. He slides off the clip and counts out a thousand dollars. He hands the money to Karen.

Lucy, the blonde girl, gets the same.

"What's this?" Karen says.

"A little spending money," Buck says. "Enough to help with the rent, your studies, a new pair of shoes. Nowhere near enough for a good lawyer. You know what I'm saying?"

Lucy shakes her head.

"We appreciate your silence," I say.

The girls seem to get it. Keep the story out of the media or face a lawsuit.

"Alright, scram," Buck says to the girls. "There's a woman outside who'll drop you off at home."

As the girls leave, taken in hand by Christine, Buck slides open a wardrobe door and comes out with a brown, pre-packed Louis Vuitton holdall. "I had Christine prepare it after the last time," he says. "He didn't even know it was in there."

I go soft and easy with the kid, lifting him off the bed by the arm and leading him out of the bedroom, being careful to steer him around the glass.

As we climb in the SUV, Buck is already on the phone, instructing the cleaners who look after the house. Seeing him in action, I've gotta admit, I have a whole new respect for the guy. I think we're gonna make a pretty good team.

17

Rehab. The luxury surrounds of Serenity Valley. A kind of reform school where burnt out stars are sent by their studios and record labels to get back in shape. The biggest star of 'em all sits up in bed. Pale, drawn, small in a pair of white pyjamas. He's sweating, squirming and puking it out. More cold turkey than the day after Christmas. But it's not too long before he's back on his feet again, shuffling around the clinic in his complimentary white dressing gown and slippers.

Of course, not only does Josh have to go through rehab —so do I.

For his protection. And maybe just so he's not the only one suffering.

I've got a room down the corridor from his. Not as big or fancy. Just a box with a bed, a tiny window that looks out onto the car park.

But on the plus side, there are three square meals a day and other things like a recreation area, a cinema, a gym and a pool. A bit like prison, really, except the food doesn't taste like cardboard and there's no one trying to stab or bum you in the shower.

The grounds are beautiful. Lawns, lakes and zen gardens. We go for walks around the place in the morning sun. Do the basket weaving and the meditating, which isn't as airy-fairy mumbo jumbo as I thought it'd be.

The spa and pampering session is a bit weird. Something about lying on a bed getting a facial. If my old gangland enemies could see me now . . . But the session I really struggle with is impulse control.

The resident shrink reckons Josh has an addictive personality. He has a tendency towards compulsive behaviour.

The shrink reckons it's part genetic and part chemically induced.

Whatever the reason, I end up sitting in a semi-circle in front of a session leader, listening to the problems of various A, B and C-listers. We're sat in an atrium. Light pouring in. Big wooden fans spinning slow and silent overhead. Tall plants creeping up the walls. And wicker chairs with thick cushions which some of the assembled crowd cross their legs on.

Everyone cradles a mug of something or other in hands, except me.

I asked for a cup of tea, but they only had that herbal stuff that tastes like you're drinking a cup of pissed-on flowers.

So I said I'd settle for a coffee.

But caffeine isn't allowed. Too much stimulation.

So I said I'd have a pint. That was out of the question too. Turns out everyone's part of the same twelve-step program and you can't put anything in front of 'em that might tempt 'em.

So I sit and listen, chewing on a stick of gum.

Josh talks about his ongoing fight with booze, drugs and more mood swings than Dr. Jekyll.

Others talk about other addictions. Fame, gambling, sex, violence, porn and prescription medication. Even social media likes and selfies.

They all talk until I'm the last one who hasn't said anything.

"Charlie..." the session leader says, turning in his seat to face me. His name is Brian. He looks like an old hippy, with long white hair, glasses, a baggy white linen shirt and beads around his neck.

I try to avoid his eye, but he's locked on like a heat-seeking scud.

"Is there something you'd like to share with us?" he asks.

"Oh, it's alright," I say. "I'm just sitting in."

"Everyone has to share something," Brian says. "That's the rule."

"Yeah, Charlie," says a big fifty-year-old black guy I recognise off comedy films.

"It's okay Charlie," a young blonde woman says. I know her from somewhere too. I think she's a pop singer. Looks different with her hair straggled and tied—plain, pale face free of makeup.

"I really don't struggle with anything doc," I say to Brian. "I have the odd pint now and then, but who doesn't?"

"What about mood swings?" Brian says.

"Yeah, but everyone gets arsey, don't they? Not like I'm an addict like you lot—" I stop myself. Realise I've put my foot in it. "Shit, sorry."

"It's okay Charlie," Brian says. "Addiction is a sliding scale. We all display signs of addictive behaviour."

"Like getting fish and chips every Friday?" I say.

"Yes, like fish and chips," Brian says, "Or anger ... What does it feel like when you get angry?" Brian asks me, acting like he knows me.

"What does it feel like?" I ask.

"Yes," Brian says.

"Well, usually I wanna lamp someone."

"Lamp someone?" Brian says.

"Yeah, you know. Deck 'em. Chin 'em. Spark 'em out." I look around the group. "But I only do it if it needs doing. It's not like I enjoy it." My mind drifts back a few nights, to Carlos. "Well, sometimes I do."

"And when you get these violent urges—" Brian says.

"I didn't say they were urges."

Brian rephrases. "When you find yourself in a violent situation, how do you express it?"

"Express it?" I say. "I'm not bloody Picasso."

"He means how does it come out?" the pop star says. "What do you use?"

The rest of the group make eye contact. They urge me on by the way they look at me.

I shift in my seat and check the corners of the ceiling for CCTV. "This isn't being recorded, is it?"

Brian shakes his head.

"Then I suppose, all kinds of ways," I say. "And all kinds of things ... Fists, feet, elbows ..."

"That's it," Brian says, "list them all, get it all out ..."

"Well, uh, I guess, guns, knives, baseball bats." I hear a few sharp intakes of breath, but I'm on a roll. "Cricket bats, tyre irons, belts, scissors, fire extinguisher, hot poker, giant bottle of champagne ... What are those things you use to moisten a bird in the oven?"

"Turkey baster," Josh says.

"Yeah, and a turkey baster. . . Everything but a cuddly toy." I let out a big sigh. "That felt pretty good."

The rest of the group exchange glances. They look away. One of 'em hard swallows. Another scratches his nose. The pop star pulls a face at the floor.

Brian clears his throat. "I think that wraps it up for today."

I've never seen a room clear out so fast. The door to the atrium swings shut, leaving me and Josh alone in our wicker armchairs. He looks at me and raises his eyebrows.

"Hey, he asked," I say.

18

We pull into the long, sweeping driveway of Silver Hills. It sits in Bel Air and is the home of a grand old white mansion lit up and crawling with celebrities and media. The driveway is lined by prim evergreens and lit by glowing white balls every twenty feet. The grounds are vast and the drive itself lined with limos parked up either side like we're on our way to a state funeral. Josh is in the 458. To my surprise, he bypasses the valets outside the mansion entrance and around to the far end of the vast gravel driveway. He parks the Ferrari on the end of a line of limos and supercars. I pull up alongside. I'm about to get out when the passenger door opens. Josh climbs in and shuts the door. He's back to his usual California glow, perfect hair and designer suit and tie combo. Though his right leg jigs a little and he breathes deeper than usual.

Outside the mansion, there's a red carpet, a pack of photographers and a couple of TV presenters with microphones and lone cameramen by their sides. Josh is the biggest name at the party. A showbiz fundraiser thrown by Art Solomon's wife to help disadvantaged kids.

It's Josh's first outing in public since his private meltdown. A gentle reintegration at a party with a strict ban on anything white and powdery—Solomon's orders.

"Everything alright?" I say.

"Yeah, just need a second," Josh says, psyching himself up.

"You sure you're up for this?" I ask.

"I'll be fine when I get in there," Josh says. He turns to me and looks me in the eye. "Thanks Charlie, for everything."

"It's part of the job."

"No it's not." he says. "You're the only one who gives it to me straight. Probably 'cause you're the only one who isn't trying to squeeze me for something. You don't know how rare that is. Or how much I needed it."

I take off my seatbelt. "You're a good lad," I say.

"You sure about that?" Josh says, shaking his head. "After the way I talked to you, I—"

"Listen, I've worked for some prize wankers," I say. "I mean, vicious fucking bastards. " I turn to Josh and put a hand on his shoulder. "You're not an arsehole, Josh. You've just gotta stop acting like one."

Josh nods and lets out a deep breath. "Okay, let do this."

We share a fist-bump and he gets out of the car.

Josh fastens a button on his charcoal blazer. He strides over to the red carpet that runs up the wide stone steps to the mansion entrance. I see him pose for shots, flashing a smile brighter than the chattering flash bulbs.

I walk around the side of the mansion and enter through a secretive door held open by a burly ginger guy. I show him my security pass and walk in through the staff entrance, straight into a grand kitchen where chefs prepare fresh canapés and waiters and waitresses zoom in and out with silver trays, picking up posh nibbles and tall, slim flutes of champagne.

I pick my way through the manic scramble to the rear of the kitchen, where a few other private security guys hang around. They're guarding Hollywood celebs too. And just like me, they've been ordered to give their A-listers some space in front of the cameras.

We hang around and talk for a couple of hours, picking off a big plate of leftover sandwiches with the crusts cut off and posh tarts and pastry envelopes. There's a kettle and some mugs so we can make our own brews. Better still, they've got proper tea bags here. None of that weird stuff that tastes of potpourri. I rest back against a counter top, sip on my mug of tea and look around the kitchen.

The madness has quietened down a little. But it doesn't stop a young waitress getting an earful from an ageing woman in a long gold dress and pearls. They enter the kitchen on the far side. I can't see properly because of other bodies in the way, but the waitress is a slim young woman with blonde highlights in her long, curly hair. They're arguing about something. The older woman's been in and out all night bossing people around. She must be in charge of putting on the show. She's furious about something and the girl seems to be at the centre of it. The girl's got her back to me, trying to explain something or other. The woman rants and raves. The girl grabs her coat and bag. I know a sacking when I see one. God knows, I've been on the end of enough of 'em.

I shake my head and go back to my brew. A few cold canapés later, my phone vibrates inside my jacket pocket.

I answer.

It's Josh. "We good to go?" he says.

"Done already?" I ask.

"Yeah, heading out of here now."

"Right behind you," I say, hanging up.

"That's me done," I say to the other security guys.

"Lucky bastard," one of 'em says. "I'll be stuck here to the bitter end."

I shrug, smile and leave through the side entrance. I walk across the impromptu car park, an empty space where Josh parked his Ferrari. I look around. Hear the familiar growl of the V12. See the tail lights in the distance at the far end of the driveway.

Typical Josh.

I unlock the SUV. The lights flash and I'm about to jump in and get going when I notice the front left has a flat.

Bollocks. Don't remember hitting anything. Must have been a slow puncture. I take out my phone and call Josh. It rings out. Goes to voicemail. I tell him to pull over and call me back. At least if he moans, I'll have left the message.

The best thing I can do now is change the tyre as fast as I can. So I run around the back and pull the equipment out of the boot. I remove my jacket and roll up my sleeves. I take out the spare—a full-size thank Christ. Next, I take off the trim and unscrew the lug nuts. Then, jack up the SUV. I pull the flat off and dump it on the ground. Pick up the spare and slide it on. I screw on the lug nuts, lower the SUV, tighten the nuts up good and replace the wheel trim. I throw the jack and the flat in the boot.

I'm behind the wheel in a flash, starting her up and pulling off along the driveway. I speed out of Silver Hills, connecting my phone to the Bluetooth. I call Josh up again.

No bloody answer.

I put my foot down. Yeah, I know he's heading up the hills and not like anything's gonna happen to him between now and home, but I've really got into the bodyguard mindset now. It's hard not to get jumpy when your client's out of your line of sight.

Especially when he's whizzing off into the night and not answering his phone. Although I have to admit, nothing new there. And the kid gets bored easy. Probably gave me twenty seconds to catch up and then gunned it.

I take the exit onto the road up into the hills—a lot of sections almost pitch dark. As the hill road snakes and rises, the twinkling city lights come into view. I'm halfway up on a clear stretch. No mansions—just trees, bushes and a low-lying steel barrier separating road from hillside.

The road narrows. No markings and barely enough room for two cars to get by each other.

I approach a steep hairpin turn up to the right. A speed limit sign saying twenty.

As I slow for the turn, something catches my eye.

Tyre tracks on the ground.

A missing section of barrier.

And are those taillights, over the edge, deep in the darkness?

I slam on the brakes. The SUV comes to an emergency stop. Shit, they *are* taillights. Someone went over the edge. I pull the SUV over tight to the left side of the road on the bend. I jump out and run to where the barrier oughta be. I peer down into the darkness.

It's a sports car on its roof. Taillights and number plate upside down. But I know that number plate upside down and backwards.

I break into a run down the hill. Slip to my arse on the rocks and dust. Pick myself up and control-slide my way down the steepest part of the slope, through long grass and thick, thorny bushes. And into a run as the hill flattens out and the terrain gets easier.

I make it to Josh's Ferrari. Round to the passenger side. The engine's still running, the driver window smashed and gone. Josh upside down in the seat, bleeding from the head and an arm draping loose out of the window.

The first thing I do is turn off the engine in case there's a fuel leak. The second thing I do is call Josh's name. He doesn't answer.

So my third act is to check his pulse. I didn't really need to. I've handled so many in my time, I can tell by the sight of a body if it's dead or not.

Even more by the temperature of the skin.

No pulse and no breath.

I'm too late.

Josh is dead.

19

The Ferrari cabin is all bent out of shape. The steering wheel column shunted out a foot and tight to Josh's chest. It'll be hard to get him out of there, the way everything's twisted. His body included.

But that doesn't stop me grabbing hold of the driver door. I pull with everything I've got, over and over and over. The best I can do is prise it open a couple of inches.

It's no good. The damn thing is stuck fast. It'll take the jaws of life to get it open. They'll have to flip the car and cut the poor lad out.

I rise to my feet and bang at the car in frustration.

I lean against the Ferrari and hang my head.

This is all my fault. I should've insisted we drive in the same car.

Should have spotted the flat earlier.

But why didn't you wait for me, Josh?

Why did you have to drive everywhere like a maniac?

I wonder whether he was lying to me. Whether he was drinking and snorting behind my back at the party. Was that why he wanted his space?

Fuck!

And just when the kid was pulling himself together.

I work on pulling *myself* together. I look out over the city. See and hear distant sirens wailing.

Gotta call it in.

I reach inside my pocket for my phone. Realise I've left the damn thing in the SUV.

As I set off up the rise, I notice a stranger further up on the hill, smoking a cigarette and watching my every move.

They toss the cig and jump in their car. As I run up the hill, the stranger's car heads back down the road, driving fast with only the right headlight working. It speeds off down the hill.

I scramble up the steepest part of the rise and back onto the road. I jump into the SUV and fire up the engine. I swing around one-eighty and set off after whoever it is I'm after.

As I turn on the headlights, a figure comes out of the bushes by the side of the road. A pretty mixed-race girl with blood all down her front and shock all over her face.

It's only a flash. Did I imagine it? I can't make out shit in my rear view and I'm not gonna stop. Instinct tells me the stranger had something to do with the crash. A hit and run? Too suspicious to let 'em get away.

I give it beans down the hill road. It twists and turns tight through residential streets. The SUV wants to roll. I fight it, swerving between cars parked up on the side of the road.

A white Mercedes comes the other way and we almost collide head on. I brake and squeeze through the gap at the last second. I pull around a tight, blind bend curving to the left and accelerate down a straight stretch of tarmac.

I see the stranger's car ahead. At least I think it is. I wind down my window and listen out. Yeah, that's the same one. The same roaring engine. Don't get many road cars that kick out a noise like that one. I'd say it's been custom-tuned. Not your everyday road car. I wind up the window and settle down at a steady speed. Whoever it is in front, they don't know I'm the guy from the scene of the crash. And I'm not gonna give 'em reason to think that. All they're seeing is a set of headlights cruising a safe distance behind.

As we roll down the hill, I'm about to call 911. But flashing lights and wailing sirens are already on their way, blasting on by.

I'd bet any money they're headed for the scene of the crash—crime isn't exactly big around here. Which means someone must have noticed and called it in.

Maybe the stranger called it in. But why would they do that and then flee the scene? Maybe they felt guilty. They were involved but didn't want to stick around for a breathalyser and a day in court.

Either way, they're still fleeing the scene, and I'm not about to let 'em go that easy.

So I tail 'em down the hill. We come to a T-junction. The stranger heads right. So do I. They take a left turn. Me too. We cruise for another half a mile, then . . . *bang*.

They accelerate away, catching me cold.

Shit, that car is fast, too, whatever the hell it is. There's no plate or manufacturer's badge and I don't recognise the back-end. Only that it's a modified saloon with fat tyres and twin exhausts. And that it looks a dark-grey under the occasional streetlight.

I step on the accelerator and give chase. The road winds down the hill. More tight bends. I brake hard into each corner, the SUV skidding sideways on a bend that snakes right to left. The stranger can bloody well drive, I'll tell you that. But I keep 'em in my sights as we fly towards a crossing highway.

I wonder if he'll stop for the lights.

Fat chance, Charlie.

His brakes light up, but he sails through a dead-ahead red and makes a hard right onto the highway. A car switches lanes at the last second and leans on the horn as it cuts around him.

I bust through the red as well, but without slowing down early. I spin the wheel and slide into the turn.

I slide a little too far.

Make that a lot too far.

Into some oncoming traffic in the opposite lanes. I swerve around a truck and a car and pull back onto the right side of the highway, heart like the clappers and hands sweaty around the wheel.

But I make up vital ground. I'm right on the stranger's tail now, with traffic ahead stopping him from pulling away.

Yet there's not much I can do until we stop and get out of our cars. Not like I can ram 'em off the road. They know that. I know that. That's why they filter through a set of lights in a line of cars heading left.

The further towards the centre of the city we go, the denser the road system and the heavier the traffic. After a couple of minutes cruising, the stranger pulls out of line and around the cars in front. I react and do the same. We cut through a narrow gap between traffic passing in either direction, large office buildings on either side of us now, everything the colour of streetlights.

The car steers right between a pair of glass buildings.

I make the turn as well. But there's a woman crossing the side road to my left. I brake and swerve around her as she steps out. I bump up on the kerb as

I turn in. It costs me time. I lose sight of the car in front, but there are only two ways the road goes. One is a gated delivery entrance straight ahead. The other, the opening to an underground car park, glowing with yellow light to the left.

I turn into the car park and down a ramp.

The car park is swish and only a third full. The tyres of the SUV squeal as I drive between rows of cars. I slow the SUV and wind down my window. I listen for the sound of the other car's engine. The screech of its tyres. The car park spans out long and wide, all on a single basement.

I roll at a snail's pace under the dull light of the car park. Hear a squeal of tyres in the distance, to the right, beyond a double line of cars. I accelerate fast to the end of the row, brake hard and turn right, then right again, into the next aisle. But there's no sign of a dark-grey car.

So I roll again, looking left and right for anything that might resemble that car. I see nothing. Have they left already? Did I miss 'em somehow?

I drive to the end and pull a couple of left turns, into the next aisle along. I creep towards the end, scanning both ways. It's darker in this part of the car park. A couple of the lights on the blink. I hear the squeal of tyres echo deeper into the car park. An engine with a powerful sound.

I step on the gas and chase the sound down. As I'm heading for the far end, I catch sight of a car coming out behind me in the rear view. A deep growl. A dark-grey rear without a plate.

I slam on the brakes. The car in the rear view accelerates away, engine roaring. I slam the stick into reverse and back up the SUV as fast as it'll go, gearbox whining.

The stranger turns right at the end of the aisle. I brake and make the turn, too. The stranger then screeches left and up the exit ramp. I follow close behind, but in reverse. I fly up the ramp and bump out onto the road. I step on the brakes, stopping inches short of the building across the side road. The stranger pulls away, turning right, back onto the main drag.

I switch gears and take off front-ways. I make it to the main road, but a white box truck cuts across my path.

I slam on, pull out behind and then accelerate around the damn thing.

But as I do, I see the one-headlight car flying down the road in the opposite direction.

Shit, they did a U-turn at the lights. I get caught up at 'em. Wait for a red to go green and then do the same U.

Yet by the time I get a mile down the road, the stranger is gone.

20

The stretch of road is closed. Lights, cones, police tape and a cop in uniform standing guard with a torch, turning the traffic around.

I ditch the SUV short of the scene of the crash and walk up the hill.

"Sorry Sir," the pig in uniform says. "The road's closed, you'll have to follow the diversion signs back there."

Note to self—I must stop calling 'em pigs. They're not the enemy anymore. Even if I don't like 'em any more than they like me.

"I'm the bodyguard," I say.

"Whose bodyguard?" he says.

"The young lad you've got down the hill," I say. "Josh Speed."

The pig—I mean, police officer, shines his torch up and down me.

"You don't have to play dumb," I say. "I'm not with the media. I was the first on the scene. Well, one of 'em. I might have some information."

The copper eyeballs me a few seconds. Talks into a radio

on his lapel. "Sir, I've got a guy here. Says he's the deceased's bodyguard. Says he might have some information..."

"Yeah, let him through," a guy says on the other end of the radio.

The police officer steps aside. I stoop under the tape and walk by an ambulance, fire truck, two squad cars and an unmarked silver Ford with a flashing blue and red light on the parcel shelf. A pair of detectives stand in grey suits. They look down the hill, where a CSI team works, a fire crew standing by with the jaws of life, ready to cut the poor bastard out of the Ferrari.

One of the detectives, a rangy dark-haired guy with thick sideburns and a face with deep creases, peels a pair of white latex gloves off his fingers. The other, a trim, cleancut black guy around five-eleven, smokes the end of a cigarette.

They turn to me as I approach.

"You the kid's bodyguard?" the guy with the sideburns asks.

"Yeah," I say, staring down the hill, still kicking myself for letting all this happen.

"I'm Detective Roach," he says. "This is Detective Thomas."

"You said you had information," Thomas says, ditching the cigarette butt. He breathes a last sigh of smoke and pulls a notebook and pen from a blazer pocket. He clicks open the pen. "You see anything?"

"Just the aftermath," I say. "I got here just before you guys."

Roach folds the gloves over one another into a ball. Shoots me a look. "Then where the hell have you been?"

"Yeah, and why didn't you call it in?" Thomas says, making a note.

"I was gonna," I say. "But there was someone up around the next bend, standing and watching."

"Looking down at the crash scene?" Thomas says.

"Yeah," I say.

"What were you doing down there?" Thomas asks.

"Trying to save the kid's life, what do you think?" I shake my head. "I was too late, but the point is, there was someone watching up there. Smoked a cigarette, got in their car and drove down the hill."

"And?" Roach says.

"And I went after 'em, but they gave me the slip."

"You chased someone downtown for smoking a cigarette?" Thomas asks.

"They were watching me," I say.

"No crime in watching someone," Thomas says.

"Besides," says Roach. "People stop and stare at auto wrecks all the time."

"Who knows, maybe he was some sick fuck jerking off up there," Thomas says, "like in that movie..."

"Or maybe they were involved somehow," I say. "Can't hurt to check it out."

"Okay then," Roach says. "You get the plate?"

"Uh, no, it didn't have one," I say.

"The make of the vehicle, then?" Thomas asks.

I shake my head. "They must have peeled that off, too."

"Before or after the cigarette?" Roach asks.

Thomas consults his notes. Reads from his own scrawl. "So we've got a stranger in the night smoking a cigarette and driving a car with no make, no plate and only one headlight."

"Which they could have picked up in a collision with Josh's car," I say.

"Or which could have been sustained anywhere," Roach says.

"Added to the fact this was clearly an accident," Thomas says.

"What makes you so sure?" I ask.

Roach points to the tarmac behind us. "Skid marks on the road. A broken barrier. A young kid going too fast in a car he can't handle on a hairpin notorious for fatalities. You don't think we know an accident when we see one?"

"The other driver could have gone into him," I say. "Could have rammed him off. That would explain the broken headlight on the left of the car."

"And where's the glass?" Thomas asks, whirling around on the spot.

I scour the road. "It's dark," I say with a shrug.

Thomas produces a torch from an inside jacket pocket. He flicks it on. Raises an eyebrow. Flicks it off again.

"We already checked the road," Roach says. "No sign of anything other than tyre tracks."

I stare at the crash site. "Then why does anyone flee the scene like that? They ran a red just to get away."

"Oh, I don't know," Thomas says. "Maybe 'cause they were being followed by some random guy and wanted to get away?" He looks up a few inches at me. "You're not exactly Bambi." Thomas writes something on his pad. "But I'll make a note of it anyway." He looks up at me again. "You know where Speed was coming from?"

"Yeah, a fundraiser at Silver Hills, run by Art Solomon and his wife."

"He had a drink?" Roach asks. "Maybe something stronger?"

"Not that I know of," I say. "He's only been out of rehab a week."

Thomas makes a note of it.

"Oh, and I forgot to mention," I say. "There was a girl out here wandering around the hill roads, covered in blood."

"Did Speed have a date for the fundraiser?" Thomas asks.

"No. Definitely not."

"Probably a domestic," Roach says to Thomas. "Or a coked-up hooker. Who knows?"

"You wouldn't believe some of the shit that happens up here," Thomas says to me.

"Oh, I believe it." I say.

"I'll put it in the report," Thomas says, making another note. "What did you say your name was?"

Before I can answer, a blast of light and rotor noise fills the air. The three of us cover our eyes and look overhead. It's a news chopper. Channel 9. It hovers over the crash site in a circle.

"Ah shit," Roach yells. *"Someone fuckin' leaked it."*

I step out of there before they ask my name again. Not too hard for them to find out my assumed persona, but I don't see why I should lend 'em a hand. Besides, I'm not a big fan of having my face plastered all over the TV news channels. By the time they turn around again, they'll be talking to fresh air.

21

I stir awake after a horrible night's sleep. I lie under the luxury white cotton covers, hoping it was all a dream. A nightmare. At first I think it is. Then I turn on the flatscreen on the wall and watch the breakfast news.

Joshua Speed Dead in Horror Crash. That's the headline and it isn't going away.

Reporters stand in front of police tape only a couple of miles away from Josh's home. Helicopter footage shows the crash scene at night. Police and fire units. CSI in white outfits scouring the hill.

I look out of the giant bedroom windows and see the dot of a chopper in the sky. It floats left and right in silence, the whir of the rotors blocked out by the soundproof glass. It'll be madness around here for some time.

I sit up and hold my head. An empty feeling. I pull off the sheets and force myself out of bed, into the luxury shower. I dry and dress and wander around the house. Out onto the sun deck, around the pool, into Josh's room, along the hallways and downstairs.

I keep expecting the kid to come jogging through a door

with a chicken smoothie in hand. He doesn't. All that's left are ghosts.

Seeing Josh's face on those Nightburner posters on the wall doesn't help. Especially when they start talking to me from behind their masks.

"Why did you let me take the Ferrari?" the first one says in the deep growl Josh used to put on for the role.

"You knew I was fragile," the second Nightburner says.

"Where were you?" says the third Nightburner along.

I wanna talk back, but I keep walking. I know I'm hallucinating again. Roll on the appointment I've got with that renowned neuro specialist. It was arranged by Josh. Part of my healthcare package. I made up some bullshit about memory issues. Not in the habit of telling anyone I talk to the walls.

I find Christine in the kitchen, a tissue to an eye. She hides it behind her as I walk in to get a drink of posh mineral water from the fridge. She sucks up the faintest glimmer of a tear.

"You'll have to leave," she says. "Now that he's . . ."

"Don't worry, the last thing I wanna do is hang around here," I say, chugging on my water. "Place feels haunted."

"The second half of your fee is redundant now, I hope you realise that," Christine says.

I put the bottle down on a counter top. "Why, because I failed?"

Christine stares anywhere but at me.

"It's okay, you can say it. He was my responsibility."

She doesn't say it. Doesn't have to.

"Don't worry, I don't want the money," I say, finishing the water. I toss the bottle in the recycling. "I'll be out of here by ten."

* * *

I'M out earlier than ten, bag packed and keys handed over to Christine. I leave with the other staff after they're done cleaning the house and cutting the grass. We make our way across the courtyard and out through the gates to a sleek grey people carrier Christine arranged.

Efficient as always, even with her employer dead and gone.

Outside the house it's a feeding frenzy. Media all over the place. Flowers and messages laid out along the pavement, up against the perimeter wall. Superfans weeping and wailing and reporters talking into news cameras.

A couple of network choppers hover overhead. I slip on my Wayfarers and climb into the people carrier after the others. I slide the door shut and the driver nudges his way through the scrum at two miles an hour. It takes ten minutes just to clear the mess. And then there's the diverted route, still-heavy morning traffic and the drop-offs along the way.

All I wanna do is get home. Two hours later I get my wish. And when I trudge up the steps to my condo door and open it up to a tiny, stifled room, all I wanna do is get out of there.

So I go grocery shopping, grab the local paper. Look for another job. Don't need the money right now, I just need to keep busy. Move on. But it's hard when it's wall-to-wall coverage of Josh's death. On TV, on the internet, on the front page of all the papers. Crying tragedy. Tinseltown mourns. A week ago they were baying for the kid's blood. Now they act like they were his biggest supporters.

Then there's the Skype call with Cassie and Mandy to deal with. Both of 'em sit on Mandy's living room sofa, red around the eyes. Cassie sobs into her sleeves.

"I can't believe it, Dad. He's gone. It doesn't seem real."

"I know," I say, not knowing *what* to say.

I've never seen Cassie like this. Not since what's his name dumped her at age fourteen.

I've seen Mandy like this plenty of times, of course. Hamming it up. Getting her digs in. Where was I when the crash happened? Why didn't I check my tyres? Like she cares.

"Poor Jake," she says.

"You don't even know the bloody lad's name," I say.

"I might not know his name," Mandy says. "But I knew his soul."

I break into laughter. "Knew is bloody soul . . . What from, watching those Nightburner films?"

Mandy pulls a face at me.

"Thanks Mand, I needed that," I say.

"How can you laugh at a time like this?" Cassie says. "You should be in mourning. Are you going to the funeral?"

"I'm not invited," I say. "A-listers only."

Cassie shakes her head and pulls another tissue from a box. "What am I gonna do now?"

"You'll figure it out," I say, not wanting to tell her it's mass hysteria. The only explanation for a smart, got-it-together girl crying over a guy she never even knew.

"What are *you* gonna do now?" Mandy asks. "Get another job?"

"Dunno," I say. "I might do some digging."

"Roadworks?" Cassie says.

"No, *digging* . . . You know, look into Josh's death."

"What for?" Mandy says, forgetting she's supposed to be upset and shoving a crisp in her gob.

"Maybe the crash was an accident," I say. "Maybe it wasn't."

"What are you saying?" Cassie asks.
That's a good question. What *am* I saying?
The truth is, I'm not ready to say anything just yet.
I end the call and pull on my shoes.
I've got work to do.

22

The first place I head for is Grant's dealership. Sure, it's close by and convenient. But mostly, I wanna see the look on the guy's face. I walk in with the Ray Ban Wayfarers, the dark tailored suit, black tie, white shirt and expensive leather shoes Christine bought to spruce me up.

After all, when you're guarding a Hollywood star, you have to look the part.

I head straight for the red Chevy Camaro.

In the mob world, it'd be seen as ostentatious. Drawing attention. In these parts, it's called fitting in.

Besides, the money I'm spending is straight money. The old rules don't apply.

Grant hops up from behind his desk, ditching a half-eaten sub. He realises he's got a napkin tucked into his shirt at the last moment, rips it from his collar and screws it up in a pocket.

He doesn't recognise me in this get-up. "Hello Sir, how may I be of assistance?" he says with a big smile. One personality for his customers. A whole other one for everyone else.

I skirt around the car running my fingers over the bodywork I used to polish. I take off the shades. "I'd like to buy this car."

Grant double-takes. *"Charlie?"*

"Problem, Grant?"

"No, uh, you sure you can afford it? I mean—"

"I'll pay full price, in cash. How soon can you have it ready?"

"Uh, pretty much straight away," Grant says. "Just gotta do the paperwork."

Grant's been trying to shift the Camaro for over a month. But one of his former lackeys dropping back in to buy one of his showroom stars? He doesn't know whether to laugh or cry.

Still, he fills out the paperwork, I make the transfer and drive the Camaro off the forecourt, waving to Rakesh and leaving Grant scratching his head in my rear view mirror.

The Camaro has GPS. I find the Los Angeles County coroner's office in a part of town called Boyle Heights.

It's a grand, red-brick building with a steep set of steps leading up to the front doors. But I don't go in through the front. Instead, I park up along the side of the building and walk up to a black railed security gate. I hear a truck engine revving up behind, so I lean against the side of the gate and pretend to be on my phone.

After a minute or two, the gate creaks and slides open. As the truck drives out, I spin around the gate and into the delivery area.

I spot a side door open with a white box truck making a delivery. Yellow fluid in plastic see-through containers. A tall, skinny black guy stacking 'em onto a two-wheel trolley and a bald security guard who sounds Polish. He holds onto a clipboard and talks about basketball with the delivery guy.

I slip inside unseen, into a maze of corridors under artificial lights. There are two people in white coats chatting in the corridor. A man telling a story about the previous weekend. A woman throwing her head back and laughing.

I snatch the security badge and ID off the guy's belt. He doesn't feel a thing. Years of pickpocketing practice, when that was my level in life.

I follow the signs on the corridor walls to the morgue. There's a thick steel door that slides open into another corridor with a lift.

The only problem is, it's locked.

I notice there's a key attached to the security pass. I turn it in a keyhole on the door and the lift opens up. I ride it down to the crypt. As the lift descends, I take a tissue from my trouser pocket and tear off a piece. I roll it into a bud and wedge it up my right nostril. I do the same with the left.

Not that it makes a whole lot of difference. As soon as the lift door opens, I'm hit by the smell. And this is just the warm-up. I open another door into an area with a desk full of paperwork and an empty gurney. There's a giant steel door to my left, with a chunky green push button on the wall to open it.

I push it.

The door slides open to the left.

Boom, the smell really hits. And the cold, too. Like walking into a fridge full of rotting meat.

It's like a dead body warehouse inside. They're stacked high and wide, front to back. Toes with tags and naked as the day they were born, wrapped up snug in white plastic sheets. Rich or poor, famous or anonymous, they're all mixed in together now. And I don't think they have a pecking order as to who goes on top.

I reckon there's four hundred bodies in here, easy. I shake my head over the task in hand, only to see a gurney to my left with a body with tanned skin and a head of dark hair. I walk over to the gurney and check the toe.

It's Josh. And there's a report in a thin brown file resting on top.

I pull the sheet off the body. *Ah, Christ.* What a mess. There's more stitching on the lad than a leather handbag. Some of it's bound to be post-mortem, but they could've at least set his limbs the right way. I pick up the coroner's report and have a quick leaf through.

And here are the highlights:

There's reference to a blunt trauma to the back of the crown, sustained during the crash. That would explain the head injury.

There's also mention of bruising around the neck. I take a closer look at Josh's body and find black and purple bruises around the front of his neck, including the throat.

Strange, but the report seems to breeze over the head trauma and the bruising.

Maybe 'cause there are so many other injuries to the body. You've got fractures, lacerations, broken bones and a twisted spine. Whether Josh died from internal injuries or external blood loss, the report doesn't seem too clear. He had an eight-inch shard of glass sticking out of his chest, so it could've been either.

What it does conclude is that his death was accidental and occurred almost immediately—either during the crash or seconds after it. I pull out my phone and take a few snaps of the report. I do the same with the body. I move to cover Josh up with the sheet.

"Hey, you. What are you doing in here?"

A man's voice. A stocky guy with grey hair and moustache in a purple shirt and glasses. He stands inside the door.

Bollocks. How do I explain this one?

23

"I ... I can't look at this," I say, throwing the sheet back over Josh's body. "They're not paying me enough for this shit."

"Who are you?" the man asks.

"Look at this," I say, motioning to the kid. "Now I know why they picked me to come down here. I thought I must've made a good first impression, being chosen to pick up Joshua Speed's belongings. *The* Joshua Speed . . . Always wanted to meet the guy. Then I end up on his security team and now here I am. Well, I guess I got my wish."

"Yes, and now I'm calling security," the man says.

"Please don't do that. It was an honest mistake."

"How do I know you're not breaking in?" he says.

"Why would I do that? No offence, but who would wanna break into a place like this?"

"You'd be surprised," the man says, picking up a phone on the wall.

"Hey pal," I say, "Go easy will you? It's my first week. They send me down here. I take a wrong turn. See the young lad's body . . . I thought maybe he had his phone and watch on him."

"On him?" the man says, pausing with the phone in hand.

I hold out my hands. "You tell me, I don't know how any of this works."

The guy hesitates, phone in hand.

I pull out my wallet and approach him, taking out a few notes. "Look mate, I'd really appreciate you turning a blind eye to this one."

"You trying to bribe me?" the man says, as if offended.

"I would never do that," I say. "I hate bribes. And the people who accept 'em."

"Yeah, me too," the man says.

"Just a little compensation for your time, that's all."

Now I'm closer, I get a look at the ID clipped to his waist. *Geoff Schulz. Medical Examiner.*

I'm thinking I picked the wrong guy to bribe. But he starts to wobble.

"I just wanna get the lad's stuff and get out of here," I say. "And don't worry, I didn't slip a finger up him or anything like that. I'm not one of those weirdos."

Schulz wobbles some more.

I blow air out of my cheeks, laying it on thick. "Boy, am I gonna get in trouble for this. And I need this job, too. What with my daughter's operation coming up . . ."

Yeah, I will sink that low.

I give Schulz a pleading look. He finally relents. He puts down the phone. I walk over and slip him the money on the sly. He takes it and trousers it. Next thing, he's leading me back to the upper levels and along a corridor. He opens a door and flicks on a light. It's a small, narrow room full of shelves. Every slot on every shelf is wedged full of brown envelopes.

All of a sudden, they start to beep. There's a few buzzes, blips and pings, too.

"What's that?" I say at the sound.

Schulz runs a finger across the ends of the envelopes. "Phones, watches," he says. "The watches are still set to mark the hour and the phones, they're still getting texts, calls, updates, you know?"

"Man, that's morbid," I say.

"You get used to it," Schulz says, his hand stopping on an envelope. "Here we go."

He pulls the envelope out of its slot.

I reach out to take it off him. He's about to hand it over when he pauses and pulls it in close to his chest.

"How do I know you're not some journo? One of those gossip bloggers? That your bodyguard story isn't phoney?"

I think for a moment and take my phone out of my jacket pocket. "Here, I'll prove it to you."

I call Josh's number. I hear his ringtone inside. It's the Nightburner theme tune. Bass drums and dark violins.

I hang up and the music stops.

"Alright," the guy says, handing the envelope over. "But you'll have to sign for it. Name and full address, relation to the deceased."

"Anything you want," I say.

He hands me the envelope. Then there's a separate clear plastic bag with the clothes and shoes Josh was wearing during the crash.

Schulz leads me into an office—a desk stacked with paperwork and metal filing cabinets either side.

He picks up a tablet. Hands it over. "Type your name and address in here," he says.

I tap in Grant's name and the address of his dealership, leaving out the name of the business. I gave Grant a fake name when I took the car cleaning job, so I know the cops won't be able to trace me from there.

"Sign with your finger," Schulz says, pointing to a new screen on the tablet.

I scribble out an illegible scrawl. Schulz leaves the tablet on the desk and offers to show me out.

"So, you examine *all* the bodies that come in here?" I ask as we walk through to the front reception.

"Some of them," he says.

"Did you examine Mr Speed?"

"Uh-huh," Schulz says. "Why?"

"Just that he had a knock on the back of his head. I noticed you put it down to the accident."

"Of course, the car flipped over several times."

"Funny, I'd have expected the injury to be to the front, or the sides of the skull," I say.

"Are you an expert in these matters?" Schulz says, fixing me with a raised, wiry grey eyebrow.

"No, I guess not."

Schulz frowns at me. "A person can sustain all manner of injuries from a crash like that."

"I guess you're right," I say, as Schulz walks me across reception to the main entrance.

He opens one of the glass doors and waits for me to leave.

I pause halfway out. "Can I ask you one more question?"

Schulz sighs. "Sure."

"The bruising around the neck..."

"No, that wasn't from the crash," Schulz says. "The bruising would have been sustained before."

"What do you think it was from?" I ask.

"You tell me," Schulz says. "You were on his security team, right?"

"Yeah, but I didn't notice the bruising before."

Schulz thinks a moment. "The police detective, um, Thomas I think it was. He mentioned the boy did his own stunts. Had he been filming that day?"

"Yeah, in the morning," I say. "Some action scene or other. Working a closed set."

"Then that would explain it," Schulz says.

"Surely I would have noticed," I say.

"It depends," Schulz says. "Bruising doesn't tend to show right away. And if he was at a public event, he may have had a make-up artist cover them up. You'd be amazed what they can do with people, dead *or* alive."

"But wouldn't you have found that on the skin?" I ask.

"Not after we'd cleaned off the blood," Schulz says. "Besides, he was wearing shirt collars on the night of the crash. That could have disguised the bruising if buttoned up high enough."

"Oh yeah," I say. "Guess that's possible."

Schulz looks at me suspicious. "What's your interest in all this?"

"I'll be honest," I say. "I'm a bit of a CSI nut. I like the procedurals, you know?"

"Everyone's a detective," Schulz says. "Goodbye."

He lets the door swing closed behind me. I walk down the steps and around the side to the Camaro. I dump Josh's stuff on the passenger seat and swing the car around. I find the nearest drive-thru. I order a chicken salad and a juice.

Yep, Josh may be dead, but some of his habits are still alive inside of me. My taste buds may be complaining but my waistline sure isn't. So I park up and eat, I take out Josh's phone. The screen is cracked, but it still works. There's life in the battery too. But just as I thought, the damn thing's locked by a numerical code.

I move onto his wallet and clothes, finding no signs of anything that might connect to a suspicious death.

What am I looking for, exactly? I dunno. But if you don't look, you don't find, as my mum used to say.

I finish my food and drive back to Grant's dealership. Rakesh's shift finishes right about now and there he is, by the bus stop.

I pull over.

"Need a ride?" I ask him.

"Wouldn't say no," Rakesh says.

"Then don't," I say.

I throw Josh's stuff in the back, except for his phone. Rakesh jumps in the passenger seat. We take off along the road.

"So what the hell happened to you?" Rakesh says, his usual toothy grin on his face.

"You wouldn't believe me if I told you," I say. "How's life under the regime?"

"Brutal," Rakesh says. "But not for much longer, my friend. I got a job in Silicon Valley. Software startup."

"Wow, finally," I say, slapping him on the arm. A little too hard. There's not much on him and he rubs it when he thinks I'm not looking. "When do you start?" I ask him.

"Next week," he says.

"Then why are you still here?"

"Need the extra cash for the flight," Rakesh says.

"How much are we talking?"

"I'm a hundred short," says Rakesh.

I pick up Josh's phone off my lap. "How would you like to finish a week early?"

"What do you mean, Charlie?"

"You know anything about phones?"

"Like what?" Rakesh asks.

I toss him Josh's phone. "Like how to crack a code, hack a voicemail account, that kinda stuff."

Rakesh turns the phone over in his hand. "If you're asking if I've done it before—no."

"I'm asking if you can figure it out."

"Sure," he says.

Rakesh lives in a condo the same as mine, only a five-minute ride from Grant's dealership. I pull up outside. "I'll give you three-hundred if you can get me inside that thing. Four if you can hack the voicemail."

"Give me a few hours," Rakesh says, getting out of the car.

"I'll pick it up when you're done," I say, pulling out of there.

Next stop: the scene of the crash.

24

The LAPD have moved on. The media, the fans, the gawkers and rubberneckers too. Now it's just a hill. Not just any hill. It'll always be the hill that Joshua Speed crashed his Ferrari on. Where he flew off the road and tumbled to his doom. In a few days, it'll be on the Hollywood star maps and stop-off spots where tourists can get off a bus and take a selfie. But right now, it's just a hill.

So I take advantage of the calm. I park the Camaro on the bend and walk slow along the side of the road. I'm looking for something specific. I don't find it. Not on the road, anyway. So I step over the barrier to the right of the broken section. I push my way into the bushes. I don't find anything in there either.

I walk a little further down the road. I step over the barrier and into the bushes again, pushing the long grass and leaves out of the way.

Huh, no signs of—Hang on. What's that?

Something catching the light. A fragment of something. I stoop and pick it out of a clump of grass.

It's a shard of glass. And not any old glass. It's frosted white. A piece of headlight for damn sure.

I hear the voice of Detective Thomas in my head. A broken piece of headlight by the side of a busy road. Could have come from any car, at any time, at any point in the last however many years.

I take his imaginary point. But I keep the glass anyway, carrying it back to the car. I wrap it in a dust cloth and tuck it away in the glovebox.

Returning to the road, I check out the skid marks the Ferrari made before it went over the edge. They're fat and long.

Obviously the kid knew he was in trouble. He must have slammed on hard. Yet I've been in that Ferrari and tested the brakes out for myself. They stop you dead in no time. That means the kid must have been going at a real click. And that's going uphill heading towards a bend. Yeah, I know he drove like a loon, but he knew the roads. It's almost like he was *trying* to kill himself.

Another thing about those tracks . . . They seem too straight to me. No left or right turn of the wheel. I back up and squat down behind the point at where the skid marks begin. I squeeze an eye shut and line up the tyre marks with the missing stretch of barrier, which I reckon must be little more than a car-length wide. Especially a wide car like the Ferrari.

I hold out an arm with my hand pointed flat down the centre of the black rubber tracks.

Interesting.

I stand and walk backwards from the end of the tyre marks, staying in line with the space between the two tracks. I keep going until I reach the edge of the road. My calves bump up against the barrier.

Just as I thought. The skid marks don't line up straight with the gap in the barrier. They head in a straight line, but the trajectory ends a foot to the right of the gap. You add the fact the tyre tracks end short of the edge of the road and things are starting to make a whole lotta no sense at all.

Did the kid turn left at the last second? Panic and lift off the brakes? Maybe he hit a patch of dust or dirt and slid the last foot or two.

I guess it's all possible.

I take out my phone and go on the internet. I bring up the Ferrari website and scroll through to the latest model of a 458, the one Josh was driving. The sales copy on the site says the car will stop from 62mph in thirty-two metres. I pace out the length of the tyre marks, toe to heel. A rough estimate gives me twenty metres.

That meant the car had to only be doing around forty at most. Nowhere near enough to lose traction or cause the kid to veer out of control. Not unless he was accelerating fast and then pulling on the handbrake.

You get instant bite on those tyres. Laying down rubber at that speed just doesn't make any sense.

I step to the side of the road as a dark-blue Bentley cruises by. I walk on the inside of the barrier, trampling over the long grass. As I reach the gap in the barrier, I notice the edge is smooth where the section is missing. Almost like it was cut. I walk across the gap and run a finger over the steel where the barrier starts again.

The steel was definitely cut. But maybe it was cut after a previous crash. The detectives did mention it wasn't the first fatality here.

Could mean something, could mean nothing.

I take a couple of photos of the tyre tracks and tread carefully down the stretch of hill. There are only a few fragments of debris left from the crash. Nothing of use. I look back up towards the road. Try to imagine the trajectory of the Ferrari before it went off the road. The nose must have dipped and it flipped over lengthways two or three times with a couple of spins to the right before landing on its roof.

I look out over the city. Back up to where the stranger was standing and watching. I look left and right. Where the hell did that girl come from?

None of this makes any bloody sense.

25

Charlie, why don't you just leave it? Move on. Use the money and take a step up in the world. Into a bigger and better place. Maybe do a course. Learn a skill. Relocate somewhere quiet and off the radar. Why've you gotta go digging around, doing things you're not supposed to? You're inviting unnecessary heat. An event this public. You should be running like the wind to get away from it. Not rocking up at the cop shop looking for trouble.

That's what a nagging voice inside of me keeps saying.

But there's another, even more annoying voice. It keeps telling me something isn't right. It's that same little voice that moralises, guilt trips, eating me up until I do something about it.

I guess I'm a nosey bastard and I've gotta know, if only to silence the damn voice. So here I am, at the local police precinct. I walk up to the front desk. There's a duty officer stood behind it. An out of shape redheaded guy filling out paperwork.

"Can I help you, Sir?" he says.

"Yeah, I'm with Lifestar Insurance, on behalf of Solomon Studios. I've got a loss adjustment to make on a Ferrari 458. The claim says it's a write-off in L.A. County possession, but they've neglected to tell me the location. Any chance you'd have that information?"

"You sure you've got the right precinct?" the officer on the desk asks me—probably a test.

"I believe so. The detectives who attended the scene were Thomas and Roach."

"Yeah, okay," the officer says. "Then it'll be kept at this address."

He scribbles something out on the top of a notepad. He tears off the top sheet and hands it me over across the counter.

"Thanks, buddy," I say.

"That the Speed case, huh?" the officer says. "The kid must have one hell of an insurance policy on him."

"I guess so, though I'm just here about the car. Gotta check it's as written off as they say, you know?"

"Didn't you see the pictures?" the officer says. "The only thing left intact was the badge."

"Yeah, but procedures, you know what I'm saying?"

"Tell me about it," the officer says, going back to his paperwork.

I turn away from the desk and walk towards the entrance. The precinct is large and busy. Brown marble floors and stone walls. Cops in uniforms roam back and forward, heading in and out. Members of the public mingle in too, along with plain clothes narcos. A couple of 'em manhandle a guy with blonde dreads in a bright-blue tracksuit. He's proclaiming his innocence. Whether he is or he isn't, he's gonna come in handy.

The detectives are two medium-build white guys dressed in jeans and dark t-shirts. They've got him cuffed, but struggle to move him through the door. There's a kerfuffle. A couple of uniforms get involved. The detectives trade insults with the perp. On my way out, I make sure I get caught in the middle of the pushing and shoving.

"Hey, get out of here," one of the plain clothes guys says.

I apologise and fight my way out. I also rip the badge and ID off the detective's belt—fast and clean. He's too distracted to notice. I pocket the ID and badge, returning to the car.

I drive around the block to a stationery store, take a photo of myself in a booth and buy a pack of laminate pouches.

I head home, take out my iron and ironing board—Grant liked his workers in creaseless overalls.

I slide the detective's ID card out of its fake leather holder and rest it flat on the ironing board. With the iron heated up, I hold it flat over the card until the lamination comes loose. I peel the laminate covering off the card, cut one of the passport snaps of me down to size and line it up over the photo of our friend, Detective Brooks.

I glue it down and place the card inside the laminate pouch. I wrap the card in an old t-shirt and hold the iron over each side for thirty seconds. I pull the card out and we're good to go. There's a slight bump where the new photo is, but no one's gonna know. I slide the card inside the holder and pocket the badge and ID.

The address the duty officer wrote down for me goes into the GPS on the Camaro. A cross-town drive later, I'm pulling up at an L.A. County car pound. I flash the badge to the guy on the security barrier and he lets me in. I park in a visitor spot and walk through into reception.

I flash the badge again. "Detective Brooks. Here to see a Ferrari 458. Is it still here?"

"Ah, the Speed wreck. I thought you guys were done with it," a plump Latino woman says over the top of a pair of reading glasses, her hair grey and tied back hard in a bun.

"Detective Thomas missed a few details," I say. "Can't blame the guy. It was a feeding frenzy out there."

"Getting sick of the coverage," the woman says. "Surely there are other things going on in the world."

"Try working on the damn thing," I say.

The woman chuckles to herself and types something on a keyboard into a computer. She consults a screen. Her eyes lock onto something. "Here we go. It's in Unit Four. Behind reception, directly across the way. Door should be open." She pushes a visitor book my way across the counter.

I sign in and walk around the back of reception. I cross a vast sea of cars. Some impounded. Some with collision damage. The door to Unit Four is unlocked. I slide the heavy steel door open to the left. The sunlight breaks in and illuminates the red Italian wreck in the centre of the storage unit. It's crumpled to shit, half the roof torn off, the front-right wheel twisted at a wrong angle and the headlights and windows smashed out. The front and rear number plates hang off and the front end is squashed into the cabin.

I walk around it. Peer inside. The driver-side door is missing. The same for the steering wheel and the driver seat. I lean in and look around inside, then move around the passenger side again. I bend over low and walk from back to front, running a hand over the paintwork. My hand brushes over a series of grooves in the front wing. They look like horizontal claw marks, rough to the touch. I take a closer look. Angle my head so I can see better in the light.

The scratches are dark-grey. I dig a finger inside one and flecks of paint come away—definitely from another car.

The sun winks off one of the scratches. I brush a finger over the spot and feel a pinch. I feel a pinch. Check the finger. A tiny blood-red prick on the tip. I suck off the blood and take a closer look. Dig a thumb in and prise out a shard of glass the size of a nail clipping. I hold it to the light between thumb and finger. Pull out the cloth in my jacket pocket and open it out on the floor. I pick up the fragment of headlight I found by the side of the hill road. I compare the two shards, side by side.

We've got a match in colour and material.

But how many other headlights are made of the same stuff?

I slide the small fragment of glass inside a credit card slot in my wallet, wrap up the larger shard in the cloth and pocket both. I take a few photos of the car, including a close-up of the scratches down the side.

I can't think of how the Ferrari would have picked up those kind of scratches on the way down a hill. From the bushes? The barriers? Not with dark-grey paint and glass caught in the bodywork.

I stand up and look around the car one more time. There's definitely something going on. There was nothing in the news reports about a collision, so the cops obviously haven't changed their verdict on the crash.

Could this have been an accident? I just don't buy it . . . But who would run the kid off the road?

Maybe it was a hit and run. But hit and runs don't smoke a cigarette and admire their work.

As I stand there and stare at the car wreck, there's a ringing in my pocket. It's Rakesh calling about Josh's phone.

"I'm in," he says. "Man, you should see some of the selfies he's got on this thing."

I exit the lockup and slide the door shut behind me. "Don't tell anyone, don't show anyone," I say. "I'm on my way."

26

I park the Camaro with the top down on a quiet street. I kill the engine and the lights. Put on a pair of thin black gloves. Slip on a plain black baseball cap and pull the hood of a lightweight black sweater over the top. I open the door and step out into a mild, still night.

It's late. Crickets chirp and the drone of the freeway is a whisper at most up here.

I don't lock the Camaro. Don't want the sidelights to flash.

I walk up the hill roads. A couple of blocks. A few twists and turns left and right. Past garage doors and mansion walls. Zero traffic and no one out on the streets.

My legs feel the burn as the road rises steeper. I move fast and quiet. Turn at the sound of a can hitting the floor. Relax as a raccoon scurries down the side of a wheelie bin, the can rolling away down the hill.

The racoon looks at me. Big eyes glowing in the orange streetlight, body low to the pavement. It scoots off across the road and into a line of bushes. I continue on my way. Come to a stop at the bottom of a high stone wall.

There's a streetlight close to the wall. I put my foot on the base and give myself a boost. I dig the sides of my soles into the pole either side and shimmy upwards until I'm eight feet off the ground.

At this height, there's a creeping vine that starts crawling up and over the wall. I lean out and grab the end of it with my left hand. I wrap it around a few times in a fist and pull it tight. The vine holds firm. I stick a foot out and plant it against the wall, count to three and let go of the streetlight.

I swing away like a crap Tarzan. I bounce off the wall, but grab the vine with the other hand and steady myself.

With both feet against the wall, I lean back and walk upwards, pulling myself up with the vine, hand over hand until I'm high enough to haul myself up onto the top. I look down below me to street level.

Shit, this is high.

I roll over the other side of the wall and use the vines that smother the inside to climb down into the trees and bushes. I pick my way through and across the snooker table lawns around the back of the mansion. The front entrance is a no-go 'cause of CCTV. The ground floor is out as it's wrap-around glass. Solid stuff you can't make a hole in without a laser cutter.

The middle two floors are pretty much the same. Which leaves one option.

I look up to the top floor. That's where I'm headed. The easiest way that I know in.

Lucky for me, this place is designed like a kid building with bric-a-brac. Boxes stacked on boxes. Square edges. Funny angles. I put a foot on a low white wall and start climbing. I use everything from an air duct to a steel drain pipe to shimmy up to the first floor balcony. I step up onto a thin stone ledge, gripping onto the bottom of the third floor and haul myself up. I throw myself over the wall onto the balcony, then step out onto the ledge again.

I look up at the top-floor balcony. It's further up this time. I'll have to jump a little. And I'm no Michael Jordan.

Shit, this is dicey. I must be forty feet up at least. The height of the hill itself only adds to the vertigo. And it's a long time since I did any breaking and entering.

The thought of it gets into my head. Affects my balance. I wobble on the ledge, catch my balance and take a breath.

Ever get yourself into a situation where you don't wanna go forward but there's no way of going back? Ever wondered how the hell you got there or what the bloody hell you were thinking? This is one of those occasions.

Okay, Charlie, you'll only get one shot at this . . .

I steady my weight, bend at the knees and jump. I catch hold of the balcony wall above. Fingers gripping tight, legs kicking. Adrenalin sees me haul my weight up. I get an elbow on the balcony wall. Another elbow. I pull myself over and collapse in a heap on the floor. This was so much easier when I was twenty-one.

I pick myself up and skirt around to the sun deck. The infinity pool is lit by solar-powered lights. I move to the window wall that folds open. Take out a credit card and jimmy open the latch.

You can have all the sophisticated systems in the world, but there's always a weak point. And one of the first things I did here was run a check for 'em.

I told Christine to get the landscaper to clear the wall vines. I also told her we needed extra security right here where I'm gaining entry. I said we needed CCTV and alarms on the top floor too. Lucky for me, Josh didn't want another invasion of his privacy and Christine thought I was being ridiculous about the vines.

I slide the glass wall shut behind me. The latch isn't broken and no one will know. Slipping the credit card back inside my wallet, I take out a pen torch and work my way through the top floor living area into the hallway. I pull the hood down from my head and remove the cap a moment. The air is stale and warm. I rub the sweat off my brow with a sleeve and replace the cap on my head.

I walk straight to the master bedroom at the end of the hallway, listening to the sound of my own breath, my heart still bouncing from the climb.

As I'm moving towards the door of the bedroom, something catches my eye

I flash the torch over the wall and jump out of my skin.

Shit, it's just a modern art painting of a bull with demonic red eyes. I hate that bloody painting. Gives me the creeps.

I return to the task in hand, turning the marble knob on the door and stepping inside. Josh's room doesn't just have a giant ensuite attached. It has an adjoining office through a panel door.

I slide the panel open and shine the torch over the room. Like everything else in the Speed mansion, it's super-sized. There's a large white desk like an architect would use under a tinted skylight, a coffee-coloured L-shape leather sofa in a corner and a small section of a basketball court, complete with a full-size hoop and backboard. You can add a mini-cinema screen to that and a bank of wide, narrow wooden drawers against the back wall of the room.

Josh also has a director's chair with his name on it and blown-up photos on the walls of him with a bunch of other icons—Scorsese, Spielberg, Clooney, Streep, you name 'em. Then there are the framed prints of him clutching a Golden Globe and the Oscar he won when he used to do serious acting stuff in his late teens. Before the franchises got hold of him.

I find a MacBook laptop on the desk. Notice a green light on the power cable. A white light on the front of the machine suggesting it's been left plugged in and left on all this time. I open the thing up and press the space bar. The screen wakes up and shines bright in the dark. I try the same password he used on his iPad—*Nightburner1*. Hardly unbreakable.

The background is a picture of Josh smoking a Cuban in the Nightburner costume. I open a minimised browser. The kid's email account is open. I scan through the recent activity.

After Rakesh hacked Josh's phone, I went through his voicemails, his recent call activity and social media accounts. I soon realised his social media was handled by someone else and aside from a star-studded list of speed dial numbers, didn't find anything of interest.

I also took the time to delete the more personal photos on there. Especially the naked cocaine orgy ones.

Email after email, nothing flags up any potential grudge or enemy within the Hollywood community. Most of the emails are back and forths about the Nightburner franchise. Power struggles and wars of words between directors, producers, agents and the big-name actors in the franchise. Most of 'em demanding more money and a greater say in the script.

I shut the laptop and turn my attention to the wooden bank of drawers.

But hang on, Charlie, you might be thinking. What about Carlos? He was threatening the lad. Tailing the pair of you. Planning a hit on Josh. And you were probably next.

Well yeah, that was my first thought, too. But then he'd

have a hard time lighting a cigarette, let alone driving in the state I left him in. And his crew would have had an even tougher time, being six feet under.

Of course, my next theory was that Carlos might have paid a third party for a hit on Josh, with me next on the list.

But for one thing, I'm still breathing. And unless he hired a complete idiot, professional hits are professional for a reason. They do it quick and clean and don't hang around the scene of the crime when they're done.

Which leads me to think there could be other potential enemies. The boyfriend of a girl he was sleeping with. Or a small-time coke dealer who didn't get paid.

I put the torch in my mouth and roll open the top drawer. It's full of all kinds of paperwork.

I find a new contract signed last year for the Nightburner franchise. A three-movie extension. Eighty million a movie, plus a percentage of the gross box office take. And that's not to mention image rights and the cut of merchandise sales. It's signed personally by both Josh and Art Solomon.

There's a few other things, like copies of insurance documents and certificates taken out by the studio against their prized asset in case of injuries, delays and the like. And there's a screenplay for Nightburner 4. I skim through it—a giant robot squid attacking New York?

Come on. What a load of—Shit, what's that?

I hear a noise. Where from? Inside? Outside? I listen out. Don't hear a thing. Go back to the script.

Then a thud, like a heavy door closing. Faint, distant, but sounds like it could be coming from the ground floor. I put the screenplay back in the drawer and slide it closed as quiet as a mouse. I close the laptop screen and step out into the bedroom, flicking off the torch. I slip the torch inside a trouser pocket and slide the panel door to the office closed. I stand in the darkness and silence and listen.

Someone is definitely in the house. The hairs stand up on the back of my neck as I creep out of the master bedroom and pull the door closed. I turn the knob as slow as it'll go. The door clicks, but quiet. I make my way along the hallway to the main staircase that winds its way down to the ground floor.

Someone is inside and bundling around. Not as careful as me. Not expecting company.

How did they get in without tripping the alarm? Did Christine forget to arm the security system? Don't tell me I climbed all the way up the side of the house, risking life and limb for nothing.

Unless they've got serious skills, it could be neighbourhood security, armed and licensed to shoot.

I hesitate a moment. The way I see it, I've got three options. Slip out and climb down the side of the house. I don't fancy that for one second. My original plan was to lower myself down using tied-together bedsheets, but that's not gonna play out now.

So the second option is to hide and wait until the intruder leaves. But I'm too curious for that. And what if the intruder did have something to do with Josh's accident? I could be passing up my one chance to find out. Knowing what I'm like, the thought of it would chew me up.

So I guess it's the third option. I start down the stairs. One soft step after another, tracking the sound of the intruder's feet.

I'm guessing the fact they haven't activated the lights means they aren't supposed to be here. I wonder if it's the same person from the scene of the crash. The cigarette-smoking stranger. But what would they be doing here?

Whoever they are, they're walking along the ground floor hallway. I'm on the first floor landing now and I hear 'em coming towards the staircase.

The footsteps are solid.

A guy.

A heavyset guy who breathes loud and wears hard-sole shoes. The slap of his soles go one way then another. As if he's either lost or looking for something.

A chair is knocked over. Something fragile shatters on the floor. The guy curses to himself. He's moving towards the stairs again, where I wait around the corner.

I ready myself. He's probably armed. Gotta time this right.

I hear him coming closer, closer and closer still . . . *and I move.*

27

I rush out from around the corner. See a broad dark figure in front of me.

"Holy shit!" he says, turning to run.

I throw myself at him and tackle him to the floor. We hit it hard. He cries out in agony. Tries to scramble away. But I've got the bastard.

I roll him over onto his back, whip out my torch and shine it over both his hands. Empty, flapping. His waist—no weapon.

The inside of his navy suit jacket—unarmed. Not even a holster or a blade.

Finally, I shine the torch in his eyes.

"Don't kill me!" he yells, eyes shut and hyperventilating.

"Buck?" I say.

"Charlie?" he says, "is that you?"

"What are you doing here?" I ask.

"Looking for the damn light switch," he says.

"There isn't one," I say, turning off the torch and slipping it in my pocket.

"Lights on," I say, clapping my hands.

The entire ground floor lights up. I blink into the brightness.

Buck opens his eyes slow. "Why are you in Josh's house?"

I get off him and pull him to his feet. "You okay, Wyndall?"

"Nothing a spinal surgeon won't fix," he says, holding the small of his back. "You didn't answer my question."

"Looking for evidence," I say.

"Evidence of what?" Buck says.

"Grudges. Enemies. Anyone who might have killed the kid."

"The crash killed the kid," Buck says, straightening himself out. "Or haven't you been watching the news?"

"Something's off," I say. "It doesn't add up."

"Then your math must be shaky," Buck says. "Ferrari. Nose dive. Car all smashed to fuck. Ain't too complicated a sum."

"You weren't there," I say. "Someone was watching."

"Yeah, the cops mentioned that."

"They talked to you?" I ask.

"I talked to them. Wanted to know the toxicology before the reporters did. Check he wasn't, you know . . ."

"Off his tits?"

"That's one way of putting it," Buck says.

"So, did you speak to Thomas and Roach?" I ask.

"Roach," Buck says.

"Did he tell you about the car with the broken headlight?"

"Yeah, he mentioned it."

"The girl in the bushes?"

"Sure."

"How about paint scrapings down the passenger side?"

"Could have been a hit and run," Buck says.

"Except the other driver didn't run. They stayed and watched. I chased 'em downtown."

Suddenly Buck seems interested. "Did you catch them?"

"You think I'd be here if I did?"

"How about a plate number?" Buck asks. "Something to go off?"

I shake my head.

Buck leans his weight on the arm of a large stone-coloured sofa in the living area. "Those are some loose ends, alright. But if we don't know who this someone was, there's not a lot we can do . . . Did you find any evidence up there? Anything untoward?"

"Not so far."

"How about Carlos Campuzano? That's why Josh hired you in the first place, isn't it?"

"No, I don't think it's him," I say. "I dealt with him and his crew."

"He could have hired someone."

"Pros don't take chances. Josh could have survived a crash. Too much of a lottery."

Buck throws out his hands. Slaps his palms on his thighs. He leans forward on the arm of the sofa like a thought just hit him. He stands and paces around. "Look, Charlie," he says, "maybe there wasn't any malice in this thing. Maybe the person you saw, they collided with Josh. Saw him fly off the hill. Their first instinct is to flee the scene. Then they pull up around the bend. They get out of the car in shock. Smoke a cigarette, shaken up. They're wrestling with it. They're horrified at what they've just done, but they're terrified of calling the cops. Then *you* turn up. They see you at the scene. You see them. You're a big guy, dressed like the damn secret service. So they panic. Jump back in the car and decide to get the hell out of there. They drive back down the hill, their mind flying in all directions. Then they see you in the rear view coming at them fast. They panic all over again. Next minute they're in a car chase with a scary-looking guy in a black SUV. You see where I'm going with this?"

I shrug. "When you put it like that . . . I guess it's possible."

Buck stops and gazes at his tan leather shoes. "We've all been hit hard by what happened, Charlie. The studio as much as anyone. But Josh is gone. Auto-wrecks around here are a dime a dozen. And you know Josh, he drove everywhere like he was at Daytona."

"I did tell him to slow down," I say.

"Didn't we all?" Buck says, feeling his lower back.

"So, you gonna call the cops on me?" I ask.

Buck waves it away. "Don't be an ass. I know you're only out here 'cause you blame yourself. If it was anyone's fault it was mine."

"How do you figure?" I say.

"I was responsible for keeping the kid in check. Him and others like him. I obviously didn't do enough."

"Hey, I was the bodyguard," I say.

"You had a flat. The kid left without you . . . Hell, maybe it was inevitable."

"So what's gonna happen with the Nightburner films?" I ask.

Buck lets out a big sigh. He shakes his head. "Your guess is as good as mine. But who cares about that? We had our fall-outs but Josh was like family. Art's as cut up about this as the rest of us."

I look around the living area of the house. See a broken vase on the floor. A knocked-over chair. "You come out in the middle of the night for anything special?"

"Had to come by and make a list of all the valuables," Buck says. "The later the better—no cameras, you know what I mean? Besides, who can sleep . . ."

I pick up the chair. "The house going up for sale?" I ask.

"The studio's handling it. Which means I'm handling it." Buck picks up the larger pieces of the vase. "Always a fresh mess."

"I know the feeling," I say, giving Buck a hand.

When we're done and Buck has been through the house making his list, we leave together through the front gate. Buck is parked up outside in a dark-blue Bentley convertible with a beige top.

"You know, Charlie, if you were gonna sneak in, you could have come through the front door. Security system's off and I made Christine take a vacation."

"Shit, I knew it," I say.

Buck opens the door to his Bentley. He pauses before climbing in. "The job offer's still open you know. We could do with someone of your talents. There's always another Josh Speed to look after."

I look at Buck. At the surrounding neighbourhood. "Let me think about it."

"Take your time," Buck says, climbing in his car. "You've got my number."

Buck swings the Bentley around and drives off down the hill. I take one last look at the house and leave.

28

The digital clock glows red. Says three-thirty. I toss and turn, the night of the crash, the events since, all running through my mind. I see Josh's body twisted inside the mashed-up Ferrari. See it lying there stitched up under the sheet. Smell the familiar stench of the dead inside the morgue. Try and snort it out of my nose, even though it isn't there.

It's in my mind. Part of a big, twisted movie that plays on a loop. The stranger smoking the cigarette—a bright orange dot in the night. I zoom in close and see it burn. Taste the smoke. But I can't make out the face behind it.

The girl flashes into my mind. Only a split-second glance. She looks familiar. Where do I know her from? I turn over in bed again, listening to the crack of far-off gunfire. Sirens wailing in response.

Hot and sweaty, I kick off the sheets. I sit up on the thin, springy mattress. I slide off and walk tired and wired to the fridge. I open the door and look inside for some water—you don't drink out of the tap around here. Not unless you want to puke and shit your guts out the next day.

I squint and peer inside. There's a solitary bottle of beer. I thought I had two. I tear the top off with my teeth and spit it like a bullet into the sink. I close the fridge door and take a sip.

Oh yeah, baby. I turn and stop mid-drink.

There's a figure sat in a chair in the corner by the door. "You just gonna leave it like that?" it says in a deep, growling voice.

I bring the bottle down from my lips. A hand searches for a meat knife I know is on the worktop somewhere behind me.

As I grab the handle, the figure turns on a lamp by the chair. "Don't bother," it says.

Holy shit, it's Nightburner.

Well, Josh Speed playing Nightburner. Josh Speed before the crash. He sits there in full costume—charcoal-grey including cowl mask, with the ring of fire logo and orange piping glowing in the murk.

He sips on the other bottle of beer. Sighs a tired sigh and rolls his neck, the bones cracking loud under the skin.

"What are you doing here?" I say.

"Doing what I do best," Nightburner says.

"Sitting on your arse?"

"Avenging the death of innocents. Bringing the bad guys to justice ... And the giant robot squid."

I down half my beer and hope he'll go away. He doesn't. He gets up and stretches his legs around the room. As much as you can stretch 'em around a room not much bigger than a prison cell.

"Sorry to burst your skin tight rubber bubble, pal, but Joshua Speed is dead. So is your franchise."

Nightburner lets out a low, gravelled laugh. "You'll never kill Nightburner. I'll keep coming back one way or another.

A reboot. A TV series. Right now, I'm being kept alive through you and your damaged mind."

"Yeah, well I'm having that checked out tomorrow. Spending some of my advance on a specialist."

"You really think you earned that money?" Nightburner says.

"Like I said, it was an advance."

"Oh, I'm sorry," Nightburner says, throwing out his arms. "Then you totally earned it."

"What do you want from me, Nightburner?"

"Justice," he says.

"Then go and light a fire under some criminals."

Nightburner grunts. "Unfortunately, I have to work through you now. You have to continue my legacy. At least until the next sequel."

"I've already looked into it," I say. "Buck's probably right. It was some guy who collided with the kid. Probably not even the guy's fault. He panics. He smokes. He runs."

"In a car with no plate?" Nightburner says. "Come on, Breaker."

"No one calls me that anymore," I say. "Breaker's in the past."

"Funny, I still see you wearing the suit," Nightburner says.

"It's called my skin, moron."

Nightburner grunts some more. "Maybe, but he's never far from the surface, is he?"

"What does that mean?" I say.

"In the warehouse, with Carlos." Nightburner smiles at the look on my face. "Yeah, you know what I'm talking about. Charlie's just a public mask. Your Bruce Wayne. Your Clark Kent."

"Yeah? Well if Breaker was here right now, he'd be packing his bags and getting out of town."

"Stop acting like a pussy. The kid died on your watch. That's on you."

"I know, I know," I say. "But—"

"But nothing," Nightburner says. "There's more to Speed's death than an accident. You know it, I know it."

"But the police report—"

"*Pah*. You believe those fuckers?" Nightburner says.

I shrug, unsure whether I do or don't.

"The tyre marks that don't line up right. The injuries to the kid. The car without a plate. You've been around. You feel it in your guts."

"You aren't even real," I say.

"Maybe not. But I'm right."

I sup on my beer. "What are you suggesting?"

"A full-on investigation," Nightburner says. "No more tippy-tapping around."

"I can't afford the attention," I say. "Josh's death is still global news if you haven't noticed. The last thing I need is my face in the papers."

Nightburner sighs and flaps his arms like I'm stupid. "No one will see your face, dummy."

"How do you work that out?" I say.

Nightburner nods towards something behind me. I turn and see a dark rubber Nightburner suit laid out flat on the bed.

"Whoa, I'm not wearing *that*."

"I've worn it for thirty years," Nightburner says. "Never did me any harm."

"Look at me," I say, slapping my stomach. "I'll look like a right prat."

"Wear the damn costume," Nightburner says, getting aggressive.

"You know you're a lot different than the guy in the movies," I say.

"Yeah? How's that?" Nightburner says.

"Drinking, swearing—you're not exactly a PG-thirteen."

"That's the movie version. You're talking to the original comic book incarnation, when I used to be dark and drunk and I set fire to the scum. Burned 'em alive . . . Before they turned me into some grinning choir boy dope on the side of cereal packets." Nightburner stares at me. "So, what's it to be, asshole?"

"Okay," I say. "But I'm not wearing the bloody costume. We do this my way or no way at all."

"Fine, but remember, the fate of the world is in your hands," Nightburner says, pulling at the rubber clinging tight to his crotch.

"No it's not," I say.

"Just don't let me down," Nightburner says, sitting with difficulty in the chair.

He turns off the light. I hear a beer burp and he disappears into the darkness. I turn around and see the costume on the bed is gone too. I beat my own head with the flat of a hand and down the rest of the beer. When I leave it on the counter, I see another empty bottle by the sink.

29

Dr Kwan sits in her white coat on the other side of a large oak desk, studying the results of my scans. I'd guess she's in her fifties. Far-Eastern with glasses and her dark hair cut short. She speaks with a West Coast accent. I'm getting good at telling the difference now.

"So doc, what's the verdict?"

"There doesn't appear to be any cranial damage," she says. "Can you remember when you first began to experience these hallucinations, Mr Walters?"

"I think it was fifteen, sixteen years ago."

"And had you sustained any kind of injury to your head at the time?"

"I'd taken a couple of knocks," I say. "The first one was in a car crash. A blow to the back of the head."

The doctor looks puzzled. "From someone behind you?"

"Nope."

"From a projectile then?"

"I dunno. The car flipped over nose-first. Then it tumbled a few times. The airbag went off in my face and I felt a whack on the back of my skull." I take out my phone and scroll through to a close-up shot. Blood-stained black hair and a nasty-looking swelling. "Here, I've still got the photo of it," I say, leaning over the desk with the phone.

Dr Kwan wrinkles her brow. "Resembles a blunt trauma impact. How strange, I've seen similar injuries from car accidents, but not to this part of the skull. I can't think what would have caused it."

"Me neither," I say.

"You said there was a second injury?" Dr Kwan says.

"Yeah, I took a whack from a baseball bat . . . In the forehead."

"Ouch." Dr Kwan pulls a face like she just sucked on a lemon. "You were mugged?"

"Uh, something like that, doc."

"Well either injury could theoretically have caused your condition," Dr Kwan says. "Though it sounds as if the baseball bat may be responsible." Dr Kwan lays out my results on the desk. "The hallucinations you're experiencing are the result of something called TBI—Traumatic Brain Injury. The technical term is a psychotic episode, a misperception of auditory or visual stimuli that can manifest in a hallucination. Psychosis induced by a blow to the head is caused when the brain is shaken violently inside the skull. In many cases the psychosis ends when the brain heals, but episodes can continue for a long time afterwards. Because of the striking action of the bat and the location to the frontal neocortex, I would suspect it would be that particular injury that triggered the psychosis, rather than the car accident."

"Could they be triggered by something I'm doing?" I ask.

"Quite possibly, in times of stress, perhaps. If the brain is the hardware, your mind is the software. A change in the software can trigger a change in the neural functioning of the brain, and vice versa. It's hard to know exactly. Perhaps you could try cutting down on stress. Make some lifestyle changes. They can have a profound effect on brain healing and psychosis."

"You probably think I'm crazy," I say. "Talking to people who aren't there."

"Not at all," Dr Kwan says. "Regardless of how strange or ridiculous the hallucination, you will perceive them as real."

"So even though I know I've got this condition, It still *feels* real at the time?"

"That's correct," Dr Kwan says.

"So I'm not a total nut-job," I say.

"No, Mr Walters, you are not *a nut-job*."

"That's a relief," I say, relaxing into the chair. "How do we fix this brain injury? Surgery or what?"

Dr Kwan clasps her hands together and rests them on her desk. She leans forward. Her eyes give me the truth before her mouth does. "I'm afraid there's no correctional procedure available for your condition," she says.

My head drops, my hopes of a solution close behind.

"However," Dr Kwan says, "there are a couple of options open to you, which I would be happy to prescribe, should you choose."

"Sure," I say.

"The first option is medication," Dr Kwan says.

"Those little yellow pills?"

"You've tried them before?" she says.

"Yeah, they make you wanna die. What's the other option?"

"I believe counselling could prove useful."

"A shrink? I'm not really the talking type."

"It might help you come to terms with the condition," Dr Kwan says. "To accept it as part of who you are."

I look around the office. At the busy book shelves, the

certificates and awards on the walls. "Can I think about it, doc?"

Dr Kwan hands me a card with the name of a mind-meddler on it. "If you decide to go ahead with counselling, just call the number on the card. I'll pass on your details in the meantime."

I stand out of my chair. Dr Kwan smiles and shows me out of her office.

I walk out of the hospital doors with a mix of feelings.

The head scans may have turned out to be a dead end. But Dr Kwan's reaction to the photo of Josh's head wound said it all.

She's a head injury expert—one of the best—and she was as confused by it as I was.

I don't know what it all means, but there's bullshit in the air. Ten stinking tonnes.

Nightburner was right. There's something going on here, and people are gonna start talking.

30

I come out of the hospital car park and drive through the upmarket streets of Beverly Grove.

It's not long before I notice something fishy on my tail. A dark-blue Ford saloon a few cars back. I noticed it pull out behind me after I left the hospital car park. Nothing funny about that, I'll grant you. But call it instinct, paranoia, whatever you want, it doesn't look right.

It's hanging out wide to the left of the middle lane, like it's trying to get a view of me around the cars in front.

I make a couple of unplanned turns, as I always do when I'm sniffing out a tail. It makes the same turns soon after. So I throw in a dummy. The car cruises on behind me, not reacting.

We're on a major highway, following a popular route, so it could be nothing. I need a different kinda test. A stop-off somewhere.

Lunch seems like a good idea. I can't investigate anything on an empty stomach, so I head towards a good place I know—a diner called Freddie's. It's no-frills basic. Just off the Sunset Strip and just how I like it.

As I pull into the car park, I notice the Ford saloon drift past. I stop and watch it sail into the distance with the other traffic.

I decide it's probably nothing and head into the diner.

Freddie's makes an English cup of tea that doesn't taste like steaming hot ball sweat. I'm guessing from the black and white snaps of London on the wall behind the counter there's some kinda transatlantic connection. They also do brown sauce here. I slap out a fat glob of the stuff on the side of my plate and go to work. Josh's good eating habits are already wearing off. I fill my guts with sausage and mash. While I'm digesting the food and sipping on my tea, I think over my next move.

I reckon I need to talk to someone the kid knew well. Someone I haven't spoken to yet. Christopher Lipton, the movie director would seem like a good bet and no time like the present. So I drink up and pay the bill.

As I hold the door open for an old couple walking in, I notice the Ford saloon rolling across the small car park in front of the diner.

Rather than head straight for the Camaro, I turn sharp to my right.

I walk along the front of the diner, glancing over my left shoulder. The Ford has the same plate as before. It's following me for sure, with a guy driving and another in the passenger seat.

I can't make out their faces from here and I don't intend to. Instead, I pick up the pace and hang another right around the side of the diner. But I run straight into Detective Roach. He leans against the wall, a deadly serious look on his face.

I instinctively back-pedal. The Ford mounts the curb at

speed and slams to a stop. The front passenger door flies open. It's Detective Thomas.

He jumps out and opens the rear passenger door. "Get in," he says.

"I'm good, thanks."

"Just get the fuck in," Roach says.

I turn and walk to the car. Roach shoves me in for good measure. I scoot across and sit behind the driver, another guy I don't recognise. Brawny with thinning sandy hair.

Roach and Thomas get in and slam their doors shut. The driver takes off with a screech and a bump as we pull off the kerb. They drive me out of the car park and onto the passing highway.

"It's alright lads, I don't need a lift," I say. "I've got my own set of wheels. Though you'd already know that, since you've been tailing me for long enough."

"Yeah, we do that a lot with perps," Detective Roach says.

"Sorry, I don't follow," I say, wondering if it was sneaking into the morgue or impersonating an officer that did it.

Or was it the Speed mansion break-in? That fucker Buck. I bet he double-crossed me. I bet the bastard was nice to my face—didn't wanna risk a beating. But then when I was gone, he gets on the phone to the L.A. fuzz.

"You been talking to Wyndall Buck?" I ask. "Cause whatever he says, I wasn't there."

"Who the hell's Wyndall Buck?" Roach says.

"You should know," I say. "He said he talked to you."

"Oh, the studio guy," Thomas says. "Yeah, we talked to him."

"And no, he didn't mention you," Roach says.

"Why, is there something you're not telling us?" Thomas says.

"No, but there's gotta be something you're not telling

me," I say. "Like why the hell you're harassing an innocent citizen."

"Innocent?" Thomas says, laughing. He turns in his seat and eyeballs me. "Three dead bodies in an underpass innocent?"

I shrug as if I'm clueless.

"They were Carlos Campuzano's crew," Thomas says. "The same Carlos Campuzano who was harassing your former employer."

"Gang warfare's pretty common around here," I say.

"This guy must think we're real dumb," Thomas says to Roach.

"You think we're dumb, asshole?" Roach says to me. "Cause we're not."

"We know you've been sniffing around the Speed crash," Thomas says.

"Just doing my due diligence," I say. "Trying to figure something out."

"Oh, what's that?" Thomas asks.

"Whether you guys were born stupid or paid stupid."

I'm pretty happy with my comeback. Until Roach, who isn't, punches me hard in the ribs.

"What kinda shit do you give?" I ask, coughing, a hand to my side.

"The kind that might cause us extra paperwork," Thomas says. "And for no good reason."

"Questions asked by you, mean questions asked of us," Roach says. "Like who is this guy? Why's he making fake IDs and creeping around morgues?"

"How would you know what I'm doing with my life?" I say.

"We're the fucking LAPD numb-nuts," Roach says, rapping his bony knuckles on my crown.

The piece of shit lands another punch in the same spot the first one hit. If he wasn't a cop, I'd put him through the car window.

But he is, so I don't.

"Could you not do that?" I say. "It's bad for the digestion."

Thomas talks to the driver. "Turn it around, Mickey. We need to drop off some garbage."

Mickey pulls a U-turn in the road and heads back towards Freddie's. He pulls up fast in the car park and jumps out of the car. He opens my door, drags me out by the collar and pushes me to the floor.

"Stay out of police business," Roach yells from the backseat.

"And stay away from Carlos Campuzano," I hear Detective Thomas say.

Mickey puts a swift, sharp boot into my guts. "Digest that, asshole," he says, climbing back behind the wheel.

The doors to the Ford slam shut again. I eat the smell of exhaust fumes as it drives away. I cough and get to my feet. Stomach aching, but in one piece. And at least they were good enough to drop me off by the Camaro.

I collapse into the driver's seat and start the engine.

Right, where were we?

31

Thank Christ for my own bloody laziness. I tossed my access all areas pass and parking badge in with my clothes when I packed my bag and left the Speed mansion. They come in mighty handy now, getting me through security and into the Solomon Studios car park. I slide the blue VIP badge on the dash of the Camaro and leave it in a priority space. I hang the pink access pass around my neck on a lanyard and walk through the various studio buildings—giant white boxes with numbers painted in giant black numerals on the side.

I'm pretty sure they'll be shooting in sound stage fourteen, just like before.

The studio complex is like a mini town, with offices, gym, coffee shop, spa, bar, restaurant—you name it.

Little white golf buggies zip back and forth between box trucks loading and unloading props. I find fourteen and flash my pass. The place is noisy, which means they're on a break between shooting. It's the same sound stage as when I was here with Josh, but the scenery is different. This time it's all green screen, with actors and stuntmen fixed to wires and dressed head-to-toe in shiny green lycra, with what look like white Ping Pong balls glued to their body.

I find Lipton sitting in his director's chair, headphones around his neck, eating a tuna sub. He drops a dollop of mayo on his black turtle neck.

"Ah, bollocks," he says, wiping it off with a serviette.

"Alright, Chris?" I say.

He swallows a mouthful of butty and looks up at me. A smile on his face. "Charlie, how are you doing, mate?"

"Not bad, considering."

Lipton's face drops, sadness in his eyes. "Yes, well, you have to get on, don't you?"

"You go to the funeral?" I ask.

"It was a nice ceremony. Big, of course, but tasteful. I did a reading. Tennyson."

"Who?"

"The poet?"

I shake my head.

Lipton finishes his sub. He has a sip of takeaway coffee and wipes his mouth. "So what are you doing here, Charlie? You minding another of our great and good?"

"Not here for work," I say. "Shouldn't really be here at all, if I'm honest."

Lipton chuckles. "I won't say anything if you don't. What can I do you for?"

"I was wondering if I could ask you a few questions—about Josh. If you've got time."

"Go ahead. We're on a break. Harnesses aren't working right. What do you want to know?"

Lipton waves to another director-style chair to the left of him.

"I take it you've read the papers, watched the news, talked about it 'til the cows come home?" I say.

"The accident? Yes," Lipton says.

"Well I'm not so sure it was an accident . . . Or if it was, I think someone might have been involved."

"Like what, a road rage incident?"

"Could have been," I say. "But I wanted to rule out enemies first."

"You mean grudges, feuds, something like that?" Lipton says.

"Exactly like that. Did Josh have any problems with anyone?"

"He had problems with a lot of people," Lipton says. "But who doesn't around here?"

"Nothing serious then? With another actor, or someone on set?"

Lipton looks towards the lighting rigs on the ceiling and chews on his lip. He brings his eyes back to me. Shakes his head. "Nope. Not that I can think of, sorry." Lipton sips on his coffee. "The news reports said the police ruled out any foul play," he says. "What makes you suspect anything different?"

"There are inconsistencies," I say. "A lot of 'em."

"Like what?" Lipton says, the first person who seems interested.

"The tyre tracks and the angle of the crash for one," I say. "The presence of an onlooker who fled the scene in a dark-grey car. The same colour paintwork found on the front passenger wing. A broken headlight and the presence of a woman at the scene, covered in blood."

"Surely the police picked up on these things?" Lipton says.

I shake my head. "I reckon the detectives rushed the

investigation. Cut some corners, missed a few vital pieces of evidence."

"Can't they go back over their own work?"

I shake my head. "It's as if they know they messed up and they're too embarrassed to admit it."

"Big celebrity case like that," Lipton says, "I'm not surprised."

I rub my still-aching guts.

"Something wrong?" Lipton asks.

"Talking to the detectives on the case—Thomas and Roach—gave me indigestion."

"Hey, I know those guys," Lipton says.

"You do?"

"Sure," Lipton says. "They do a little moonlighting for the studio. On-set advisors to, um, what's that show—LA Justice. They were working on the last movie me and Josh worked on together."

"I was here," I say. "I didn't see 'em."

"We only call them when we need them," Lipton says.

"You think they could have had a beef with Josh?" I ask.

"The LAPD?" Lipton says. "Why would they?"

"Yeah, I suppose it's a long shot. Maybe Buck's right. The crash was an accident, a hit and run with a panicking driver. It's just that Josh had an injury to the back of the head," I say, tapping the back of my own.

"Postmortem?" Lipton asks.

"Not unless the medical examiner whacked him on the back of the skull," I say. "The bruises on the neck can be put down to him doing his own stunts, but—"

Lipton breaks into laughter. "*Stunts?* Josh didn't do his own stunts. Who told you that?"

"Apparently it's a well-known fact."

"A well-peddled myth more like," Lipton says. "Don't believe everything you hear on The Tonight Show."

"You mean Josh didn't do any of his own stunts, *at all?*"

"As much as I loved Josh, he didn't like anyone touching his hair, never mind his face. It was guys like Jerry and Klaus over there who did all the stunt work."

Lipton points to a pair of guys in green screen suits practicing a fight routine.

"So these bruises you mentioned . . ." Lipton says.

"He had a bunch of 'em around his throat," I say.

"What do you think it could mean?" Lipton asks.

"I dunno. Something. Nothing . . . What's this one about, then?"

"The movie? Oh who the hell knows," Lipton says. "The original director was fired. I stepped in at the last minute to finish the job. Helps me keep my mind off Josh. That and they're paying me through the nose to save it."

I get up off the chair. "I'll let you crack on. Thanks for your help, Chris."

Lipton stands and shakes my hand. "Josh was like a son to me. If there's anything else I can do . . ." Lipton slaps his jeans pockets, grabs a runner—a uni age brunette wearing a headset. "Cara, go and find Charlie here one of my business cards, will you? There should be a stack on the desk in my trailer."

"Sure, Chris," she says, turning one-eighty. "This way," she says to me.

I thank Lipton again and follow Cara.

Lipton strides off towards the green screen set. *"Are those harnesses ready yet? We've got a movie to finish."*

Cara leads me outside and tells me to wait out on the street where they're filming a scene with actors and animals.

"I'll be back in five," she says, hurrying off around the side of the studio building.

To my left, there's a border collie on a lead held by a plain, middle-aged woman in a blue jacket.

"Hey, that's a nice dog," I say, bending over to stroke it.

The woman yanks the dog away by the lead. "Do you mind?" she says. "He's working."

32

Cara returns with Lipton's card, but the way I came in is blocked off due to filming. Cara gives me some shortcut instructions on how to find my way out. But it's a lot of lefts and rights and vague pointing and before I know it, I'm bloody-well lost, walking around in circles wondering where I am.

Have I been here before? It looks so familiar. Maybe 'cause all these streets and buildings look the same.

I end up squeezing through a row of cars lined up between two sound stage buildings. A couple of 'em are mock police cars. Another a New York cab and a few stunt vehicles—family saloons on the outside, stripped and caged on the inside. There are three rows of four. Some of 'em pretty badly damaged from previous stunts. I squeeze through the last row onto the street. It runs left to right across my path. As I look to my left I see the road bending around to the right.

I figure it's gotta lead somewhere.

But as I'm about to set off, something catches the corner

of my eye. A dark-grey saloon without a badge or a plate. It's parked on the end of the back row.

Surely not.

I skirt around to the left-hand side of the car. The headlight is missing, jagged the edges. Just by sight alone, the colour and material of the glass a match for the two fragments I found. I crouch in the gap between driver doors and run a hand over the bodywork.

Red paint scratches.

Shit, this is the car.

I feel the hairs on the back of my neck. But my attention is drawn by a sound. The sound of a diesel engine roaring.

I look up through the windows of the stunt car. See an electric-blue tow truck speeding towards it.

I turn and vault onto the bonnet of a black Ford Taurus behind me.

The tow truck smashes into the side of the mystery car and pushes the entire row of vehicles to the left.

I fly back and bounce onto the bonnet of the third car along, then the fourth.

I roll off the end car as the truck comes to a stop.

I rise and try to get a look at the driver, but he wears a white hockey mask over his face.

Safe to assume that wasn't just an accident.

Nope, definitely not. He reverses and pulls around the cars towards me. The way is blocked to my left, so I run out onto the road, looking for a safe place.

There isn't one.

The driver guns the tow truck. It comes right at me, fumes kicking out of the exhaust pipe into the air. The sun winking off a giant chrome grill that threatens to suck me in and run me down.

I keep going, weaving left and right, looking for a doorway, a witness, anything. But this part of the lot is deserted. Everything locked up and left alone.

The truck accelerates towards me, but the road branches off to the left. I sprint around the bend. The truck brakes and slides into the turn, rear wheels juddering. The guy can drive.

Could it be the stranger on the hill?

I dunno. Gotta keep on running, a stitch in my side from the food at Freddie's.

I zig-zag left and right onto a disused film set of what looks like old New York. The truck swings one way and the other. Knocks a fake lamppost over, ploughs through a bin and smashes a stand full of plastic fruit and veg out of the way.

The truck is closing fast.

The set is a big one.

The end of the road a long way off.

Too far off.

So I get a stupid idea.

A really bloody stupid idea.

And like most stupid ideas I get, I decide to do it without much thought.

I dive forward and throw myself to the road.

The tarmac hits me hard as I land.

The second I'm down, I lie flat to the ground. Arms out in front. Right cheek pinned to the road, teeth gritted hard.

The truck barrels over me, the undercarriage clearing by an inch. The driver brakes, twin rear wheels smoking as they catch on the warm, gritty road.

I push up off the ground and start running.

The truck sets off again, but it's too tight for the driver to swing it around.

I run it down before it can pick up any real speed. I jump onto the back of the truck and drag myself onto my feet.

The driver must have seen me in his rear view mirror, 'cause he turns his wheel left and right again, tyres screeching. I'm thrown to my right by the turn. I reach out and grab the hook on the back of the tow winch.

The arm the winch follows the turn of the truck. It swings out far to the right. I hang on for dear life as the driver swerves towards a mock store front.

I close my eyes and duck as the arm breaks through the glass window of the store.

The window shatters around me, but I come out clean of injuries.

The truck turns again and the arm swings all the way over to the left.

I look up and see the corner of a building coming right at me. A red brick wall. No time to let go. No way to escape.

This is gonna hurt.

Hell, it's gonna kill me.

33

I wait for the fatal impact.

Instead, I hit cardboard. Thick cardboard with foam stuffed in between.

But cardboard nonetheless.

Ha! The damn thing's nothing but a wobbly piece of scenery.

I tear a Charlie-shaped hole through the fake wall and keep on swinging. Over to the right again as the truck makes another turn.

I can't hold on forever. But soon we'll hit the more populated area of the studios. The guy'll be exposed.

All I've gotta do is . . . Shit, the front of the truck ploughs into a fire hydrant.

A real one.

The top pops off and a jet of water powers high into the clear blue sky.

The driver pulls left and I swing right into the line of fire. The force of the water hits me like a cannon. It snaps my right arm away and I lose my grip on the hook.

I fall and tumble over the ground. I come to a stop and

pick myself up, rain arcing and cascading down on me in a fine, ice-cold spray.

The truck speeds away and brakes for a hard right. I can't make out the plate. But I did notice one thing during my little joyride. The driver had a tattoo of a flaming skull on his left forearm.

And as the truck disappears out of sight, I see the flash of a blonde ponytail out of the back of that hockey mask.

I look up at the jet of water and stagger forward out of the spray, battered and bruised. A shrivelled old guy in a beige uniform appears out of one of the sets. He wears a tool belt, has a pencil behind one ear and a gawp the size of the Channel Tunnel on his face.

He looks at the fire hydrant and then at me. "What the hell kinda movie are you shooting?"

34

There are always ways and means in a city to get a gun. And this is one of the easiest places to get one. With or without a licence.

A couple of right questions asked on a street corner and I'm in the room of a shabby downtown hotel with worn brown seventies furniture and a small, hunched guy who dresses like he missed a few decades.

He talks me through my options. He wears a tan leather jacket past the waist and his bushy black sideburns long. He has this season's catalogue laid out in a large silver suitcase. It's opened up on the bed.

The guy's name is Yuri—Eastern European with a nervous energy and one eye on the door.

After padding me down and checking me for a wire, he hands me weapon after weapon. Automatic nine millimetres, semi-automatic pistols, the classics, the new models just in.

I'm doing things the hard way, of course. The easy way would be to report what happened to me at the movie studios to the cops. But as I already found out, the LAPD aren't too keen to listen. Quicker and easier to do it my own way. Especially now I *know* I'm onto something.

I look over the selection. "You got any Glocks? I like a Glock."

"I've got a beautiful piece right here," Yuri says, taking the automatic rifle off me. He hands me a Glock 17.

I look it over, checking inside the barrel, lining up an eye behind the sighting. I check the action, too. Gotta make sure it's genuine.

"It's last year's model," Yuri says. "Ex-military. Unused stock."

There's a reason this type of gun is popular. And that's because it doesn't have a safety to speak of. The safety mechanism is built into the gun. Which makes it quicker and more convenient to use. I check the pistol thoroughly, feel the weight and balance in my hand.

"Nice and light, heh?" Yuri says. "Yet powerful and reliable. Smooth action, too. Less of a kickback than the old models."

"Clips?" I ask.

Yuri holds up a finger. "Funny you should say." He walks over to a built-in wardrobe with a sliding door. The door is open. He takes a dark-grey suit carrier off the rail and lays it out flat alongside the case. "I'm doing a three-for-two on all models." Yuri unzips the suit carrier, revealing a spread of ammunition fastened with black tape to the inside. He runs a finger over the selection and picks out a clip, rips off the tape and tosses it over.

"How many do you need?" he asks.

"Three," I say.

"I've only got two," he says. "I can get you more."

"Two'll do fine," I say,

He eyes me for a second, in case I'm gonna shoot. A hand lingering close to the lapel of his jacket.

I aim the pistol at the carpet and nod. "I'll take 'em."

I detach the clip.

Yuri relaxes.

He tells me the damage as I tuck the gun in the back of my trousers under my suit jacket. I stash a clip in either inside jacket pocket.

I count out the money in hundred dollar bills as Yuri zips away the rest of his merchandise. I pause before giving the guy the cash.

Yuri eyes me with suspicion, hand out for the money. *"What?"*

"How about a twenty percent markup?"

"What for?" Yuri asks.

"Information."

"What kind of information?" he says.

"I'm looking for Carlos Campuzano. You know where I can find him?"

Yuri shakes his head. "Never heard of the guy."

I hand over the money we agreed. He pockets it and returns to his packing.

"An extra forty percent says you do," I say.

Yuri stops. Straightens up. "That's not a lot of money for what you're asking."

"I don't see anyone listening," I say, motioning around the stuffy little room.

"Sixty percent on top," Yuri says.

"Fifty," I say.

"Done," Yuri says, holding out a hand.

I take out my roll of hundreds and count out the extra cash. "Plus an extra hundred for your silence," I say.

"The Crazy Rat . . . You know who he is?" Yuri says.

"I don't care who he is," I say.

Yuri shrugs. He takes the money and tucks it away in a black leather attaché case. He scribbles out an address on a pink sticky note pad inside the case and tears it off the top. He hands it over on the end of a finger. "It's your funeral," he says.

35

I cruise through a Paicoma neighbourhood of brightly coloured stores, apartments and lockups, passing by buildings with colourful murals of Latin icons on the walls.

Now that's art.

I consult the pink sticky note Yuri gave me.

I roll into one of the more rundown suburbs, where kids deal on corners and supervisors and pimps sit out on stoops, looking out for custom and trouble. They watch me drive by. I notice their gang tattoos, but I don't look too close and never straight in the eye.

I drive along with the top down in my Camaro, like a rooster parading in front of a fox den, one hand on the Glock tucked in the waist of my trousers in case the car gets jacked.

After a few minutes of driving around, I come across the place. It sits on the corner of a row of disused commercial units. It's one of those auto shops where they pimp people's rides, with a handful of cars waiting their turn outside. I park out front and walk between a lime-green nineties

Cadillac and a gleaming white Mercedes with a large swoosh of fire down one side.

The auto shop is a big place. Multiple mechanics on the go. Four outlandish cars in a row, two jacked up high. The cars are having their rims and suspensions messed with, or their engines tuned and enhanced. The mechanics are all Latino, which suggests a tight-knit group in a tight-knit neighbourhood.

This isn't gonna be easy.

I stand in the large, open doorway. Smell the grease in the air. Listen to the shrill buzz of power-drills. Get the lay of the land.

And the people.

A radio plays music that goes with the surroundings.

There's an office to the back, off to the left. Windows with blinds half closed. It doesn't take long for the mechanics to start noticing me.

I guess they don't get many customers who look like I do. One of 'em sticks his head up and around the bonnet of a maroon SUV. He rubs the oil off his hands on a dirty white cloth as he wanders over. He's around five-seven with a shaved head. A string-bean with gang-style tattoos on his neck. A former con, maybe.

"Can I help you?" he says.

His name badge says Alejandro.

"Looking for a tune-up," I say.

"What kind?" he asks, getting closer, but stopping short of punching range.

"Got a valve that isn't firing right," I say.

"We don't do that kind of work here," he says, looking me up and down.

"Fair enough," I say, looking over the guy's shoulder. "Is Carlos in?"

The guy tenses up. *"Carlos?"* he says, yelling loud over his shoulder.

The other mechanics stop what they're doing, the sound of tools dying down. Only the radio playing in the background. The mechanics look over at me from the left and right. They exchange nervous glances.

Alejandro pauses a moment. "You're a long way from home, friend. Maybe you should get back in your LAPD pool car and drive on outta here, huh?"

"Do I look like a cop?" I say.

"You look like you're going to a fucking funeral," a fat mechanic with a thin goatee says. His name badge says Eddie.

I look again over Alejandro's shoulder. "Is Carlos here or not?"

"Who's asking?" Alejandro says.

"I'm a friend of Yuri's. Got some merchandise. Limited time offer."

"What kind of merchandise?" Eddie says.

"Double-ended dildos," I say. "What do you think?"

Alejandro clicks his tongue against the roof of his mouth. He turns and strolls off to the door to the back office. He disappears through the door.

I look at the remaining mechanics, left and right, going from eye to eye. I reckon they're all ex-cons. Each with their own thing going on, or taking home a cut of something more than the price of a pimped-out ride.

I start to wonder where these cars came from. Whether there are any real customers at all. Steal 'em, pimp 'em, sell 'em? Maybe.

The door to the back office opens up. Alejandro slips out but hangs back. A couple of big lads squeeze their shoulders through the door frame. They walk over. One in a red tracksuit with a matching red bandana. The other in a baggy black shirt and jeans with a silver chain hanging off the side. They stop in front of me.

"What's this merchandise?" the one in the tracksuit asks.

"Come out front and I'll show you," I say.

They look at each other.

The guy in the tracksuit is the talker. "Put your arms out," he says.

"I'm not carrying," I say.

The pair of 'em stare at me. I lift up my arms. The one in black pads me down. Finds my piece tucked away round the back.

He hands the one in the tracksuit the weapon, who raises an eyebrow. He holds up the Glock. "Why don't you load your gun?"

"Cause I can just use yours," I say.

The guy in black instantly feels for his pistol under his shirt.

I smile and hold it up for both of 'em to see.

36

The guy in red drops my Glock. He reaches for his pistol under his tracksuit top.

I shoot him in the left thigh. He collapses and yells. But still goes for the gun. He's right-handed, so I put another bullet in the same shoulder.

His mate in black wrestles me for his gun. He's a strong bastard and throws me against a purple Cadillac. He takes aim with the pistol, but I reverse the barrel in his hands as he pulls the trigger.

He puts two rounds in his own guts and drops like a sack of spuds.

But no sooner have I got control of the gun, than it's knocked from my hand by a tyre iron. My hand stings. I turn and see Alejandro taking another swing. I land a fist on his chin and he's out like a light.

I shake out my hand. But another pair of mechanics join the fight. One picks up the tyre iron. I catch his arm and slam his head against the roof of the Cadillac. I come away with the tyre iron and whack another mechanic in the head with a backhand swipe.

As he spins away, the guy in the red tracksuit gets around to taking out his gun. I smack him in the temple with the tyre iron and it's goodnight nurse.

Only trouble is, there's a mechanic the size of a wardrobe behind me.

He gets me in a headlock. A real good one. I drop the tyre iron and grapple with him.

I can't shake him off, so I run him backwards against a mustard-yellow SUV, jacked up high off its wheels.

The bastard holds on, with one remaining mechanic approaching. He's armed with a cordless power drill and a look that says he'll use it.

I try again to shake off the guy behind me. He's not letting go. His smaller friend strides towards me across the garage floor.

I notice the chrome trim is missing its nuts on the jacked-up SUV, its wheels at eye level beside me. I rip off the trim and throw it hard like a Frisbee. It hits the mechanic with the drill in the nose.

He's down, the finger on the trigger and the drill whirring away.

That leaves the guy on my back, trying to break my neck. There's a control box hanging on a wire to my right. I stretch and grab it. Push the button for 'up'.

The SUV rises another foot on the platform behind us. I drive back on my heels, taking the mechanic with me.

His head cracks on the solid steel kick plate of the SUV. I remove his arm from my neck as he sways. I flat-palm him in the nose. His head snaps back again. Hits the sill again and then hits the deck, blood pouring out of the back of his skull.

I retrieve my Glock and tuck it in the waist of my

trousers. I pick up the gun the guy in the red tracksuit dropped and make my way towards the back office.

I stop to grab the power drill and head for the door, pretty sure Carlos's guys are all knocked out, dead or on their way to dying.

And yeah, yeah, I know . . . Bodies stacking up, Charlie. But what can I say? Omelettes, broken eggs, I'm trying.

37

Carlos is still loading his pistol when I kick in the door. It swings open, splintering at the hinges. Carlos freezes. He sits behind a busy desk full of dockets and invoices—purely for show, I'm sure. He has his gold-plated Magnum in hand. A fancy-arse piece with a pearl handle. He just about gets the clip in with his chin. Loading's not easy when your left arm's in a sling.

"You pimping your guns now too?" I say, getting the drop on him. "Empty it."

Carlos detaches the clip from the gun. It drops onto the desk. I look around his office. There's a flatscreen TV with the sound turned down playing news on the wall to the right. A seven-foot steel filing cabinet behind the desk. A table with a coffeemaker and mugs behind me, along with a knee-high beer fridge underneath. Not much to note, other than a bin under the TV full of fast food wrappers.

"Toss the piece," I say, nodding towards the bin.

Carlos throws his gun in the bin. It makes a soft landing.

"And the clip," I say.

Carlos tosses in the clip.

"What are you gonna do?" Carlos says.

He's dressed casual today. A red open-neck shirt with the sleeves rolled up, revealing forearms with a devil tattoo. He has a bruised right eye and a plaster on his nose.

I take a seat across from him, moving slow, angling the chair so I've got half an eye on the office door.

"What I do depends on what you tell me," I say.

"We had an agreement," Carlos says. "I back off, you back off."

"You're right, we did have an agreement," I say.

"This ain't fucking backing off," Carlos says, pointing to the mess out on the garage floor.

"Neither's killing the kid," I say.

"Speed? That was an accident. Look at it, still all over the news."

Carlos nods to the TV on the wall. The report is to do with Josh. What next for Nightburner now the star of the franchise is dead?

"Come on, Carlos," I say. "We both know better than to believe the news."

"What the fuck does that mean?" Carlos says.

"At first I thought it was someone else," I say. "Didn't seem like your style. But now I'm thinking one of your crew did it."

"You killed all my guys, remember?"

"Not all of 'em," I say. "Seems like you've been doing some recruiting."

"And now I'll have to do some more," he says.

"You've still got the blonde guy with the ponytail."

"Who?"

"The arsehole who tried to turn me into a pancake at Solomon Studios."

"What are you fucking talking about?" Carlos says.

I squeeze the trigger on the drill. It revs into action. I drive the end into the desk and make a hole in the top. "Wonder what else this'll drill through?"

"Whatever you think I know, I don't know shit," Carlos says, glancing at his phone, face-up on the desk. "And whatever some other motherfucker tried to do to you, it's not on me."

I rise to my feet and tuck my gun in my waist. "Part of me was kinda hoping you'd say that."

I stride around the other side of the desk. Carlos goes to get up, crying out for help. I grab his head and slam his right cheekbone down on the desk. I pin his head down and hold the drill over the temple.

"You reckon this'll drill through bone?" I say, squeezing the trigger on the drill. I bring it closer to his temple.

Carlos bucks and wriggles. Saliva leaks out of the side of his mouth as he looks at the drill, eyeballs bulging.

"Fuck... I didn't do it," he says. "I don't know who did it."

"So someone *did* something," I say. "They run the kid off the road?"

"From what I heard," Carlos says. "But I don't know who or why."

I'm about to squeeze the trigger on the drill again when something catches my attention out of the corner of my eye. It's something on the TV. On the news. That something is my face. A grainy shot of me holding the door of Josh's SUV open for him as he climbs out. I got papped. I got bloody papped and now my ugly mug is all over the news.

And it gets better. What about this for a headline?

Bodyguard Implicated In Joshua Speed's Death. LAPD Issue Warrant for Arrest.

I look at Carlos. Glance at his phone. Something's up

here. Something involving him. I push his head down harder into the desk and squeeze the trigger.

"What else do you know?"

"Nothing, man," he says. "Fucking nothing."

"Bullshit," I say.

You think I wouldn't talk with a fucking drill to my fucking skull? Come on!

"Maybe I'll just make a little hole," I say, bringing the drill right up to the skin, close to the ear.

"Alright, alright!" he says. "I can give you something."

I keep the drill bit spinning. "I'm listening."

"It ain't what you want, though."

"Tell me anyway."

"It's the LAPD," Carlos says.

I release the trigger, but keep the pressure on Carlos' head. *"What's* the LAPD?"

"They've got me working for them. That's my involvement."

"Explain," I say, revving the drill a couple of times.

"They got me intimidating a bunch of movie stars."

"Why?" I ask.

"How the fuck should I know? They had me by the balls, man. First degree murder. Distribution. Three life sentences."

"And so what, you cut a deal with 'em?"

"They cut one with me," Carlos says. "Had me run intimidation on a few A-listers ... Threats, blackmail, flash a piece in their face. Wasn't gonna go anywhere."

"It was all an act?"

"Yeah, man," Carlos says. "I Pacino'd that shit up. They should've given me a fucking Oscar."

"If it was just intimidation," I say, "why the attempted hits in the club and the underpass?"

"We were gonna scare the kid," Carlos says. "To show his Hollywood friends that no one was safe. We were waiting for the right moment, when you weren't around. Then you went all Charles fucking Bronson on us."

"Why pick on Speed?" I ask.

"Cause he was hot shit and If we could get to him, we could get to anyone. It was a message."

"From you, on behalf of the LAPD? You expect me to believe that?"

"Hey, I'm not directing this fucking movie," Carlos says. "I know the whats, not the whys."

Carlos glances up at the news reports. I hear sirens wailing in the distance. Getting closer. Converging on a single spot. My current spot.

Carlos laughs to himself. "You're fucking fucked, motherfucker."

"What the fuck did you do, Carlos?"

"Yuri called me just before you showed up."

"And you called your pals at the LAPD," I say.

"Welcome to my world, bitch."

I toss the drill aside and take out my gun. I hold it to Carlos' head. "There a back door to this place?"

"Out of the office. To the right."

I let go of Carlos' head.

He peels his face off the desk. "You're a fucking dead man now—"

I slam his head into the desk and he drops to the floor, out cold.

Meanwhile, the sirens grow loud. Through the open garage door I see the flashing lights of black and white squad cars screeching to a stop. I head right out of the office and toss the weapon and clip. I throw my own away and push a fire exit door open into an alley.

I walk around the corner, thinking I'll leave the Camaro for the cops to tow away.

But there's a slight complication.

Roach and Thomas stand by their unmarked Ford police car. Roach with the right rear door open and his mouth ear to ear in a smile. Thomas leaning against the front passenger door puffing on a cigarette.

The bastards flushed me out. I stop in my tracks. Relax. Accept my fate and walk towards the car.

Roach motions for me to get in. Thomas flicks his cigarette in the gutter, leaving it to burn. I get in the car. Roach and Thomas take up their familiar places. Mickey does the driving again. He pulls the car fast out of the neighbourhood. Not the kinda place you wanna hang around if you're a cop, even with Carlos Campuzano in your pocket.

"Nice to see you again, lads," I say. "Where to this time?"

The answer is short and sharp. A punch to the jaw by Roach. I notice he's wearing black leather gloves. Mickey, too. Thomas pulls on a pair of his own.

Oh, this isn't good.

38

Mickey gets on the freeway. We're headed out of the city limits, towards the airport. The distant rush of 747 engines confirm it.

"So I'm the prime suspect, huh?" I say.

"Don't forget fugitive," Mickey says.

"You gonna throw in the stuff at the auto shop too?" I ask.

"What stuff?" Thomas says.

"Oh, nothing," I say.

"Like anyone gives a fuck about those spick bastards," Roach says.

"I'm curious," I say. "How are you selling this one in? You already filed your report. Accidental death, you said."

"Yeah, well that was before new evidence came to light," Roach says.

"What new evidence?" I say.

"That you got tired of the kid giving you shit and decided to get rid of him."

"You think it'll stick?" I ask.

"Shouldn't be too hard," Thomas says. "You've done most

of the work for us. Your fingerprints were found at the scene of the crash."

"Yeah, cause I was the first one there," I say.

"You were also seen at the county morgue, interfering with the body," Roach says.

"And in the precinct where you stole Detective Brooke's ID," Thomas says.

"Using it to tamper with evidence, no doubt," Thomas says.

"Out of some amateur attempt to cover your tracks, or just some sick fuck fantasy, who gives a shit?" Roach says. "All the media'll see is a guy with a history of mental illness and I'm pretty fucking certain a criminal record, who by the way, just had a check-up from the neck up using some of the kid's money."

"An advance payment as I heard it," Thomas says. "Which means you had nothing to lose in offing the kid."

"How did you know—"

"We paid Dr Kwan a visit," Mickey says. "Asked your buddy Wyndall Buck what he thought of you."

"He said it couldn't possibly be you," Thomas says. "But people have a way of giving away information they shouldn't."

I shake my head and laugh. "So what, you've decided to turn this into some big celebrity murder case?"

"The biggest since OJ," Roach says.

"And you three will be the ones to bring me in, huh?"

"Not exactly," Mickey says, his beady, pale-blue eyes glancing at me in the rear view mirror.

"What does that mean?" I ask.

The three of 'em go quiet on me.

I look out of the car window. We're getting off at an exit. I glance over my shoulder to see if there's a black and white following us.

No, we're on our own.

But wait, is that my Camaro?

Shit, it is. Following us all the way.

I turn to face the front, body getting twitchy, heart rate rising and a bad feeling in the pit of my guts. "So, mind if I ask an obvious question?"

"What's that?" Roach asks, looking out of his window, a cold stare on his drawn face.

"What we're doing out here? Or what my Camaro is doing back there?"

"That's two questions," Thomas says.

"And yeah, we mind if you ask," Mickey says, making a left turn.

He pulls another sharp left and we drive through some steel mesh fencing that's seen better days. We roll down a slope into a viaduct with high sloping walls either side and the odd dirty puddle at the base.

It's not exactly glamorous around here. Or well populated. A few factories, a lot of concrete and not much else.

We seem to be travelling back on ourselves. I turn and see the Camaro behind us, stuck like glue. I get a better look at the driver, too. A grim-faced guy with a deep tan that almost matches his brown suit jacket. He wears mirrored aviator shades, his salt and pepper hair dancing in the wind. He also wears a pair of gloves, the same as the others.

I guess the guy doesn't wanna leave any prints.

No, this isn't looking good at all.

* * *

I FEEL the car slowing down. Turn to the front again as Mickey brings us to a stop.

The viaduct is a smart choice. Not only is it in the middle of pissing nowhere—the high-sided walls means we're hidden from anything except helicopters. And as I peer out of the window at the clear blue sky, I don't see a bird, a plane or a chopper in sight.

Mickey turns off the engine. Roach jacks open his door. Thomas puts away the phone he's been tinkering on and gets out.

Roach walks around the back of the car. He opens my door.

I stay where I am, not making it easy for 'em. It's the least I can do.

"Don't be an asshole," Roach says. "Get the fuck out."

Roach reaches in and pulls at my arm.

I go with it, struggling up out of the car.

A lukewarm breeze ruffles my tie. The Camaro engine ticks as the fourth cop gets out and strolls over.

"Charlie, this is Detective Weiland," Roach says. "He'll be driving your car from now on."

Weiland nods. Doesn't say a word.

Mickey rounds the back of the Ford and opens the boot.

As he does so, Roach spins me round and pins me to the side of the car. To my surprise, he unlocks the cuffs around my wrists.

"Giving me a fighting chance?" I ask, thinking about who I'll swing for first.

I hear a click and see Thomas has his duty weapon pointed at my head.

"Guess not," I say, wondering what they've got in that boot of theirs. "Before you do it, any chance you can tell me what we're doing here?"

"We're not doing anything," Thomas says, as Mickey slams the boot shut. "You are."

"I don't get it," I say.

"You will in a minute you dumb shit," Mickey says, holding something in his hand. I can't tell what.

Roach pushes me around the side of the car into a clear stretch of concrete by the side of the cop car. Thomas follows close with the gun trained at my head. Roach knocks the legs out from under me. I drop to my knees. They crack on the viaduct floor. I suck it up. Don't wanna give the pigs any more of a good time than they're already having.

Thomas holds the gun to the back of my skull as Mickey comes over with two long loops of black rubber tubing. I'm trying to think of some way out of this when all four cops surround me. Roach grabs my right arm and holds it up. Before I can fight him off, Mickey slides a length of the thick, black rubber tubing around my forearm.

Thomas digs the barrel harder in the back of my skull. "Struggle or not, this is it, Charlie."

"Yeah, enjoy the California sunshine," Detective Weiland says. He catches a second tube tossed over by Mickey.

Next thing I know, it's being forced over my body, pinning my left arm to my side, only my right arm free.

I feel the barrel of Thomas's pistol return to the back of my skull. They work as a unit, slick and fast. Like they've done this before.

I struggle, of course, but there's four of the bastards and they've got all the leverage. Mickey loops the tubing over itself so it's wound tight around my right wrist. He and Roach force the arm in at the elbow and around my front.

They pull the remaining part of the loop over my head and shoulders so I'm trapped.

They're trying to put a gun in my hand..

As Mickey pulls on the tubing behind like reins on a horse, Roach reappears with a gun wrapped in a dark-blue cloth. He stuffs the cloth in his pocket and preps the weapon.

I fight against the inevitable harder than before. But there's nowhere to go. Roach tries to force the handle of the gun into my right hand. I clench my fingers tight into a fist so he can't prise 'em open.

"I can't get it in," Roach says.

"You don't need to," Thomas says to him. "Give me that," he says holstering his own weapon and stepping around the front of me. "Just keep his arm in the right place. We'll pry the fingers open later."

Thomas takes the pistol from Roach and half-squats over me. He aims the barrel under my chin. I fight left and right. Weiland grabs my head by a tuft of hair. He tilts it back, exposing my chin.

I fight some more, but not to escape. This time I just wanna get onto one knee.

Just give me one knee, universe. One fucking knee.

As the four of 'em wrestle me into a stable position, I sink lower on my shins. I drive up with everything I've got. I pull my right foot out from under me and plant it on the ground. I throw my head forward and feel a clump of my hair rip clean out of my scalp.

It stings like crazy. Mickey and Roach fight to keep me under control.

Weiland laughs a deep laugh. "His fucking hair came right out."

"Stop jerking off and grab the other tube," Mickey says.

Suddenly I feel the resistance double. No wrestling out of it. But I've got a foot on the ground. And my head free to move. Before they restrain it again, I relax my body and let out a sigh.

I lift my chin, inviting Thomas to take the shot.

"Finally, the guy sees sense," Thomas says.

"Just take the fucking shot already," Roach says with a snap.

"What's eating you?" Mickey says.

"We're out in the open," Roach says. "And I'm hungry."

"Yeah, yeah," Thomas says, angling the gun into my chin.

Thomas lines up the shot, taking care to get the angle just right to fake my suicide.

He's got one shot at this.

And so do I.

39

I can't see the guy's finger on the trigger. But I can tell in a man's eyes when he's gonna shoot.

When I think his finger's about to squeeze, I move my chin to the right.

I drop it fast to the side of the barrel.

Bite down hard on the guy's tendons.

Thomas cries out. His trigger finger squeezes. The gun goes off. The bullet blows a hole in Mickey's face.

Blood sprays into the air, his body collapsing.

"Holy fuck!" I hear Roach yell through a ringing in my left ear.

I spit a mouthful of Thomas's blood in his eyes. It blinds him. He pulls the gun away. I head-butt him flush.

He hits the concrete floor. I rise up to my feet, driving off my planted foot.

Weiland tries to pull me back and Roach yanks at the tubing tied around my right wrist.

As Thomas wipes the blood from his eyes in a daze, he aims at me with the pistol.

I kick it from his hand. He pulls his own duty weapon. I boot him in the head, knocking him out.

I run backwards, taking the two remaining cops with me. I run until I hit the unmarked car we came in.

This way no one can get leverage behind me.

Weiland lets go of the tube and draws his weapon.

But I've got my left arm free. I grab him by the throat and ram his head into the roof of the car. I swing a left as he bounces back and knock him for six.

I take a punch from Roach. Another. He kicks my right leg out behind the knee and goes for his weapon.

I yank his left leg by the calf and he staggers back against the car.

I'm up fast, blocking a right hook and hitting him hard to the body.

A right elbow driving downwards into his jaw gives him the jelly legs. He spits out a tooth.

I draw the gun from his holster and back up, training the barrel from man to man with my free hand.

I peel the rubber tubing off my right arm with my teeth. I shake off the tubing and backpedal between the Camaro and the cop car.

I climb in the Camaro, switching hands with the gun, keeping it trained on Detective Roach.

He could go for one of the other cop's guns, so I'm taking no chances. I glance down and see Weiland left the key in the ignition. I start the Camaro, knock the car in reverse and spin the wheel to the right.

I switch hands again, holding the gun in my left around the side of the windscreen.

Roach doesn't move. He watches me go. Mickey lies in a pool of blood as Thomas and Weiland scrabble around on the ground.

They're soon in the distance. Tiny figures left in a mess on the viaduct floor. I put the safety on the pistol and rest it on my lap.

I spin the car one-eighty and drive fast out of the viaduct, aquaplaning through standing sewer water and taking an exit ramp out onto the stretch of highway we came in on.

I notice Weiland changed the bloody radio channel. Now all I've got is a talk show about baseball.

Though I guess in context it's not the biggest problem I've got.

Roach will have been on that police radio like a shot.

Fugitive sighted.

Cop killer.

APB all units.

No doubt about it.

40

I check the sky for whirlybirds and my wing mirrors for distant flashing blue.

No sign yet, but soon. I reckon I'm twenty minutes out from the city. Clear of the viaduct but in need of cover. I spot a black dot in the sky. Getting bigger. And I think I hear the churn of helicopter rotors, the ringing in my left ear easing off.

Yep, looks like a chopper. A few miles out. And are those blue lights back there in the far-off distance? The freeway is coming up. I can't afford to take it.

Yet all is not lost.

I see an underpass under a small bridge with a bunch of homeless guys camping out beneath it. One is trying to hitch a ride into the city using a battered piece of cardboard. It says L.A. In crude brown lettering written in something I don't wanna imagine.

I pull off the highway, down into the underpass, where police choppers can't see. I slam to a stop alongside the homeless guys and honk on the horn. I wave the hitcher over. He turns and shuffle-runs into the shade of the underpass.

The rest of the homeless stare at me and the car. Some lying in sleeping bags. Another rooting through a trolley full of rubbish. And one staggering over with an almost-empty bottle of gin, his body withered and face haggard like a rotting skeleton under a grey beard. He mutters something I can't make out, swaying on the spot.

I leave the engine running and eject the Neil Diamond album I've got in the CD player. Can't leave old Neil behind. I pocket the CD and take a spare windscreen cloth from the glovebox. I wipe down the car the best I can and open the driver door.

The hitcher is a black guy with wild afro hair. He's in better shape than the man with the gin bottle and twenty years younger, but covered in dirt and skinny and crooked under a long army-green coat. He wears military dog tags around his neck.

"That's a sweet ride," he says, sounding like he's from somewhere else. Another state. Detroit? Atlanta, maybe? "You heading into the city?" he asks.

"Nope," I say, opening the driver door. "But take it for a spin. It's yours."

"You serious?" the guy says.

I climb out of the Camaro and hold the driver door open for him. "I'm bored of it, anyway. Feel like a stroll. Go on, get in."

He climbs in behind the wheel, wondering what the catch is.

"It's best driven fast," I say, closing the driver door.

"No doubt," the guy says. He wraps his hands around the wheel and smiles. He steps on the gas and the Camaro bullets out of the underpass in a whirl of tyre smoke and exhaust noise. He takes a hard right and disappears, bound for the freeway into L.A.

The homeless guy with the beard and the gin bottle sways on the spot in front of me. His eyes grow to the size of pool balls as he points a long, bony finger at me. *"You're wacko!"*

"Probably," I say, taking out my wallet. I hand him a twenty. "Here, get yourself something to drink. You didn't see me or the Camaro."

The guy nods and smiles. His mouth opens wide and black with rotten teeth and gums. I sidestep him and walk out of the underpass, checking the sky for that helicopter. It's elsewhere over the city. The sirens have been and gone. They'll no doubt be locking onto the Camaro's tail when they spot it haring into the city.

But I need a ride myself. As I emerge up a ramp onto a slip road, the perfect opportunity appears. A white Chevy people carrier, a hire car by the looks of the sticker in the rear windscreen. It's parked up, carrying a young family. Two kids in the back and a husband and wife stood outside of it consulting a roadmap. The husband is slim and ginger. Forty or so in jeans and a white polo shirt. The wife is pale and pretty in a summery green dress —freckles and mousy hair that curls around her ears.

"I told you we should have gone for the GPS," the wife says.

"At ten bucks extra a day?" the husband says. "I don't think so."

I straighten my hair and do up my tie, dust off the knees of my trousers and hope I don't look too threatening. I pull my jacket over the butt of the stolen gun at the front.

"Hey, can I help you?" I say.

The husband looks up at me from the map. Doesn't say

anything.

"You lost?" I ask.

"We're looking for the 405, I think," the wife says.

"You staying in the city? A hotel?" I ask.

"The Imperial," the husband says.

"I'll make you a deal," I say. "You give me a lift into the city. I'll direct you to the hotel."

"You local?" the wife asks.

"For my sins, yeah."

"You don't sound local," the husband says.

"I'm adopted," I say.

The husband drops the map to his side. The kids stare at me through the glass.

"Hey buddy," the husband says, "Thanks for the offer and all, but—"

"I get it," I say. "I'm a stranger, coming at you from out of nowhere. You've got a family to look after. I'd feel the same way. But my car was stolen back there by a homeless guy. Can you believe it? He's lying by the side of the road. I stop and get out to help him. He jumps up, assaults me and takes off with my car. I don't know if you saw the guy. The car's a red Camaro. A convertible—"

"Hey, we did see that," the wife says.

"Guy in a green coat. Looked like a bum. Thought it was odd," the husband says.

I flap my arms. "Well. I've got some walking to do, so . . ."

I go to walk past 'em, but stop and look over the husband's shoulder at the map. "You wanna take the next slip road onto the 405, then onto 110. That'll take you right in."

"Thank you," the husband says.

"You're welcome," I say with a smile. "Enjoy your stay."

As I turn to leave, I see the wife giving the husband the

eyeballs. She throws an elbow in his side.

"Hey, buddy," the husband says.

I stop and turn.

"I've forgotten all that already," he says. "Why don't you get in and we'll give you a ride?"

I breathe a sigh of relief. "You're a lifesaver."

"So long as you don't mind sharing a car with a couple of little terrors," the husband says.

"What? I love kids," I say. "Got one of my own. She's at university now, but she'll always be my little angel, you know what I mean?"

The wife nods and smiles. "Awe," she says, a hand on my arm. "You're so sweet."

The parental schmaltz seems to relax the pair of 'em a bit more. Seeing as I won't need to flash my piece to intimidate 'em, I button up my jacket over the butt.

I climb in the back with the kids. There's a flame-haired lad playing some kinda game on a phone and a girl with the same hair as her mum singing to a pop tune.

Neither of 'em can be more than eight or nine.

I tell the husband where to get on the freeway and which lane to take.

The little girl looks up at me from the middle seat. "I'm Reagan. And you're not wearing your seatbelt."

"Oh, sorry," I say, pulling my belt across and clicking it in place.

Reagan points at the knuckles on my right hand. "You've got ketchup on your hand." She leans forward and points at the tip of my right boot. "And on your shoe . . . *And* on your suit."

"Oh, I, uh . . . It was at the drive-thru. The sachet burst."

"Oopsie-whoopsie!" Reagan says.

"Yeah, oopsie-whoopsie," I say, licking a finger and trying

to remember whose blood it is I'm wiping off my knuckles.

"Here," the wife says, handing me a wet wipe from up front.

I take it and clean my hands, then the toes of my boots. I rub at another bloodstain on the lapel of my suit jacket, scrunch up the wipe and stuff it in a pocket.

"That's better," Reagan says. "All clean."

Damn kids. Too bloody perceptive.

I smile at Reagan, thinking she might be a little bit mental—paranoid she might spot something else.

Another song comes on the radio. "Ooh, this is my favourite." She squeals like a rat stuck in a blender, singing along at a pitch high enough to make a dog's ears bleed.

We roll towards the city, traffic starting to get heavier, a smoking car wreck a mile ahead. On the way in, we roll past the Camaro. It's parked on the hard shoulder across the freeway, the hitcher cuffed and bent over the bonnet by a pair of cops in uniform.

I hold my breath as we ride on by, unbuttoning my suit blazer. If mum and dad notice, or either of the two sprogs chirp up about it, I'll have to bring the gun out and threaten 'em with it. The last thing I wanna do with kids in the car.

I also keep my fingers crossed the couple up front haven't seen the news in the last few hours. And that the cops aren't stopping traffic.

But it's all clear up ahead. I relax as we leave the Camaro behind. Even more when a train of squad cars speed by in the opposite direction, sirens flashing and wailing. I notice that police chopper in the sky, leading the way. I realise they're headed to the underpass—the hitcher probably telling the LAPD where he got the car.

I sit back and take my hand away from the gun. "Next exit," I say to the husband.

41

Home is a no-go and the airport is out.

Maybe I could take a Greyhound out of town, or a Metro rail ride out to the valley. Make my way out of the state from there. Head south across the border, into Mexico.

I slam back a drink as I plan my next move. Thr first of two stiff ones lined up alongside a beer.

I wear my suit collars up around my neck and my tie slung low. The gun lies dismantled down a grid somewhere. If they eventually catch up with me, I can't be found carrying Roach's piece. And I'm not about to get into a shootout with the LAPD.

I sit in a booth to the back of a dingy downtown hole I know. A place where the only question asked is *what'll it be?*

The booth is tight and high, with brown padding with the stuffing showing. The bar is long and narrow like a train carriage. The light barely creeps in through dirty street-side windows and the bar to my right runs long and busy with drinkers on stools and bottles of all kinds on the shelves.

There's no entertainment here, other than a boxy TV

perched high behind the bar. It plays some kind of daytime soap opera about a hospital. No sport on at this time and the primary concern of most people in here is getting to the bottom of the next glass.

I'm gazing into my own when a deep voice talks to me. "Drinking, at a time like this?"

"Oh, for fuck's sake," I say to myself.

I look up from my glass. Josh Speed as Nightburner sits across from me in the booth. He sips a chicken smoothie out of a tall glass through a straw.

"What you need is protein," he says.

"What I need is for you to fuck off."

"A little touchy, aren't we?" Nightburner says, a white film around his top lip.

"I'm wanted for Josh's murder and probably the murder of an LAPD detective now, too, so yeah, I've got things on my mind."

"What's your next move?" Nightburner says, sucking on his smoothie.

"Drink this," I say, pointing at the glass. "Drink that," I say, pointing at the bottle of beer. "And get the hell out of here."

"Leave town?" Nightburner says.

"You got it, pal."

"But you're in the middle of an investigation," Nightburner says.

"A dead one," I say.

"Things are just warming up," Nightburner says.

"How do you figure that?"

"The bruises around the kid's neck," Nightburner says.

"With no clear idea of how he got 'em," I say.

"The attack at the studios," Nightburner says.

"Could have been anyone," I say.

"How about the deal between Carlos and the cops? There's something big going on here, Charlie. Real fucking big."

"Too big," I say. "A lot bigger than one man with a criminal record and a face all over the news."

"It's not a clear picture," Nightburner says. "Sure, you recognise your own face, but how many people on the street would know it's you?"

"Forgive me for not taking any chances," I say. "The only question left is what's my safest route out of town."

Nightburner grunts and shakes his head. Sucks on his smoothie.

"What?" I say.

"There you go again, putting yourself first," Nightburner says.

"You've gotta know when to fold," I say. "The reason I'm in this mess is 'cause I don't quit when I'm behind. Well I'm starting to learn." I neck the remainder of the double whiskey and slam the glass down. I wrap my hand around the slippery-cold brown beer bottle.

Nightburner grunts some more. He slurps the end of his chicken smoothie and puts down the glass. "Did I quit when my parents were burned to death by drug dealers? Did I take a step back when I faced Mongoose and Battering Ram in Nightburner 2: The Return? Did I cry like a big fucking baby when Rancid threw Marcy-Jo West off the top of the Chrysler Building?"

"I dunno, I fell asleep during that one."

"You fell a-fucking-sleep?" Nightburner says, taking it far too personally.

"I'd been up all night, a situation needed cleaning up. I only went to see it 'cause Cassie wanted to go. And that's only 'cause she fancied the arse off Josh."

Nightburner leans over the table and puts his face in mine. "No, I didn't quit," Nightburner says with a snarl. "Shit no motherfucker. I jumped off that roof and saved Marcy-Jo with a laser-guided grappling gun."

"Good for you," I say. "But without any hard evidence or witnesses, it's all conjecture. My word against the LAPD's . . . I'm not even sure they're involved in Josh's death. Only that they're covering their own mistakes."

"And you think they're gonna stop pursuing you just because you leave town?" Nightburner says.

I take a slug of beer. Another, another.

"There's only one way out of a hole this deep," Nightburner says.

"Oh, what's that, Einstein?" I ask.

"Keep digging," Nightburner says.

I keep drinking, closing my eyes and hoping the guy'll go away. But he keeps talking, his hot breath and specks of his spit showering my face.

"None of this is real," I repeat to myself. "None of this is real."

"So you're a Descartes fan, huh?"

I open my eyes. Look up and see a waitress in jeans and a white top with an empty tray. She's got her dark-brown hair up and big looping ear rings. She's good-looking and chews on a stick of gum.

"A what?" I ask her.

"Descartes? I'm studying Descartes at college. He said that nothing can be known to exist for certain other than the mind."

"Yeah, can't get enough of the Des—what's his name," I say, glancing up at the TV over the woman's shoulder.

My eyes catch and lock onto the screen. A glance turns

into a stare. I count her out a couple of notes. "Excuse me," I say. "Keep the change."

"Don't worry, I will," she says, a little confused, but glad of whatever ridiculous tip I just left her.

I move over to the bar.

The barman, a guy with three chins and a flush-red face the colour of his shirt picks up a remote and changes the channel.

Suddenly we're on one of those auction shows.

"Do me a favour," I say. "Turn that back over, will you?"

The barman stops and stares at me. "You wanna watch Hope Medical?"

"Yeah," I say. "It's my favourite."

"Yeah, well no one else wants to watch that shit," he says, laughing.

I reach over and grab him by the collars. "Put on Hope Medical or I'll beat the belly fat off you."

"Hey, let go of him," a fellow drinker says. A stocky bald guy with a ruddy nose says.

"Or what, motherfucker?" I say to him, giving him the not-today eyes.

The drinker looks the other way.

I tighten my grip on the barman.

"Alright, alright," he says, picking up the remote. He changes the channel back to the medical soap on TV.

I let go of him and watch the TV.

It's a scene with two doctors talking in a corridor. One with grey hair and one with dark. Both stupidly handsome and tanned. They argue over something. A woman, I dunno. The guy with the grey hair strides off thinking he's gotten the better of his colleague.

The dark-haired doctor turns to the screen and stares into space off-camera. *"You think you've got the upper hand,*

Hamilton?" he says to himself. *"You think Valerie is yours . . . But you're wrong. You're dead, dead wrong."*

"Doctor!" a nurse says, rushing onto the scene.

Boom, there she is again. Pretty and slim with hair dyed a mix of light brown and dirty blonde.

And that face. It's burned into my mind. No longer in the glare of my headlights, but framed by the TV.

42

"*What is it?*" the dark-haired doctor says.

"*We've got a code blue in ward three,*" the nurse says. "*It's little Jimmy. We're losing him!*"

"*Little Jimmy?*" the doctor says in horror. "*Oh my God.*"

As the doctor processes the news and the nurse nods up and down with mock tears, the episode cuts to the closing credits. I watch 'em like a hawk.

"What a loada shit," one of the drinkers says behind me.

I ignore 'em. Eyes glued to the screen. The credits roll fast.

Nurse in Corridor - Naomi Jones.

There we go. Must be her.

I grab a paper napkin off the bar top. "Got a pen?" I ask the barman.

He hands one over. No arguments.

I scribble down the name. "Sorry for my aggressive behaviour. I've had a rough day." I slip him a ten dollar bill and tell both guys I threatened to have a drink on me.

"And can I keep the pen?" I ask.

"Whatever," the barman says.

I snatch the napkin off the bar top and head outside through a fire escape door, into an alley. I cross the alley and stand next to a coffee shop that has free wi-fi. I piggyback the signal and hop on the internet. I tap Naomi's name into Google and get a result. She must be an unknown actress, because she doesn't have a potted bio or a Wikipedia page. I do find her on iMDB, though—a brief list of the odd appearance here and there. An advert, a TV show. Roles like 'Pretty Girl in Mall' in another soap and 'Second Dancing Smiling Girl' in a fizzy drink advert.

At the bottom of her list of roles is the number of a talent agency she's signed up to.

I dial the number.

A woman with a forty-a-day throat answers. "Hello. Can I help you?"

"Hi, I was wondering if you could put me in touch with Naomi Jones."

"Who's asking?" the woman says.

"I'm a casting director. I work for Solomon Studios."

"Oh, uh, hello," she says, perking up. "So you're interested in seeing Naomi?"

"Yes, as soon as possible," I say. "We're shooting a movie. A big one. But we need to re-cast the, uh, the best friend of the romantic lead."

"And you want Naomi?"

"I just saw her work on Hope Medical," I say. "Outstanding."

"Really?" the woman says.

"Yes," I say. "But she needs to screen test today. Do you have a number I can call her on?"

"Sure, but she's at an audition right now," she says. "The lead in an independent movie, as it happens."

"Do you know where?" I ask. "I'll meet her there when she's done."

"Uh, yeah, one second," the woman says.

She comes back with the details. I scribble down the name of the production company and the address, trapping the phone between shoulder and ear and holding the napkin up against the concrete wall of the coffee shop. "Thank you very much, madam. You've been a great help."

"Call anytime," she says. "I've got a roster full of talent."

I cut her off during mid-pitch, memorise the address and pocket the pen and napkin. I head out onto the street and flag down a cab. I jump in the back, give the cab driver the address and sit low in the backseat, keeping my head down and my eyes from connecting with his.

"Told you the case wasn't dead," Nightburner says, sitting alongside me.

43

Hornblower Productions is small. Unassuming. Tucked away in the suburbs. A flat, two-story brick building with a bunch of different production offices all lined up in a row.

We're not in tinseltown anymore. More like tinfoil town, Bentleys replaced by second-hand Beamers in the car park out front. I press the buzzer and wait. No one answers the voice box, but the door buzzes back at me and clicks open. I push on through and find an entrance hall with a bank of beaten-up metal mailboxes. There's an arrow on the wall pointing up a staircase to Hornblower. The dark-red paint on the stairs is chipped and the black bannister wobbles when I use it for leverage. I stride up the stairs and find myself in a reception area with a smoky-pink carpet. There's a small desk without a receptionist.

"Hey buddy, you here for the audition?"

I turn to find a guy slimier than a sea cave rock. Long black hair slicked back over his head with a chip-pan worth of grease and a baggy yellow shirt from the nineties tucked into a pair of brown suit trousers. He wears big white trainers and a gold chain around his neck. "Lost your tongue, buddy?" he says. "Hope not. You're gonna need it."

"Uh, sorry, yeah," I say.

The guy strides up to me. Pokes me in the biceps and slaps me on the shoulders. "Well you're the right kinda size." He looks at my face. Circles his own with a finger. "And you've got the whole rugged thing going on . . . Come on through."

I follow him down a corridor that could do with a lick of paint. We head into a pokey office swamped with screenplays.

"The name's Aaron," Aaron says, throwing himself into a brown velour, high-backed swing chair that looks as if he dug it out of a skip.

The visitor chair isn't much prettier. A blue one with a dubious ringed stain on the seat cushion.

Aaron tosses me a tattered screenplay, open at a page with a few lines marked in yellow highlighter pen. I look around the office. The desk has a name plate that says *Aaron Zweltsmann, President & Executive Producer*. The posters of previous productions are printed big and framed on the walls.

I get the impression this isn't the kinda place you're gonna find De Niro or Scorsese dropping in to pitch ideas.

On the walls, we've got:

Apocatits

Apocatits 2

Zombie Pussyeaters 3

"You make a lot of pornos?" I ask.

"You mean post-apocalyptic adult erotica horror?" Aaron says. "Yeah, that's our speciality."

"And what's the film I'm reading for?" I ask.

"Apocatits Three," he says. "Now, you're playing the role

of Hades, the bad guy's chief henchman. You'll be wearing a metal mask and a chainmail suit, so there's a chance your face won't appear on camera, depending on edits. That okay with you?"

"Sure," I say.

"You get your cock out in the third act—some anal, of course," Aaron says.

"But of course," I say.

"There may or may not be a money shot, followed by a group orgy. We wrap up with Taylor, the lead, cutting your head off with a chainsaw."

"Uh, okay," I say.

"Sooo," Aaron says. "We'll read a few lines and then I'll need to see the goods."

"The goods?"

"Your cock," Aaron says. "And I'll need to see it hard. Make sure everything's working' right. Sound good?"

"Uh—"

I'm about to blow my cover and start questioning Aaron about Naomi, when I catch a glimpse of her picture on his desk. It's a glossy black and white headshot print with a white mug resting on top that says *Suck My Dick*.

I lean forward and point at the photo. "Who's the girl?" I ask.

Aaron picks up the photo from under the mug. "Who, this chick? We've got her in right now, auditioning."

"For this film?" I ask.

"Sure. She's playing the lead," Aaron says, "And before you ask, no, she's not a star name. That's not our style at Hornblower Productions. We like to get 'em ripe, you know what I'm saying?"

"I'm not sure," I say.

Aaron leans forward as if he's confiding in me. A smirk

on his face. "We put these free ads out online looking for new talent, you know what I'm saying? We say it's an indie picture, some romantic bullshit, whatever . . . They come in and read for a part. A phoney script about a small-town girl seeking love in the big city—something they can relate to . . . Then we tell 'em maybe they're not right for the part. But maybe they'd be perfect for another picture we've got on the boil."

"Oh yeah?" I say.

"Yeah. And this is the best part . . . These girls are desperate for a break. And fresh, too. Especially this latest one. Man, you should see the tits on this girl. She's gonna rock the wet titty scenes . . . Man, In this one scene, she gets dunked upside down in a barrel, a torture scene, you know what I'm saying?" Aaron stops rabbiting for all of two seconds to suck on his own bottom lip. "Oh, I can't wait for that one. You like a pair of wet tits? I love a pair of wet tits, man. Nothing I like more than seeing a pair of sopping wet tits hanging upside down. It's a Hornblower speciality, you know what I'm saying?"

"I think I get the picture," I say. "You auditioning her right now, you said?"

"Yeah, she's in with Guy,"

"Guy?"

"Guy Meddles, the director. He's got firsts on this one, lucky fuck. We take turns, you know what I'm saying? But I'm next in, you get me?"

"Yeah, I get you," I say. "Which room have you got her in?"

"Why, you want a turn?" Aaron says. "Hey, sorry man. We've got a reading to do here. Besides, female auditions are strictly producer and director, you feel me, brother?"

"I think I'm about to," I say.

Aaron cocks his head. *"Huh?"*

I launch forward over the desk. I grab him by the neck and pull him up off his seat, drag him over the desk. Up close he stinks of cheap aftershave. His neck bulges and his face turns purple.

"Where's the audition happening?" I ask, loosening my grip a little.

"Who the fuck are you, man?" he says, wheezing.

I grab a fistful of shirt with my spare hand, pull him all the way over the desk and throw him against a bookshelf full of DVDs. He hits the office carpet. Scrambles to his feet to get away, slipping on a mass of DVD cases.

I yank him up by the back of his shirt collar and pin him against the nearest wall.

"Don't make me ask again," I say.

44

I leave Aaron to cough and splutter. I stride down the corridor, straight to the director's office at the opposite end. There's a laminated paper sign hung on the door that says *Audition in Progress. Do Not Disturb.* I hear muted screams from behind the door.

I try the handle. It opens. As I walk into an office with a desk, a black leather casting couch and a video camera on a tripod, I find Guy Meddles pawing at Naomi. He has a wild island of receding brown hair and a face like a pig.

Naomi scoops her handbag off the casting couch and backs away from the guy.

Meddles grins like a maniac and grabs at her dress. "Don't play hard to get, baby."

She kicks Meddles in the balls. He doubles over but seems to enjoy it. The girl makes a beeline for the door.

"Hey," I say, reaching out to grab her. Probably not the best move. Now she thinks I'm one of them. The girl body swerves me and takes off out of the door, into the corridor and down the stairs.

"Who the fuck are you?" Meddles says, holding his crotch.

I ignore the guy and head out of the door after Naomi. I hit the stairs, but she's fast and frightened. I barrel down the staircase after her, almost falling arse over tit.

I jump and miss the last few steps. The girl throws the door open and disappears. I catch the door as it swings shut and see her running across the car park.

"Hey! It's okay!" I yell.

Either she doesn't hear, or doesn't care, digging her hand in her bag on the run. Looking over her shoulder. Bringing out a set of keys. Slamming on the brakes next to a beaten-up old pale-blue Beetle.

I run to catch up. Her hand shakes, but she jams the key in. She jumps inside and pushes the lock down. I reach the car and bang on the window.

She panics, gets the key in the ignition and turns the car over.

"I just wanna talk," I say, hands on the driver window.

She turns the ignition again. The Beetle coughs and starts. Smoke kicks out of the exhaust and she pulls away. I bang on the window, but she's off.

I whirl around.

Need a car of my own. Something easy.

I spot a bronze nineties Honda Civic. A saloon. I run over, slam an elbow through a window and open the driver door. I rip the cover off the steering wheel column and hot-wire the car in seconds. I step on the accelerator and spin the Civic out of the car park. I fly out of the entrance, cutting up an oncoming car.

I get the Honda going as fast as it'll go. See the girl's Beetle a hundred yards ahead. I slow to a cruise and gradually make up ground, sitting low in the seat. Don't want her to know it's me.

I tail her a good half an hour across town, into a rundown area in San Fernando Valley. The girl pulls into a suburb where the homes are small, boxy apartments with secondhand cars missing wheel trims, nose to tail on the streets.

I hang back as she parks up outside a white apartment block and gets out of the car. I see her fiddle with the lock on the car door and then make her way up a set of brick steps to the apartments. She drops her handbag on the way. It spills open. She squats and scrabbles to pick up her things, then makes her way in through the front door.

I pull up directly across the street from the apartments.

I hope no one notices the broken window on the Civic. Though around here, I doubt anyone cares. I slide lower in the driver seat and notice a light going on in the front room of a ground floor apartment to the right of the main entrance. Naomi hurries around inside. Closes the venetian blinds over all the windows. Is she calling the cops? I guess we'll soon find out.

* * *

Night falls fast, but time ticks slow.

I find a bottle of half-empty coke in the glove box. There's a pack of nacho crisps and a Hershey's bar. I eat the nachos then ration out the chocolate and remaining coke.

There's no sign of activity from inside the apartment. No sniff of a visit from the LAPD. Why didn't she report it? Maybe she didn't wanna cause a scene. Create a rep for herself. Movie people know other movie people. All that bullshit.

At around eleven, the lights go off behind the blinds in Naomi's apartment. The streets are quiet except for barking dogs and the odd passing car. Around midnight, my eyelids get heavy. I fight it for a while, but in the end I figure what's the point? Not as if she's going anywhere. And I'm not gonna approach the girl until the time is right. Until she's calmed down. Had a good night's sleep. Then I'll make my move, slow and subtle.

Not like before, where I ran after her and banged on her car window like a crazed maniac.

No, it's like approaching a deer in the forest—no sudden movements. She's gotta know I'm not a wolf.

So I ease the seat back, rest my head and let myself drift.

45

It's that time between night and dawn. Where it's dark, but not as dark as it was. Where you can see what you're doing, but not quite. Where it's a new day, but no one's up.

I stir and feel the chill of the air through the window on my bones. Pull the lapels on my jacket tighter to my neck and shudder. I try to sleep again, but I'm too awake and in a funny position on the driver seat.

It's a few seconds before I realise it's a noise that woke me up. The sound of a low-humming car engine and the slow roll of tread over tarmac. The slight creak of a set of brakes as it comes to a stop. And the yellow glow of dipped headlights in the far corner of an eye.

I turn slow in the seat to face the driver-side window, my side aching and my hip bone giving me all kinds of grief. I peer out over the door sill and see a big, tall shadow of a man climb out of a black SUV.

He's dressed in dark clothes—jeans, boots and a bomber jacket, a baseball cap and gloves.

He shuts his door as soft as he can. Walks quiet up the steps to the apartments.

The guy could be a resident. But my gut says no. Call it an old fixer's instinct.

The lack of a fob or a key in the man's hand confirms it. He takes out a lock-picking screwdriver tool and gains entry. He slips inside with a glance over his shoulder.

The guy could be there for someone else, to rob an apartment. But it's a mighty coincidence. And even so, am I gonna let an intruder break in like that?

I pull my seat upright and get out of the car. I walk off the stiffness as I cross the road, into a light jog. Up the steps and in through the door, I push through without a sound.

There's a staircase up to the left. The door to an apartment to the right—apartment 1A. The door is ajar. Another lock picked. Again, I go in slow. The apartment is close to pitch-dark. I creep inside and down a narrow hallway.

I turn right into a room. The living room. I knock a magazine off the arm of a sofa. I'm lucky. It lands on a shagpile rug.

I back out into the hallway, eyes adjusting to the dark. A shadow moves at the end of the hall. In through a door. I move along the hallway after the intruder, right hand clenching into a fist.

I get to the door. Step inside. Pale slits of light break in through the blinds and over Naomi, asleep in bed.

The intruder's so focused on the girl he hasn't sensed me coming in behind him. He picks up a spare pillow off a bedside chair. Naomi faces the window. White bed covers half-off. Mouth open and prone to an attack. The guy stands over her with the pillow. Leans in towards her, the pillow nearing her face.

I dart forward. Grab the guy in a headlock and pull him

away. He yells, crashes into the bedside table and staggers backwards, fighting me off.

Naomi wakes and screams. The intruder is bloody strong. Shoulders like boulders and desperate to break my grip. He runs me against a wall. An elbow in my ribs. A punch thrown over a shoulder, right in my face. He slams me against the wall as I try and apply a sleeper hold.

The entire apartment shudders. The guy weighs more than an elephant. My hold on him comes loose. He drives a knee into my guts.

Can't see much, but I sense the draw of a pistol. I fight him for it. There's a silencer on the end. A couple of shots plug into the wall behind me, missing by an inch.

I twist the guy's wrist. The gun is on the floor, but lost to the darkness.

Naomi keeps on screaming. Screaming at us to get out. Not a loud scream, the fear stealing most of her breath. More of a squeal and a gasp.

Meanwhile, we grapple back and forth. Two burly figures in the dark, the girl sitting up frozen on the bed.

The intruder's had training. Self-defence, hand-to-hand holds. He gets me in a good one. An arm-lock. He bends me over.

A knee driven between my collarbones. I take it. Drive a fist into the guy's balls.

He loses some of his grip.

He reaches for something—the gun off the floor.

I stoop low and grab hold of his thighs. I lift him off the ground and drive him into the floorboards on his back.

He drops the gun. I hear it slide over the wood. I'm on top of the guy before he knows it. Driving a fist in his face. Another. Another. He goes limp. You know when you've thrown a clean KO. You can feel it. In the connection. In the other guy's body—looser than a sack of spuds.

As I get to my feet, a bedside lamp clicks on. Naomi is off the bed. Scissors in hand. She points the sharp ends at me, shaking like a leaf.

"Get out!" she says. *"Get the fuck out!"*

"Calm down," I say, trying to make an approach, hands out in peace.

"Don't come near me," Naomi says. "Stay away!"

"You realise I just saved your life?" I say, taking a step forward.

"Stay away," she repeats.

I point to the guy on the floor. "I know you're scared, but this man was gonna kill you. He was gonna suffocate you in your sleep with a pillow. Maybe put a bullet in your face. I stopped him. Now give me the scissors. I'm not here to harm you."

"How do I know *you're* not the guy—The guy who was gonna kill me," she says, backing up against the wall.

"I guess you don't," I say.

She squints into the light, focusing on my face. "I recognise you. From the production company. You're one of those sick perverts. They sent you to get me, didn't they?"

"No, no," I say, edging towards her.

"Get out! Get out or I'll call the cops!"

I'm close to her now, but I stop and hold up my hands. "Okay, you win. I'm going . . ."

Before she can react, I snatch the scissors from her hands. She backs up against the wall. I slide the scissors under the bed. "Like I said, I'm not gonna hurt you."

"Then what the hell are you doing in my apartment?" she says. "And what the fuck is going on? I mean, who are you? Who's he?" she says pointing to the intruder.

"I don't know who he is. I was parked up and saw him breaking in from the street."

"You were stalking me?"

"Staking out," I say.

"What's the difference?"

"I only want information," I say. "I saw you on TV and found out who you were, where you were gonna be—"

"You *are* stalking me," Naomi says.

"No," I say. "That didn't come out right . . . Did you watch the news today?"

"No," she says. "Why?"

"No reason," I say, moving over to the intruder. "I'd suggest you put on some shoes. And some proper clothes."

"What for?" Naomi asks.

"So we can get out of here," I say.

"You're the one who needs to get out," Naomi says. "And take your friend with you."

"Listen, I haven't got time to argue . . . Or get rid of a body. It's not safe here," I say, searching the intruder's pockets. I find a wallet in an inside jacket pocket. An ID inside the wallet. Clyde Tunney. DMZ Security. The same security firm Solomon Studios hires to look after its VIPs and movie stars.

The guy starts to groan. Comes to, but slow. He tries to sit up. I pop him in the jaw. He's out cold again. I look at the ID and look at him. He's a bull of a man with a grey buzzcut and big facial features. "Come to think of it, he does look familiar," I say. "One of Speed's old minders."

"Speed?" Naomi says. *"Joshua Speed?"*

"Yeah," I say, pocketing the ID and returning his wallet.

"You knew Joshua Speed?" she says.

"Yeah," I say, recovering the pistol with the silencer. "I

was his bodyguard. Took over from this guy and some other clown. I don't know what the hell he's doing here, though."

"Why don't you ask him? Force it out of him?" Naomi says, "Seeing as you're so good at beating people up . . ."

"Because he's carrying a nine millimetre semi-automatic pistol with a silencer attachment. Which means he's almost certainly not operating alone. And I for one don't wanna be around when the cavalry shows up, do you?"

Naomi shakes her head.

"Besides, I've got a better idea," I say. "Now put on some clothes and grab your car keys."

46

I take the wheel of Naomi's clapped-out Beetle, pushing the seat right back so my knees aren't up around my ears. I put the key in the ignition and turn. A cough and an apology from the engine. I turn again, get nothing.

"You have to let the choke out," Naomi says.

Christ, the choke. I haven't had a car with a choke in years. I try again and it's third time lucky.

The sun is on the rise and the dawn growing lighter. I pull the Beetle away from the kerb and head towards the end of the street.

At the end of the street, there's a crossroads wide enough to swing the car around one-eighty. I make the turn and head back where we came from. But only a short distance. I pull in sharp to the kerb on the right-hand side of the street and bring the car to a stop.

"What are you doing?" Naomi says.

"Waiting," I say.

"For what?"

"For the guy to wake up."

"I don't get it," Naomi says. "I thought you said we had to get out."

"Out of the apartment," I say. "Not out of the neighbourhood. Pretty soon he'll come around. Then we'll follow him for a while. See where the road takes him."

"Hey, whatever you wanna do," Naomi says, hands up in surrender. "Just don't include me."

"Too late for that," I say. "Seems like you've got a price on your head, just like me. We're gonna tail him and get some answers. In the meantime, I want some answers from you."

"Answers about what?" Naomi says.

"I saw you, up in the hills the night Josh died. You were there. You must have witnessed something."

"Is that what all this is about?" Naomi says. "Look, I went to the police. They wouldn't listen . . . I should never have got in that car."

I'm about to give Naomi a grilling when I see Tunney stagger out onto the street and into his SUV. He pulls away from the kerb and comes our way.

"Get down," I say, slumping low in my seat and pulling the girl with me. The SUV cruises past slow—I notice him on the phone already as he passes by. He swings the SUV around the same way I did and comes past us again. I keep hold of Naomi's arm.

As soon as Tunney clears us by a reasonable distance, I slide up in my seat and pull the Beetle clear of the kerb.

"Okay," I say. "How about you fill me in on what you know?"

"How about you fill *me* in?" Naomi says, crossing her blue-jean legs and folding her arms, with sleeves pulled over hands in a baggy white sweatshirt that matches her trainers.

I crank up the heater. After a stiff drink or a hot cuppa, it's the next best thing I can do to help alleviate the girl's shock.

"Fine," I say, turning out of Naomi's street and following the SUV onto a main highway. "Let's see . . . The kid hired me as his bodyguard after our friendly intruder was getting outmuscled by a local hood by the name of Carlos Campuzano. I took care of Carlos and everything was going great, only for the kid to suffer a breakdown and go into rehab. Anyway, he sorts himself out, checks out of rehab and we're at this charity fundraiser at Art Solomon's mansion . . . Now Josh likes to drive himself around—doesn't like to be nannied. He calls me up and tells me he's leaving. I head out to my car, so I can follow behind. Only I get a flat. I change the tyre and play catch up on the roads. But by the time I'm caught up, he's lying dead and upside down in his Ferrari at the bottom of a hill. I see a stranger watching in a car with only one headlight. They get away and the cops don't seem too interested. So I sniff around a little. Find inconsistencies at the crash site. Injuries to the kid that don't make sense. Three of the LAPD's finest tell me to leave it alone, then a mystery man in a tow truck tries to run me into the ground on an old movie lot. With no other known enemies, I think maybe it's Carlos Campuzano after all, getting revenge on me and the kid. So I make a few polite enquiries and he tells me the LAPD are forcing him to threaten Josh and a bunch of other Hollywood royalty. Next minute, the LAPD have made me the prime suspect in what's now being billed as a murder case. They drive me east of the city and try to fake my suicide. Except the bullet misses. I get away. And I'm sitting in a bar about to give it up and skip town when I see your face on TV."

"What, me?" Naomi asks, eyes lighting up.

"Hope Medical," I say.

"What did you think?" she says. "Was I good?"

"Not sure about the rest of the show, but you were great," I say.

Naomi smiles and does a little fist pump. She composes herself. "Sorry, carry on."

"So I Googled your name. Your agent told me you were auditioning at Hornblower. That's when I found you with Meddles."

"Ugh, the director. What a creep. My agent said it was an indie movie. A romantic lead, but it was some horrible—"

"Post-apocalyptic erotica horror, I know . . . I was gonna warn you, but then you kicked Meddles in the bollocks and ran off. That's when I followed you to your apartment."

"Yeah, equally creepy," Naomi says.

"Hey, I was gonna wait until morning," I say. "I thought you'd have called the cops."

"Not after my last experience," Naomi says.

The traffic is as light as the pale-blue morning sky, so I stay back a distance—as far as I can without losing the SUV. Tunney seems to be heading towards Hollywood. Back to his day job, minding stars? I dunno. I keep following. Tell Naomi it's her turn to talk.

"Well," she says, "I guess it all started at Silver Hills. At the fundraiser."

"You were there?"

"Oh, I was there," Naomi says, laughing. "Small town girl playing actress, working as a waitress. Cliché or what, huh?"

"Cliché or not, don't spare me the words," I say. "I wanna know every detail."

"*Every* detail?" Naomi says.

"*Every* detail," I say.

"Well, there I was," she says, "wearing my best smile and carrying a tray full of champagne, struggling not to let either one drop..."

47

It was my first job with the catering company. They turned me down when I first applied, but then someone called in sick and I was parachuted in. No idea what I was supposed to do or say or what the drill was.

"Just smile and hold the tray," Mrs Leibowitz said to me and the other staff. She was this beehived nightmare in a stiff gold dress, the party planner for the night. "When the tray's empty, come and get a refill," she said. "But don't touch the guests. Don't talk to the guests. Don't stare at the guests. And *strictly* no selfies."

So Mrs Leibowitz, in her stiff gold dress, sent us out of the kitchen armed with our trays. I was hoping for canapés, but someone handed me a tray of champagne flutes. Which seems pretty easy, until you realise how heavy the tray is . . . I've only got skinny wrists, you know? And it's not like waiting restaurant tables where you can prop multiple plates with your arms—But . . . You want me to get on with the story, don't you?

Okay, so I was walking around with this champagne,

swerving around guests as they moved left and right, throwing elbows and arms and hair and jewellery. And my wrist was killing me—I mean, man—but I was getting the hang of it, you know? Getting used to mixing with the stars—my God, I've never seen so many faces off the TV and movies before, and directors, too. For a minute, I was thinking about introducing myself. Doing a scene from A Midsummer Night's Dream. A little number, maybe. Then I thought, *jeez get a hold of yourself, Naomi. How desperate are you? Just hand out the champagne and keep your mouth shut*. So I got rid of all the flutes and I'd just returned to the kitchen to pick up some more champagne when I was handed a big glass of vintage red to take to Francis Ford Coppola, because apparently, his other great passion in life is wine. So anyway, I was told to go and find him in the party and hand him the wine. And I was relieved because my wrist was aching so much. I mean, my whole arm had gone dead, you know?

So I went back into the main part of the house looking for *the* Francis Ford Coppola, shaking my right arm out and carrying the glass of red in my left. I went around in circles looking for him, telling myself to keep my mouth shut when I did and reminding myself not to stare. But I couldn't see him, so I decided to stand still and do a three-sixty. But while I'm stood there flexing out my fingers, this old guy with white hair—well, he took a bite out of a caviar canapé. He screwed up his face and said, "What *is* this crap?"

"Caviar, dear," his wife said, in her shimmery silver gown.

"Tastes like cat shit," he said, looking around.

Anyway, the next thing I knew, he was grabbing my wrist and spitting the canapé out into the palm of my hand.

I thought, *what'll I do?* I didn't know *what* to do. So I smiled and said, "Thank you."

The man wiped the spit from his chin and turned away. I didn't have anywhere to put the canapé, so I just held it in my palm and went looking for Coppola. He wasn't downstairs, so I went upstairs. Up one of two huge staircases that curved up along either wall and met in the middle on this grand landing under a chandelier. Mrs Leibowitz had said we were banned from going there, but she'd also said to find Mr Coppola and get the glass of red to him right away. So I went upstairs, seeing some of the guests milling around up there, looking at all the art on the walls. But I was getting lost the place was so big. I couldn't find Coppola or even the main staircase back to the party, and before too long, I found myself wandering down these huge luxurious corridors—like Buckingham Palace or something. And one of them led out onto this veranda with a stone bannister decorated with little fairy lights. He wasn't out there, either. And neither was anyone else.

That's when the wind picked up and the french windows blew shut on me. They locked from the inside and I couldn't get them open. Fortunately, the veranda ran on past a couple of other rooms, but with little stone walls dividing it into separate, smaller balconies.

That meant I had to hitch a leg and slide over two of them until I reached another set of french doors. Which, of course, meant my tights ripping right up one side.

The good news was, I didn't spill any of the vintage wine, and I soon found my way into a bedroom. From in there, I heard chatter and music, so I thought, *great I'm back on track*. But as I passed by a full-length mirror, I noticed my tights were hanging in strips off my legs.

There's no way I could re-enter the party looking like that and I still didn't have anywhere to put the mushed-up canapé. I was too scared to leave it on the polished furniture in case it made a mess, so I put down the wine on a doily on an old antique desk, straightened my hair and blouse and slipped off my black heels I'd been told to wear.

I pulled my tights off, got in a tangle and fell over onto the carpet. I wriggled out of the tights, got to my feet and realised I'd ripped my skirt up the side, as well, showing way too much leg up the left thigh. But what the hell, you know? So I rolled the tights into a little ball and stuffed them down the front of my blouse. It made the right boob look bigger than the left, but I decided to go with it.

I picked up the wine and headed out of the room, into the hallway. I followed the chatter and music back to the main balcony and looked down over the party. I spotted the top of Coppola's head from a sea of guests and headed down the staircase to my right.

When I got to the bottom, I lost sight of him again. I weaved my way through the crowd until I spotted him a few feet away. I swallowed my nerves and started my approach, practicing my line in my head. "Excuse me, Mr Coppola, here is your wine," which I'd do with a nice little smile, you know?

And I was almost there, on my little approach, when this fat goddamn guy with a brown toupee came out of nowhere and barged into me in a head-on collision. The wine went over me and over him, soaking my white blouse and staining his tux. He went nuts at me, calling me a "Clumsy bitch," saying "Do you know how much this suit cost?" I tried to wipe the wine off him with one of my sleeves. He batted me away and called me a few things I'm not gonna repeat. And meanwhile, Francis Ford Coppola still didn't have his wine.

So I was thinking, *oh jeez I'm in trouble now.* What a first night, right? Yet, as the guest was berating me and everyone's staring, Joshua Speed entered stage right. *The* Joshua Speed.

48

Josh handed me a silk handkerchief from his suit pocket while taking the guest by the elbow.

"Come on, Lenny," he said with a smile. "You've got a wardrobe full of those things."

"The bitch should watch where she's going." Lenny said.

That's when Josh tightened his grip on Lenny's elbow. I heard him speak low in this Lenny guy's ear.

He said, "You talk to her like that again and the only thing you'll be writing is a Christmas card."

"You can't do that," Lenny said.

"Wanna bet?" Josh said.

"I'm a two-time Oscar winner," Lenny said.

"And a two-bit asshole," Josh said.

At that point Lenny stormed off in a huff, muttering something about leaving anyway.

Josh turned to me, shook his head and said, "Screenwriters . . . Smart as hell, but no social skills."

I kinda stood there in shock. Josh was a lot more handsome in person. Charming, too. Like everyone else, I assumed he was some obnoxious celebrity who used to be a *real* actor. But I guess I was wrong, because he smiled at me and apologised on Lenny's behalf. I didn't know what to say, and technically I wasn't allowed to say anything, so I just stood there staring at him.

"What?" he said to me with a smile. "I got something on my face?"

"Uh, I'm not allowed to..."

"What?" he said.

"We're not supposed to talk to the guests."

"Well it's too late for that," Josh said.

As he looked around the party, I instinctively messed with my hair. Only I'd forgotten about the canapé the old man spat out in my hand. Next thing I knew, I had caviar, spit and pastry stuck in my hair. I tried to get it out but I just made it worse, rubbing it in along the strands. That's when Josh turned back around. I pretended to act cool.

But he noticed straight away. "Do you know you've got shit in your hair?" he said.

"Oh, that's just food," I said, fiddling with it, making it even worse. "It's been in someone's mouth, so..."

Josh looked at me like I was crazy. And as if that wasn't bad enough, he pointed at my chest. "And one boob is bigger than the other," he said.

"Hah!" I said, laughing like a douche and digging a hand down my blouse. "That's just a rolled-up pair of tights. I had nowhere to put them."

"How about on your legs?" Josh said.

"I tore them climbing over a wall." I looked over my shoulder and saw Mrs Leibowitz staring at me from across the room, face like freaking thunder. I looked back to Josh. "I gotta go," I said. "Francis Ford Coppola needs a glass of wine."

I was about to bug out, when Art Solomon appeared in a

white tux and red bow tie with a giant cigar in his mouth. He took Josh by the arm. "Joshy-boy, great to see you doing so well. There's someone I'd like you to meet."

"Sure, Art," Josh said, taking the tights from my hand. "I'll hold onto these for you," he said to me, winking and tucking them away in a trouser pocket as he went.

I didn't know if he was being a gentleman or a tight-sniffing perv. But I hurried back to the kitchens to get a replacement glass of red and try and do something about my blouse. Maybe I could pull some kind of apron on over the top, I thought. But as soon as I got inside the kitchens away from the party, Mrs Leibowitz tore right into me. Called me a disgrace, a mess and told me I was fired.

I tried to explain, but she wouldn't hear of it. Worse still, she said I had to get out, there and then. And make my own way home. They'd ferried us in on a mini bus, see. It was late and I didn't have any money for the real bus.

She told me that was *my* problem. She had enough of her own. Then she stormed off.

So I put down Francis Ford's empty wine glass, grabbed my bag and jacket off the coat hooks on the wall and walked out of the kitchens.

Mrs Leibowitz had told me to leave through the back, but I thought *screw her*. I'm leaving through the front. I'm gonna stare at the other guests. Maybe even take a selfie or two, you know?

So I pulled on my jacket and grabbed a couple of those caviar canapés off a tray, along with a flute of the expensive champagne on my way out. I drank half the champagne and stuffed one of the canapés in my mouth. As I was passing the old man who spat one out in my hand, I opened my mouth and stuck a tongue full of caviar out at him. I did a little impression of him. "Tastes like cat shit!"

He shook his head. His wife tutted at me. I brushed through on my way towards the door, wondering where the hell I could get a bus from around there. Not like many people caught a bus where the Solomons lived, you know?

Anyway, I drank the other half of the champagne, ditched the glass on a passing tray and put the other canapé in my mouth.

"Hey where are you going?" I heard a voice say, a hand on my arm.

It was Josh.

49

"Home," I tried to say. Only I had a mouth full of caviar and pastry, obviously.

"What?" Josh said.

I held up a finger, chewed the canapé and swallowed it down. "Home," I said, wiping pastry flakes from around my mouth.

"How come?" Josh asked.

"The party planner fired my ass, that's why."

"For the wine spill?"

"For a lot of things."

"You want me to talk to her?" Josh said.

"Thanks, but I don't need saving," I said, grabbing his arm and leaving caviar on the sleeve of his gazillion dollar suit. "Oh no, sorry about that," I said, trying to wipe it off but rubbing it deeper in.

"It'll wash out," Josh said, not seeming to care.

I slapped a hand to my face. "Look, I'm having a bad night."

"Yeah, me too," Josh said. "This party sucks."

"Must be hell for you," I said, unable to control my own sarcasm.

Josh just laughed. "Why don't you stick around for a while as my guest?"

"I don't know," I said. "I think I'd better leave, I mean . . ." I pointed to my hair, my skirt, the wine-stained blouse sticking to my skin."

"Don't forget about the caviar on your face," Josh said.

"Oh great, where?" I asked.

Josh wiped it from my cheek with a thumb and sucked it off the end.

I think it was the most surreal, romantic, confusing moment of my life.

But then I burped. "It's the champagne," I said.

"Have another glass with me," he said, grabbing a pair of flutes off a passing tray. A glass of champagne and another filled with orange juice.

He put the champagne in my hand whether I liked it or not. "So what are you, an actress?"

"I'd love to say yes, but . . . Well, I guess so, yeah."

"And you're from . . . Iowa, right?" he said, squinting at me.

"Is it that obvious?" I said.

"When I first got here from Idaho, I waited tables and pumped gas for two years. In between, I was doing auditions and sleeping on a mattress in a room with two other actors, cooking together, getting wasted together, picking up, um, chicks together . . ." Josh seemed to go off into another time. "Way better actors than me. Bigger, taller and just as good-looking."

"Surely not," I said, slapping a hand to my cheek.

"Yeah, can you believe it?" Josh said, laughing. "Now one of them's in sales, the other's still a waiter."

"So what was your secret?" I said. "Why were you the one who made it?"

"I didn't give up," Josh said with a shrug. "You know, that was some pretty funny shit you pulled on Mandlebaum back there."

"Huh?" I said.

"Sticking your tongue out at one of Solomon's top yes-men."

"That guy was—? Oh great. The latest in a brilliant string of career moves."

"Ah, don't worry about it," Josh said. "The guy's a corpse. He retires in a couple of weeks."

Josh smiled at me a few seconds, not saying anything. It made me feel uncomfortable. Felt like I needed to break the silence.

"Your eyes are *really* blue," I blurted out.

"And your eyes are *really* brown," he said, gazing into them as he sipped at his orange juice.

That's when his phone rang. He excused himself and turned away from me to take the call. "Yeah... Yeah... Sure, Bucky, that'd be awesome... I can swing by right now." Josh came off the call. "Listen, I've gotta go. Where are you headed after this?"

"Straight home," I said, pinching my blouse away from my skin. "Where else?"

"You need a ride?" Josh said. "I've gotta go."

I hesitated. "I dunno..."

"Come on," Josh said, tucking away his phone. "What's the worst that could happen?"

50

I didn't want to say it. I didn't have to.

"It's my reputation, isn't it?" Josh said.

"I'm not one of those girls," I said.

"I know, that's why I'm offering," he said.

I danced around it in my head. Didn't even make a decision before "Um, yeah," came out of my mouth. "If you're sure."

"Totally," Josh said, taking my champagne glass from me. He handed them to a waiter carrying an empty tray and took me by the hand. "Right this way, madam."

As we walked through the party together, everyone was staring. I've never felt so self-conscious in my life. Not since wearing that little Wonder Woman costume on the Walk of Fame.

"And I'm not one of those guys by the way," Josh said, leaning into me. "Not anymore."

That's when it dawned on me. "We're going out of the front?" I said. "Where all those photographers are?"

"You want Hollywood to know your name?" Josh said. "You'll be the talk of a thousand gossip blogs by morning."

"I don't want it that way," I said, messing with my hair. "Especially not looking like this."

Josh stopped. He turned to me and smiled, I don't know, as if he was surprised. "Then meet me out in the driveway."

So we split up. I headed through a side door and started walking down the drive. Not long after, Josh pulled up in a gleaming red Ferrari.

As I climbed in, he was on the phone, the hands-free. "It's Josh. We good to go? . . . Yeah, heading out of here now," he said, before ending the call. "Sorry, that was the bodyguard," he said, rolling us down the driveway. "Gotta tell him what I'm doing."

"Don't you want to wait for him?" I asked. "Isn't that the point of a bodyguard?"

"He'll catch up," Josh said. "He always does."

As we pulled out of Silver Hills, Josh accelerated away.

"He's not catching up now," I said. "I thought you'd, you know, get driven around the place."

"Are you kidding? This is the only freedom I get," Josh said. "Speaking of which," he said, putting his phone on silent as it rang out.

Then he looked at me. "Hey listen, how about we get a coffee? I know a great little place, low profile, open late."

"I've got fish crap in my hair," I said.

"So, you can wash it out first," Josh said. "The night's young. And so are we, if you hadn't noticed."

"Uh, okay," I said, "Why not?"

"Cool," Josh said. "But we'll have to swing by the hills first, if you don't mind."

"This isn't some ploy, is it?" I said.

Josh laughed. "I've gotta pick up a screenplay, that's all. You can wait in the car. I'll be straight in and out."

"I guess I'm being ungrateful, huh?" I said.

"No. you're right to be careful," he said. "There are some real predators in this town."

Josh put some chilled-out indie music on the stereo. We cruised through the streets towards Beverly hills and stopped at a red. That's when a car pulled up alongside us. I couldn't tell what kind it was.

"Here we go," Josh said, looking across. "We've got a contender."

"Just ignore him," I said, but I could see Josh watching the lights, tightening his grip on the wheel.

The car next to us revved up loud, like it had a different engine put in it, you know? Anyway, its tyres started to smoke as it got ready, the car lurching forward like it was a dog on a leash. The lights turned to green. The car next to us got the jump and pulled away in this cloud of white smoke. Josh gave him a second and then stepped on the gas. I couldn't believe the speed of the Ferrari. My head snapped back and my whole body was pinned hard against the passenger seat. It was kinda scary. I definitely wasn't a fan, but Josh had a huge smile on his face. Especially when the Ferrari caught up with the other car. We flew past it in no time and left it for dead.

I rolled my eyes at Josh, flexing my neck and shoulders.

He shrugged back at me. "What's the point of owning a Ferrari if you can't smoke some asshole at the lights?"

Josh slowed the car down. I looked at him again in the pale glow of the dash. "Why me?" I asked.

"Why what?" he said.

"That party was full of beautiful women. All those gazelles walking round in their sparkly dresses. Why are you taking *me* out for a coffee?"

"Why not you?" Josh asked.

I messed with my curls again, the caviar stuck firm liked

dried poop. "Look at me. I'm a no one. I look like an animal took a shit in my hair."

"Yeah, but you're real," Josh said. "You talk to me like I'm a person, not a product . . . The only other one who talks to me like that is Charlie. I feel like I can be myself around you guys." Josh gazed ahead, as if giving a monologue from a play. "I've been acting most of my life. Most of it off-camera. At high school I acted like a jock to avoid having my ass kicked for doing drama. Since making it big I've been acting like a real jerk."

"Why?" I asked.

"I don't know. I guess it's easier to be a persona than a person . . . Remember when I used to be a real actor?"

"Before Nightburner?" I said. "No offence."

"I'd like to get back to that version of me," Josh said, as we started up the hill roads. "Fuck it. That's what I'm gonna do."

"Can you just switch like that?" I said.

"Sure, I'm swinging by Bucky's right now to pick up the screenplay for the next Nightburner. I'll just tell him the deal's off."

"But I thought—I read somewhere you had a contract."

"Three more movies," Josh said. "But the studio don't want it, I don't want it and from the box office numbers, the public don't want it either. This way everyone can take a break and reboot. The franchise, the fans, my career. Hey, maybe we could do a play together, off-Broadway. Or an indie movie."

"You barely know me," I said. "You've never even seen me act."

"Nah, you've got it," Josh said. "You've got presence."

Josh breathed a big sigh, like a weight had been lifted. A decision had been made, you know?

"Hey," he said. "I never even asked your name."

"Naomi," I said. "Naomi Jones."

"A pleasure to meet you, Naomi Jones," Josh said with a smile, only for it to drop from his face.

"What the fuck—?" he said, glancing in his mirrors.

I looked over my shoulder. It was a car, headlights flashing at us and a honking horn, right up the Ferrari's rear fender.

Josh sped up as we made our way up the hill, but the car stuck with us. It pulled out and roared alongside us, close to the passenger side.

"Is that the same car as before?" I said.

"Yeah," Josh said, as we headed towards a tight bend. "What does the asshole want?"

"Slow down," I said. "Let him past."

Josh seemed to be wrestling with his own ego. He glanced across at me and eased off the gas. The other car shot past us, but then the brake lights went on and it slowed down too. Next thing I knew, we were making the turn side by side up a steep rise.

The road snaked around in left and right bends. I was getting scared. There were no road markings up there and the car squeezed in on the right-hand side, forcing us towards the left. We were risking a head-on collision from a car coming the other way. But things got worse. The psycho in the mystery car suddenly turned into us. It was on a straight stretch of road rising high above the city lights to our left. I felt a shunt as the cars collided. It wasn't that hard a collision, but Josh seemed to be just as scared as me.

"What is this guy doing?" he said, before I saw fear turn to anger in his eyes. *"Fuck this,"* he said.

Josh stepped on the brakes and let the other car fly by.

He swerved to the far left on the side of the road, where there was space to pull over.

The other car reacted, pulling over only a short distance in front.

"What are you gonna do?" I said.

"Tell this asshole to go fuck himself," Josh said, all his composure gone.

"Don't," I said, grabbing at his arm.

Josh shook me off. "I'm gonna sort this guy out," he said, opening his door. "Stay in the car. This'll only take a second."

I didn't know whether to do as he said, or get out and try and diffuse the situation. In the end, I stayed put, frozen in my seat, thinking of calling the cops. But then the rest of it all happened so fast.

* * *

JOSH STRODE out towards the other car. The driver got out and met him halfway, in the headlights of the Ferrari. He was a big guy. A mean-looking guy in black with a blonde ponytail.

Josh yelled at him, throwing his arms around. Seemed like he knew him or something. But the guy walked straight up to him and swung a fist.

Josh ducked and threw a punch back. I didn't know how to work the phone in the car, so I fumbled inside my bag for my own cell. But when I looked up again, the other driver had Josh by the throat.

He was wearing a pair of black leather gloves and choking him to death. Josh fought back. I went to dial 911, but I'm on a shitty cell and a shitty plan. Couldn't get a good enough signal.

I was about to get out and do something. But the driver

of the other car pulled one of those leather saps from the back of his belt.

He flipped Josh around and hit him on the back of the skull with the sap. It had to be filled with lead or something, because Josh went limp.

The guy hit him again and again in the same spot. Josh dropped to the ground.

I caught my own scream with both hands.

The driver tucked the sap in his belt. He bent over, took off a glove and checked Josh's pulse. I couldn't tell if he was making sure he was dead, or alive. But he wiped Josh's neck with the hem of his t-shirt where he'd touched his skin and slipped the glove back on.

He looked towards the Ferrari. I realised I'd be next if I didn't act.

Now, I didn't know if he could see me, but I thought maybe not, because of the headlights, you know? So I took off my heels. I slipped off my seatbelt and opened the passenger door, slow and quiet. I slipped out through the tiniest gap in the door while the driver was moving Josh's body.

I squatted low along the side of the car and pushed the door shut so it clicked. The driver left Josh's body on the ground, close to his own car.

I looked around for someone, anyone passing by. But it was late and there was no one else around.

Then the driver started walking towards the Ferrari. If I didn't move, I'd be dead.

51

I turned and ran low around the back of the Ferrari.

My only chance was to make it into the bushes by the side of the road.

I couldn't afford to wait. So I went for it. Running and jumping over the metal barrier. I dove into the bushes. I turned and looked back at the road. The driver paused and peered into the darkness, like he thought he'd seen or heard something, but couldn't be sure.

It was dark and the car engines were loud, even idling in neutral. I prayed he hadn't seen or heard anything.

He turned away and climbed behind the wheel of the Ferrari. He reversed fast down the road. Then accelerated up towards the bend again, as if he was gonna fly right over the side of the hill. But he hit the brakes, skidding and screeching and stopping a few feet short of the edge. The air smelled of smoking rubber. It got right up my nose. The driver jumped out of the Ferrari and jogged over to Josh's body. He picked him up under the armpits and dragged him back to the car. I saw him put Josh in the driver's seat. He seemed to be arranging his body somehow. Then he shut the door, ran around the back of the car and started to push.

I watched on from the bushes. Frozen in fear. Stifling my own whimpers. The driver pushed with everything he had and the car rolled forward until the nose tipped over the edge of the hill. The driver pushed some more and the Ferrari rolled away, through a gap in the barrier and down the hill. I saw it tumble over and over. There was a horrible crunching, smashing sound as it went. It came to a stop on its roof. The red taillights upside down.

I couldn't believe it. Josh must have been dead. If not from the leather sap to the head, then from the crash.

The driver looked over the side of the hill, glanced around and started towards the bushes, where I was hiding. I wanted to run. Couldn't move. But the driver stopped mid-tracks. He turned and jogged back to his car and got inside. He waited there a moment. A yellow BMW came up the hill, went around the bend and disappeared up the next rise.

The driver revved the car, which at this point I could make out was dark-grey. It didn't have a number plate and as it swung up around the bend, I noticed it only had one headlight. The other must have broken when it rammed into us.

I was going to make a run for it, down the hill, call the cops. But the car stopped up around the next bend. The driver got out. I thought at first he was looking for me, from a higher position, you know? But then he lit a cigarette and smoked it.

That's when a black SUV showed up. A man jumped out and looked over the hillside.

He skidded down the hill, fell over, got up and ran down to the Ferrari. Josh's killer stood and watched, smoking his cigarette.

I tried my phone again. Still no bars. So I watched the other man reach inside the Ferrari. I was trying to get a look at the guy's face, but it was too dark. He pulled at the door, but couldn't get it open. He got frustrated. Banged the side of the Ferrari. Stared a moment out over the city, then patted himself down as if looking for something. He started walking back up the hill. Then he looked up. He stopped. I realised he was staring at Josh's killer. The killer tossed the cigarette and got in his car. He turned it around and came back down the hill. I crouched lower, out of sight of the lone headlight.

I saw the other driver scramble up the hill, as if giving chase. I realised he wasn't with the killer. So as the man jumped in the SUV, I stumbled out of the bushes and climbed over the metal barrier. I tried to flag him down, but either he didn't see me or didn't care. The headlights of the SUV almost blinded me as it sped away after the killer.

I thought the best I could do was run down the hill road and knock on doors, try to get a signal, something like that. But on my way down, a couple of cop cars flashed by me up the hill. I tried to get their attention. They ignored me, but I saw them stop further up the hill where the Ferrari had gone off the road. An ambulance was next. And an unmarked police car. By the time I'd walked back up the hill, they were cordoning off the road, a fire truck on the scene and a police helicopter overhead.

I couldn't believe how fast they'd gotten there. Even the CSI showed up within a few minutes. I explained what I'd seen to a pair of detectives—Roach and Thomas. They got a squad car to take me home, rather than to a precinct, which I thought was strange, you know? Anyway, they'd told me not to say anything to anyone. If I did I could be prosecuted, can you believe that?

After I saw the news reports, I gave Detective Thomas a call on a card he'd given me. I asked him if he'd seen the news. That the media had got it wrong. They thought it was an accident. Thomas told me he'd come out to see me to explain.

Next minute he and Detective Roach knocked on the door of my apartment. They pushed their way in and sat me down on the sofa. They said whatever I thought I saw, I didn't. That Josh's death was an accident. That I was suffering from PTSD. I told them I was shaken up, but I know what I saw. Detective Roach told me to keep my mouth shut. I mean, the way he said it—it sent shivers down my spine.

Then they left, saying they'd be keeping an eye and ear on me.

I wanted to say something to the papers, to speak out. But I thought they were bugging me, following me. And that if I said anything . . . Well, who knows what they'd do? So I kept my head down, went to work, auditions, the usual stuff.

I've felt guilty ever since. Then I wake up in the dark and find a pair of strangers in my room. One of them was you. And I guess it was you on the hill, in the SUV. And that's what happened.

Was that enough detail?

52

"Yeah, I think that was enough," I say, as we tail Tunney across the city. "Don't think I needed to know about the canapés."

"Hey, you said not to leave anything out," Naomi, says, looking out of the passenger window. "My mom tells me I talk too much. Says I'm a chatterbox. Once you get me going, there's no shutting me up—And I'm doing it again, aren't I?"

"A little bit," I say, struggling with the stubborn gearstick on the Beetle.

"So what do you think?" Naomi says.

"I think I was right," I say. "Josh was killed and the LAPD are involved. I just don't know how or why."

I keep following Tunney at a safe distance, the Beetle chugging away, steering like sludge and a permanent vibration through the enormous wheel.

"You know, you really need to get the tyres looked at," I say. "When was the last time you put any air in 'em?"

"You have to put air in them?" Naomi says.

"Er, yeah," I say.

"Well how the hell does it get out?" she asks.

I realise she's not joking. Shake my head and notice Tunney slowing the SUV up ahead. He turns right into a drive-thru. A lesser-known burger joint open early.

I pull over by the side of the road a moment.

"What are we waiting for?" Naomi asks.

"Give it a second," I say, checking my watch. "It's early. Looks suspicious if we pull right in behind."

I count thirty seconds on my watch and pull out into the road again. I hang a right and cruise into the drive-thru lane. Tunney's already paying for his food. An arm comes out of a window and passes him a white takeaway bag. He hands over a note and pulls into the car park behind the burger place.

We roll forward onto the ordering point.

"What do you want?" I ask Naomi as I wind down the driver window. "Burger?"

"Oh no, I'm a vegan," she says.

"What does that mean?"

"I don't eat anything that comes from an animal," Naomi says.

"How do you manage that?"

Naomi stares at me like I'm thick, or mad. She starts to remind me of my daughter.

"Do vegans drink coke?" I ask.

"I'll have an apple juice," she says.

I place the order and pull onto the next window. I pay for the food and hand a warm paper bag to Naomi. She recoils at the smell. I drive out of the lane and into the car park—a single line of nine spaces facing a grass verge and a wooden fence.

Tunney's SUV is in the next-to-last space of the drive-thru car park, to the far right. I pull up in the second spot in, to the far left. I leave the engine running, just in case it won't start again.

"Ugh, the cup is almost touching your—whatever that is," she says, taking her drink from the bag.

She hands me the bag like it's fresh from Chernobyl.

I snatch it off her and take out my food. I unwrap the white wax paper and bite into my bacon double cheeseburger.

We stay low in our seats, our eyes fixed on the SUV.

"So this is it?" Naomi says, sucking on her juice through a straw. "He breaks into my apartment, gets knocked out, wakes up and thinks, hey, I'll have breakfast?"

Now, there are plenty of times I've had a long day or night doing some rather unsavoury and not exactly moral things—they have a tendency to make you hungry. At least after the first four or five times you do 'em.

Not that I'm gonna mention that to Naomi.

She'll only freak out.

But right now, I'm having no trouble chomping through my—*Hang on a minute, what have we got here?*

Another car appears at the drive-thru window. A tattooed forearm reaches out and takes a bag of food. The car is a Ford Mustang. The classic kind in dark-blue with twin white racing stripes over the bonnet and roof.

It growls out of the drive-thru lane behind us and across the car park. It pulls into the far space next to the SUV.

"Look at that," I say.

"Look at what?" Naomi says.

"Two cars parked up alongside each other."

Naomi shrugs. "Big deal."

"All these spaces free."

"Maybe the guy in the blue car is lonely," she says.

"Or maybe they're talking. The SUV reversed in. The

Mustang went in nose-first. That means the driver windows are lined up."

The windows of the SUV are tinted, meaning we can't see either driver, or whether they're talking, or just eating. I finish my burger and swallow a mouthful of black coffee.

It isn't long before Tunney pulls out of his space. I get a good look at the driver in the Mustang, his window wound all the way down.

Naomi gets a good look, too. *"Oh my God, that's him,"* she says. "That's the guy who killed Josh."

The guy is big and muscular. A blonde ponytail, deep tan and a face with fat features—nose, lips, and a Neanderthal brow. I watch him bite into a burger of his own. He hasn't noticed us yet.

"Alright," I say, tossing the end of my coffee out of the window. I stuff the burger wrapper and cup in the bag, along with Naomi's empty juice. I reverse out of the parking space.

"What are you doing?" Naomi says. "That's the guy. Shouldn't we be following him or something?"

"Trust me," I say, driving out of the car park.

"What does that mean?" Naomi says.

I ignore her, slow the car and throw the bag out of the window and into a bin near the exit. I pull out of the drive-thru and into the forecourt of a petrol station next door. I drive through the pumps and hang out by the far exit

I stop the car but keep the engine running, watching the exit of the burger joint. Josh's killer appears. He turns left out onto the road, cruising into the heart of the city. I let him go a few seconds and pull out behind him.

"Okay, you bastard," I say. "Let's see where you go."

53

I've gotta crank through the gears so I don't lose the guy, but lucky for us, there are plenty of lights, along with a silver Buick in between, giving us cover. The killer drives into the flashier parts of town, where Josh and his Hollywood pals used to hang out. We end up just off Rodeo Drive, pulling into a horse-shoe shaped avenue of glass buildings with a car park in the middle. There's an arcade of designer stores at the end, a high-end health club to the right and the biggest coffee shop I've ever seen on the left.

As I turn into the car park, I see Josh's killer get out of the Mustang.

He looks familiar, somehow. And not just the tattoo I recognise from the attack at the old studio lot. But with his phone to his ear, I just can't place the face.

"You got your phone on you?" I ask Naomi.

"Of course, I'm an out of work actress," Naomi says.

We swap numbers and get out of the car.

"Grab a seat in the window of the coffee shop," I say.

"What are you gonna do?" Naomi asks.

"Try and find out more about Road Rage Barbie over there."

"He murdered Josh," Naomi says. "What else do we need to know?"

"From what you told me, Josh's murder sounds premeditated. This guy doesn't look the premeditated type. Keep your phone on."

Josh's killer grabs a black holdall out of the boot of his car. He slings it over a shoulder and crosses the car park to the health club.

I jog after him, keeping my head down and my face away from any CCTV. The entrance to the health club is vast and the floor black marble. There's a chill-out area with white leather sofas to the right. A leisurewear store to the left and a curved reception desk dead ahead with a tanned blonde guy with superhero arms popping out of a turquoise polo shirt. The gym itself is on an upper level visible from down here in the lobby, soundproofed behind floor-to-ceiling panes of glass.

Josh's killer nods to the receptionist like he knows him. He swipes through a barrier to the left of the desk as an early gym-goer exits through another one on the right. I duck into the leisure store and grab a handful of clothes and a pair of trainers in my size. I pick a black gym bag off a hook and pay for it at the counter. I stuff the gym clothes in the bag and hurry through to the reception.

The guy behind the desk looks up at me as I approach. "Hey," he says.

"Hi, do you do day passes?" I ask.

"Sure, man. Gym-only or access all areas?"

"Gym-only," I say.

"Gym-only," he repeats to himself, scanning a card against a machine.

He tells me the damage.

"Bloody Nora," I say.

The guy—his name tag says Brad—smiles at me. "Steep, huh?"

"Steep? Makes Everest look like a speed bump."

I hand over the money. I knew I should have flashed the fake detective badge.

Brad gives me the card. Stares at me. Shit, I think he recognises me. I might have to punch his lights out. I hope not, he seems like a nice kid.

He wags a finger at me. "Hey dude, you look just like that guy on the news. The guy the cops are after for the Speed murder."

I laugh and sigh. "You're the third one who's said that today. At this rate I'll have to get a face job."

"Hey, we do those if you want?" Brad says. "You want the brochure?"

"I already saw a surgeon," I say, swiping through. "He said there's nothing they can do."

I leave Brad laughing to himself and follow a sign that leads me left to the changing rooms. I push through the door to the men's and find the poshest changing rooms I've ever seen.

I'm careful to stick to the edges of the room. As Josh's killer sits down, he turns towards me. I turn away and take a seat on one of the long, black leather benches that run back to back—polished wooden lockers skirting the edges of the room.

I keep my distance, glancing over my right shoulder to see Josh's killer getting changed. He takes off a black t-shirt, revealing a ripped upper body littered with more tattoos. I remove my tie and slip off my shoes, taking my time about it. Next off is my jacket. A quick glance again and Josh's killer is in a white muscle vest, pulling on a pair of grey jogging bottoms. As I remove my shirt and trousers, he laces up a pair of luminous yellow trainers. I snap the tags off my gym clothes and pull on the t-shirt and shorts.

Josh's killer slides his bag in a locker at chest height and closes it. He slips on a pair of black weight-lifting gloves as he struts out of the room. I bend over and lace up my trainers as he passes behind me.

As soon as he disappears around the corner, I jump off the bench, grab my stuff and bundle it into a locker.

The lockers are tall and deep with flat metal hooks either side. I check over my shoulder before ripping one of the hooks off the inside left side of the locker. I keep my phone on me and close the locker door. There's a key in the lock. I twist it and slide the turquoise band attached to it over a wrist.

While the changing rooms are empty, I hurry over to the locker the killer put his stuff in. There's no subtle way to do this, other than jam one end of the hook in the thin gap between door and locker. The hook is in a v-shape. I pull hard towards me. There's a splintering sound. The door comes loose. I root through the killer's stuff until I find a wallet. I slide out a driver's licence.

His name is Klaus Jacobsen.

Klaus—where have I heard that name before?

I memorise his home address and slip the licence back in the wallet.

I find another card. An image of him in a polo shirt the same as Brad's. He's a personal trainer here at the health club. I return the card to its slot and pull out another one. An Equity Card. The guy's an actor? I call up Naomi on my phone.

"Yeah," she says. "What's going on?"

"Google this, will you? Klaus Jacobsen, actor."

"Googling now," Naomi says. "You know, this is kind of fun in a weird way."

"Glad you're enjoying yourself," I say.

"Here we go. Klaus Jacobsen," Naomi says. "I'll check his IMDB . . . He's barely been in anything—Hold on, here we go, whoa yeah. He's more of a stuntman. Huge list of credits. Some pretty big movies."

"Any Josh was in?"

"Yeah," Naomi says. "Including Nightburner One, Two and Three. So what are you gonna do now—"

I cut off the call as Naomi rambles. I slide the card back in the wallet, take the money out of it and toss the wallet in with the rest of his stuff. I hear someone entering the changing rooms. I push the door closed and toss the cards and cash in a nearby bin. Want it to look like a standard robbery.

An old guy walks in dressed in gym stuff. I avert my face so he can't get a good look at me. I head out of the changing rooms, turning right. There are twin escalators heading up and down. I take one up into the gym and scan the surrounding area.

The main body of the gym is open-plan, with machines in the centre and a blue, two-hundred metre running track around the outside. It then breaks off into different rooms, all visible through squeaky clean glass partitions—spin rooms, stretch rooms, rooms for classes, yoga, boxing and weights. The air is chilled. The music the usual thudding travesty. The whole place lit by natural light coming in from a square skylight above almost the size of the entire gym.

It's a far cry from the old spit and sawdust holes I'm used to, set up in bricked-up old textile mills on the edge of town with a blood-stained boxing ring in the middle, equipment from the stone ages and snarling monsters injecting steroids into their necks and blocking up the one working toilet.

I look myself up and down as I pass a full-length mirror —light-grey t-shirt, black shorts and orange running shoes. I'm not exactly a stack of cushions and after living and training with Josh, I'm in much better shape than before. But compared to some of the perfect young tens floating around the place, I feel like a right old bloater.

But anyway, I start wandering round, looking for Jacobsen.

I see him run past me on the track. Jogging at a steady pace. I hit the track and follow him round at a forty-yard distance.

Jacobsen runs a couple of laps before peeling off into the weights room in the far right corner of the gym. I ease up to a walk and stroll through a set of automatic doors into the weights area. It's predictably huge and swanky, with all the latest kit. Plenty of fancy machines and a long stretch of free weights with a cushioned black floor. There are windows to the left out onto the streets and a wall of mirrors to the right.

The place is quiet at this time of the morning. Just the hardcore fitness freaks and bodybuilders in the house, pumping and grunting, or sitting and resting between sets.

I hang back far enough so Jacobsen can't make out my face too easy. I pick up a set of light dumbbells and pretend to warm up. I notice Jacobsen towards the bar end, fist-bumping a couple of lifters. Big guys in vests that show off their muscles. They shoot the shit. Look pretty chummy.

Jacobsen lies down on a bench and starts cranking out a chest press set with heavy dumbbells.

I grab a set of my own dumbbells off the long rack that runs in front of the mirrors. I put 'em down by a bench at the opposite end of the free weights area to Jacobsen.

I set up a bench at a sixty degree angle and lie down with my feet planted on the floor. I push out some upper-chest reps with a pair of twenty kilo dumbbells. Nothing too heavy, but not too light either. Wanna make it look like I'm there to work, the same as everyone else.

I'm wondering whether to keep tailing Jacobsen or wait until he gets back to the changing rooms, get him in a quiet corner and force some information out of the guy. Maybe I could get him in the boot of his own car. Drive him somewhere and get some answers. I pick up the dumbbells again to push out another few. As I do, I watch Jacobsen repping out another heavy set.

Josh versus Jacobsen in a fight—the kid never stood a chance.

"Yo, dude," a guy says—one of Jacobsen's lifting pals in a lime-green vest. "Give me a spot?" He points to a barbell rack over a flat bench across the gym floor. It's far enough away that I won't get spotted and I don't wanna draw attention.

So I say, "Sure," dropping the dumbbells.

I follow the guy over to the rack. He's already loaded up the weight on the bar and slides on his back underneath it. He wraps his fingers around the metal grips on the bar. He's around six-two with a greying crew cut, zero neck and temple veins that stick out like curly telephone wires.

I stand behind the bench, one eye on Jacobsen, now sitting up and chatting to a mate in a skin-tight red t-shirt—a young Italian-American guy with a trimmed beard and perfectly styled hair. He's around my height and not a millimetre of fat on him.

"Ready," the guy on the bench says.

I hold out my hands, palms up close to the bar, ready to grab it if he gets in trouble. He pushes out the first two, easy. The third one not so straightforward, but he makes it all the way up, his face turning red, arms shaking and body contorting. He goes for a fourth. Chews his own face off as he fights to get the bar back up off his chest. He gets halfway. I slip my palms underneath and give him just enough to complete the rep. I help him slot the bar back on the rack. He sits up and blows heavy.

"Thanks, man," he says. "Now you."

"It's fine," I say, "I'm good."

"Nah, come on man. Let's work on your pecs . . . You want me to slide some of the weight off?"

I can't tell whether he's being considerate or it's some kinda challenge. My ego elbows its way in front of me and tells him the weight is fine. I lie back on the bench and slide under the bar, looking at the thick black steel plates on either end.

It's been a while since I lifted heavy like this. I'm wondering what the hell I can press. Only one way to find out. I wrap my hands around the bar and psyche myself up. As I'm down there taking a few breaths, Jacobsen and his other gym buddy wander over. They loiter at the foot of the bench like it's a spectator sport.

Shit, what if he recognises me?

I push the bar up off the rack and bring it down to my chest.

It's even heavier than it looks, but I get it up for one rep, two and I'm going for three.

"Here, let me help you with that," my spotter says prematurely.

Only he doesn't help me lift the damn thing. He puts his hands on top of the bar and pushes it down against my chest. I fight against him, but the bar won't budge. He presses down hard. The bar digs into my pecs. Stops me from breathing right. Feels like an elephant took a sit down on top of me.

But that's not all. The Italian-American grabs hold of my knees and pins my legs down.

Jacobsen appears over the top of me. "Been following me, huh, prick?" He punches me hard in the guts, winding the life out of me.

"What now?" the guy in the lime-green vest asks.

Jacobsen checks over both shoulders. "Now he has a little accident . . . The bar crushes his throat."

54

"*You serious?*" my spotter says.

"Yeah, I'm fucking serious, Wade."

Wade keeps me pinned down for now. "But it could kill him—"

"This time of morning, lifting this kind of weight without a spot. You take your chances," Jacobsen says.

"I don't know, man," the Italian-American says. "I thought we were gonna fuck him up a little, that's all—"

"Here, I'll fucking do it," Jacobsen says, driving another fist into my guts.

All this time I'm fighting Wade. I drive up an inch, he pushes the bar back down.

As Jacobsen takes over, I manage to force the bar off my chest a few centimetres. I kick out at the guy holding my knees.

"Pin him down," Jacobsen says to Wade, forcing the bar higher towards my throat.

Wade grabs hold of my torso and pins it tight to the bench. Now all I've got to work with are my arms and shoulders.

Jacobsen has the leverage too. He rolls the bar past my clavicle. I feel the cold chill of the metal on my throat. But only some of the weight, my hands saving my Adam's apple from being crushed.

I wriggle and kick, fighting for my life. The Italian-American struggles to contain me.

Jacobsen pushes with all he's got. Wade digs me in the guts with an elbow.

But somehow I get a foot free.

I kick the Italian-American in the jaw. He lets go of the other leg. I bring both feet up and boot him in the chest. He stumbles backwards and trips over a steel plate.

I bring a knee up and crack Wade in the temple. He cries out. Lets go for a split second, a hand to his head.

I lift my legs in the air. With every last ounce of strength, I bring 'em down and use the momentum to drive up through my chest and shoulders.

I push one end of the bar up a few inches and slide out from underneath.

The bar tips over to the left and crashes to the floor. I roll off the bench to my right.

Wade takes a swing, but he's got bodybuilder arms and throws a punch like a penguin flaps its wings.

I beat him to the punch and he staggers away. The Italian-American hits me with a metal bar in the back of my thighs.

I'm down. Jacobsen and Wade putting the boot in a couple of times.

I see a stray dumbbell on the floor. I grab it and slam it down on Wade's toes. He howls and falls against the bench.

The Italian-American lifts the bar ready to nail me in the head, I roll out of the way, onto my feet.

I punch the guy in the face with the end of the dumbbell. His nose explodes and he collapses to the deck cupping the wound.

I turn and take a heavy right hook from Jacobsen. I drop the dumbbell but push him away, both hands against his chest.

As he back-pedals, I run and stoop low. I pick him up off his feet and slam him down on the edge of the bench. He rolls off, groaning.

And that leaves Wade. Limping on one leg. He gives up on the punching and goes straight to the choking. But the guy's got no real-world strength.

I slap my palms together and bring them upwards like I'm about to pray. I break Wade's hold, grab him by the vest and head-butt him with the only part of me that has any energy left.

Wade collapses, exhausted and only half-awake, a gash bleeding heavy above the left eye.

I look around. It's now or never to question Jacobsen.

But the floor where he rolled off the bench is empty. I whirl around. See him heading out to the main gym. I take off after him, chest still on fire from the pressure of the bar and arms ready to fall right off me.

Another bodybuilder enters the weights room through the automatic doors. He stops and stares, jaw hitting the floor at the sight of Wade and the Italian-American, bloodied on the floor.

"Brutal session," I say on my way out.

55

I hare through the main room of the gym. See Jacobsen flying down the escalators. As I bound down after him, he ducks into the men's changing rooms. By the time I follow him in, he's got hold of his wallet and car keys and he's heading out of another exit at the far end of the room.

I did Jacobsen the favour of breaking into his locker, of course. He doesn't have to fiddle with the key like I do, getting it off my wrist and into the slot with arms and wrists and fingers that don't want to do anything other than shake from sheer strain. Still, I get the key in, wang the door open and grab my stuff.

I call Naomi on the run. "Get the car started. He's on his way out."

"Are you okay?" Naomi says, "You sound out of—"

"Just start the damn car!" I say, cutting off the call.

I charge through the other exit at the far end of the changing rooms. Jacobsen is ahead of me, glancing over a shoulder, on the phone to someone.

Brad, the receptionist, smiles and waves at him. Jacobsen

ignores Brad and hurdles the barrier like a pro athlete. He sprints out of the main entrance. I size up the barrier and decide my hurdling days are over.

"Hey, what's going on?" Brad says, a puzzled look on his face.

I run full-pelt through the barrier. It's metal, sure, but one of those flimsy barriers you can easily push through. It snaps open and off its hinges.

"Hey!" Brad shouts after me.

I run out into the warm, bright sunshine and see Jacobsen jumping in his Mustang. He backs up fast out of his space and smokes his tyres on the way out.

Naomi pulls up in the Beetle. I open the door and jump in. *"Drive!"* I say.

Naomi puts her foot down. The passenger door swings open. I throw my stuff in the backseat and pull the passenger door shut.

Jacobsen tears out of the car park. Naomi crunches through the gears as the Beetle gets going.

"We're losing him," I say, as we turn out onto the main drag.

"I can't go any faster," Naomi says. "Besides, the lights are on red."

It's true. They are. And Jacobsen just slipped through at the last.

As we head towards the lights, I grab Naomi by the arm. "Here, switch places."

"Wait, I'll pull over," she says.

"No time, come on." I pull her out of her seat and across the cabin.

The car swerves left as we change places.

Naomi drops into the passenger seat and I get behind

the wheel, planting a foot on the accelerator as the lights turn green.

The pair of us put our seat belts on. "You ever been in a car chase?" I ask.

"No," Naomi says. "Who the hell has?"

I slip down a gear and look for a gap in the traffic to my left.

"Now hold on a minute," she says. "You're not gonna chase anyone in this thing—"

"We'll see about that," I say, pulling out into the left-hand lane. I put my foot all the way down and fast change through the gears into third. The Beetle gives me some juice. Naomi is taken by surprise by the speed I squeeze out of it.

I slalom through slower-moving supercar traffic. See Jacobsen up ahead, cruising, thinking he's clear. I gun the Beetle close to his rear bumper. He responds, pulling away. I drop a gear and give it more. Shift up and close the gap, the engine thrashing and the steering unsure of itself on thin, bald, saggy tyres. But the Beetle holds together.

We stay in earshot of the snarling exhaust of Jacobsen's Mustang. He makes a sharp left turn through another set of lights to throw us off. I beat the red this time and hang the Beetle out wide to minimise the roll.

We head down a side street lined by designer stores. Jacobsen honks a bunch of well-dressed pedestrians out of the way. He brakes heavy and makes a tight right turn into a crossroads. Cars stop dead and beep in his wake.

I follow close behind, pulling on the handbrake and spinning the wheel to the right. The rear end of the Beetle slides out to the left.

Maybe I misjudged it. We keep sliding, into a busy pavement. But the tyres bite at the last and the rear left bumps against the kerb.

I narrowly miss a parked car in front and weave through traffic left standing by Jacobsen's suicide move.

Naomi yelps and covers her eyes.

She takes her hands away. Looks worse for wear. Eyes glassy and mouth gasping for air. "I think I'm gonna be sick," she says as I race through the gears again, trying to find some extra speed.

The one saving grace is that we're on the busy roads, with morning traffic slowing Jacobsen's escape. And of course, traffic means traffic cops.

Suddenly, we've got company. A black and white cruiser heading the other way spins around as we fly on by. The cruiser joins our lane from the right and powers towards us in the rear view.

Jacobsen isn't about to stop and neither am I.

He pulls around the right side of the bus. No room for me, so I swerve around the left. The cop car takes the left lane too, right up the bloody arse of the Beetle. But when I overtake the bus, I realise Jacobsen isn't there.

I glance over my shoulder and see him spinning the Mustang round to the left in a cloud of tyre-smoke. He cuts across traffic and shoots off in a horizontal line.

"Hold onto something," I say to Naomi, braking and yanking the wheel all the way to the left.

The cop car misses us by a whisker and ploughs straight into a red pickup directly in front of us. We wriggle off across a three-lane highway with traffic coming right at us.

It's a ridiculous move to pull, but I'm caught up in the chase. And back on Jacobsen's tail.

Shit, the guy can drive. And he's opened a gap I'm not gonna make up.

But he's got a problem. Traffic is bogging down all around. He gets caught up in it. And then there's another squad car coming up behind, parting queueing cars like Moses and the Red Sea.

Jacobsen pulls left off the road. He heads down a steep grass embankment.

Naomi reads the look in my eye. "No, surely we're not—"

We are.

* * *

I SNEAK through a gap in traffic and down the embankment after Jacobsen. Only he heads in a straight diagonal down the embankment. No way I can do the same in this old heap, so I hook the wheel to the right and drift the thing down the embankment instead.

The arse of the Beetle sticks out to the left once again, the nose pointed halfway up the hill. We slide sideways at speed, with mud and grass kicking up in the air.

Naomi goes real quiet and green around the gills. The squad car follows us down, trying to take the same line as Jacobsen. But the copper behind the wheel is nowhere near the same driver. The black and white tips and rolls over. It takes a hit from a passing eighteen wheeler and spins off to the side of the road.

That leaves me free to pursue Jacobsen along the hard shoulder.

Jacobsen waits for his moment and cuts into the inside lane. I do the same and we swerve in and out of the flow of traffic.

He brakes and takes an exit ramp back up towards Hollywood.

I follow his lead and close the gap. Three or four more turns later I'm still on the guy's tail, on a quiet road that runs along the back of the Solomon Studios complex.

It comes up fast on our right. The brake lights on the Mustang flicker and Jacobsen dives into the side roads of the studios.

He's trying to lose me in here. And probably will. As he heads down one road, I split and head along another. It runs down the right-hand side of the building.

We fly fast towards a T-junction. A road cuts across us in front of another studio building.

"Shouldn't you be braking about now?" Naomi says, peering between her fingers.

"Should be, yeah," I say, leaving it late, late, very bloody late.

56

With a few feet left, I brake and yank the handbrake. We pop out of the road, sliding in a straight line on bald tyres. Jacobsen flashes past, but the Beetle clips the Mustang's rear end. I spin the wheel and careering sideways to a stop against the wall of the studio building.

It's a heavy shunt, but these old German cars are built like tanks and the clip on the Mustang is just enough to spin him around.

It's too late for Jacobsen to control the spin. He slams side-on into a stop sign pole. He tries to pull away, but the pole digs into the bodywork of the car, the sound of metal crunching.

I see his front passenger door open. I unclip my seatbelt, unbuckle Naomi's and push her door open. She sits there frozen. Shaking. I harass her out of the passenger door.

"Stay with the car," I say, climbing out of the Beetle after her.

I start running, Jacobsen up ahead. On his phone again. Who the hell's he talking to? More of his musclemen pals to come and help? Is he leading me into a trap? He ditches the phone as he runs. It smashes against the kerb and crunches under my trainer sole as I keep up the chase.

Damn he's in shape. But I'm fucking angry. This is the guy who killed Josh. And I'm gonna beat the truth out of him if it's the last thing I do.

I chase him through an open door, across an empty sound stage, the slap of our rubber soles echoing off the empty walls. The entire place is cast in darkness. We head to a square of daylight on the opposite side of the building.

Jacobsen disappears through the door, his long shadow following him out. The light is blinding as I emerge from the sound stage. I look one way, then the other. See Jacobsen running to my right.

I sprint after him again, relieved I did all that hill running with Josh and Gunnar. I gain some ground when a guy wheels a trolley out stacked with boxes. Jacobsen crashes into 'em. He stumbles forward, onto all fours, then up again.

He darts left around the corner. I'm hot on his heels. And surprised by the presence of an outdoor film set. It's some kind of historical scene. A street filled with sandbags, fake smoke and nurses in old blue and white uniforms tending to wounded soldiers in army-green fatigues.

"Cut, cut, cut!" I hear a director yell through a loud speaker as I weave my way through after Jacobsen. "What the fuck? Is this sixteen-seventeen or twenty-seventeen?" the director says.

We soon leave the film set behind, cutting through a sound stage busy with tradesmen drilling, hammering and sawing through wood as they construct a new set.

I dance between forklifts, only to lose sight of Jacobsen.

As I run past the interior of a fifties diner, Jacobsen sprints out of hiding the opposite way.

So I skid to a stop and double-back after him.

We're out on the roads of the movie studios again. Jacobsen is getting away, but I jump on the back of a white studio buggy and let it take me for a ride.

There's a fat studio exec with black curly hair behind the wheel chewing on a giant cigar. "What the hell? Get off my god-darn buggy."

"Keep driving and I won't shove that cigar up your fat fucking arse," I say.

The studio exec does as he's told. He keeps the pedal to the metal and runs a tiring Jacobsen down.

But Jacobsen sees me over a shoulder. He veers left and hurdles a thigh-high privet. I jump off the buggy and run out of control.

I bounce off a wall and crash through the privet, around the corner of another studio building straight into the middle of another film set.

This time it's a post-apocalyptic town, with a male zombie in rags lurching after a young woman in a torn white summer dress.

The set is full of bodies and litter and abandoned, burnt-out cars. Jacobsen dodges past the actors. I swerve past the woman but end up body-checking the zombie.

"Ow, watch it, buddy," the zombie says, feeling his shoulder.

"Jesus fucking Christ! Cut!" I hear another director cry.

57

After a couple more twists and turns, we run across an outdoor set filled with orange sand and a futuristic space buggy. The terrain is bumpy with little hills of sand to cut through.

It leads us straight into a dead end. A wall of brick buildings with nowhere to go. I think I've got Jacobsen cornered, but he climbs a ladder up the side of a building.

I catch my breath, hands on knees, feeling like I'm gonna be sick. I look up at the climb. It feels like someone poured molten lava down my throat into my lungs.

"What is it with me and rooftops?" I say to myself.

I shake my head and go again. Up the ladder. Onto the roof and into a run.

Jacobsen's opened up another gap. But he's tiring. The pace has slowed. And just like that zombie and the woman, it's a war of attrition.

The buildings are packed a lot tighter here. The whole lot of 'em old movie sets rubbing shoulders. Jacobsen leaps over flat rooftops.

One is a lot higher than another. He jumps and rolls like

a pro, up to his feet. I jump and tumble. Drag myself up and keep going, on my last legs, trying not to look like it.

I'm about to stop and throw up when I see Jacobsen come to a stop at the edge of the last building. He looks over the edge. Can't seem to find a way down. But there's an old medieval tower to the right, surrounded by scaffolding.

Don't you dare you bastard ... Ah, shit.

Jacobsen runs for the scaffolding and starts climbing.

I make an effort to close the gap and climb up after him. It's like bloody Donkey Kong. Running along dusty, wobbly wooden planks. Climbing up hollow steel rung ladders onto the next level.

Two wobbly levels from the top, Jacobsen turns and kicks a loose plank from the floor, leaving a hole I can't jump over.

There's no way to follow him, so he stops and smiles back at me, breathing almost as hard as I am.

"See you," he says in his Euro-American accent. He climbs up the next ladder to the level above.

I look over the edge of the hole in the platform. It's ten feet across and a hell of a lot more feet down.

Not that easily, you piece of shit.

I step up onto a pole railing and climb up the outside of the scaffolding. I try not to look down. Definitely try not to slip, shortcutting one level after another until I pull myself up onto the top of the structure. There are no guard rails up here. No more levels to climb and no scaffolding on the other side of the tower.

The tower itself is just a hollow structure made out of brick and painted to look like medieval stone.

I shake out my arms and take a breath, When Jacobsen appears up the final ladder, I'm ready for him. I grab him by the ponytail and drag him backwards across the scaffolding roof. He fights it. Twists to face the front and tackles me low to the floor.

A thick layer of dust kicks up as I land on my back on the wood. The boards creak and groan beneath us as we wrestle.

Jacobsen is on top of me. He lands a hard right to my left cheekbone. I return the favour with interest. A left hook to the jaw and a right cross that sends him rolling off towards the far edge of the rooftop.

I drag myself up and after him.

He crawls closer to the edge, dizzy from the punch, unaware of what he's doing.

"Sorry, no choreography here," I say, walking after him and getting my breath back. "There's nowhere to go, Klaus."

Jacobsen rises. I hit him with another hard right. He collapses to the floor. I boot him in the side for good measure. He spits out blood and rolls onto his back, exhausted. I drop down—a knee pressing hard on the guy's chest, twisting his left wrist into a hold.

Jacobsen cries out in pain.

"I'm gonna make this easy for you, Klaus . . . The kid. Why did you kill him?"

"I don't know what you're talking about," he says.

I twist a little harder.

His face bunches up in agony. *"Ah, fuck!"*

"Why did you kill Josh?"

Jacobsen coughs on his own blood.

"Fine," I say, trying not to notice how far down it is over the edge of the scaffolding.

Another twist of the arm gets him talking. "I killed him because . . ."

"Because?" I say, applying more pressure.

"Because they said they'd give me a part in the next Nightburner. My breakthrough role."

"You doing all this for a role?"

"You don't know how hard it is . . . breaking your bones for change while some pretty boy asshole picks up twenty million for wearing a fucking rubber suit. This deal would have made me a star, man. No more skipping meals, just so you can keep the lights on. No more endless auditions with people telling you 'no, you can't be an actor because you talk funny'. You don't know what it's like."

I'm about to moralise with the guy, then I realise—how many people have I offed just to pay the rent, keep my daughter in nappies or put her through uni? Let's face it, I can't say piss-all.

"It was harder than I thought," Jacobsen said. "After—what I did—I couldn't even drive. I had to smoke just to calm my nerves. That's when you showed up."

"Well, it can't have been that hard," I say. "Seeing as you tried to run me down with a tow truck."

"They said if I got rid of you too, I'd get a three-movie contract," Jacobsen says. "A major part in the franchise."

"Who's *they*?" I say, twisting harder. "Come on, Klaus, who's calling the shots?"

Jacobsen laughs. His eyes dart to his right. His hand on a loose pole.

There's a flash of metal.

A flash of pain.

I fall backwards and now I'm the one lying flat on the boards. The edge of the rooftop is an inch to my right. Jacobsen kneels over me. He raises the pole like a sword, ready to bring it down. Ready to stick it straight through the back of my skull.

58

As Jacobsen strikes down with the pole, I roll to my right.

The pair of us tumble over the side. I fall a level but catch hold of a rail. I swing and slam into the scaffolding. Jacobsen falls and spins all the way to the ground. He splats against a studio road, the pole bouncing and clanging and rolling to a stop a few yards away.

Bollocks.

I almost had the answers I wanted.

But if anyone asks, he fell.

With no platforms and ladders along this side of the scaffold, I climb down the outside of the structure. Slow and steady. I clear the area as quick as my tired legs allow.

I go looking for the place where I left Naomi.

It's not far. Round a couple of corners. I reckon I chased Klaus round in a big bloody circle.

I approach the Beetle from the rear. We're lucky. No one's out here on this part of the lot. No cops or onlookers. Hell, you could easily mistake the two cars for part of an action scene.

I walk round to the front of the Beetle.

I don't see Naomi.

Damn it, Naomi, I told you to wait here.

Maybe she ran. Ran to raise the alarm. Maybe she was playing along with me, until she had the chance to escape and tell someone.

Please don't say you went to the cops again, Naomi. For your own sake.

But what's this? A note on the windscreen, pinned under the passenger-side wiper. I pull the wiper away from the glass and open the note.

It's in fat black ink scribbled on white A4 notepaper. It says:

We've got the girl. Studio Seven. 11am.

Shit. Whoever *they* are, they've got me all ends up.

I check my watch and think for a second.

I grab my clothes and phone from the backseat of the car. I walk around the side of the building and change back into my shirt, trousers and suit jacket. I replace my trainers with shoes and pull a business card from inside my jacket pocket. I call up the number on the card.

"Hey, it's Charlie," I say. "Still wanna help me out?"

59

I show up dead on eleven, with a chance I'll be dead by eleven-thirty.

Studio Seven is empty. The floor is a dark-grey. Only the wall lights on, with a series of overhead rigs and gantries cast in darkness.

Three figures stand in the middle. Two men. One woman. As I walk towards 'em, I recognise all three.

Art Solomon stands to the left, smoking a fat cigar. Wyndall Buck stands to the right, a grip on the back of Naomi's neck and a snub-nosed revolver in the small of her back.

Naomi looks terrified. Solomon and Buck look thoroughly miffed.

I hear footsteps behind me. I turn and see Detectives Roach and Thomas bringing up the rear, coming out of the shadows from left and right.

I stop in the middle of the sound stage in front of Solomon and Buck. Thomas and Roach take their places a few feet behind me.

"I guess this is what they call the end of the road," I say.

"Or the final act," Thomas says.

"So what are the terms?" I ask.

"Turn yourself in and the girl gets to keep her pretty face," Roach says.

"You're gonna let her walk, just like that?" I say.

"We're not murderers, Charlie," Buck says.

"Of course not," I say. "You get guys like me to do it instead. Guys like Klaus Jacobsen."

Neither Buck or Solomon say a word.

"The way I see it," I say, "I'm either serving a life sentence or dead before it goes to court."

"Well that all depends if you're willing to play ball," Thomas says. "Doesn't it?"

"What does that mean, Detective Thomas?" I ask.

Solomon takes his cigar from his mouth. "You can cop one homicide charge, or a double."

I look at Naomi. "I'm sorry," she says. "They snuck up on me—"

I wave her apology away. "You've got a deal," I say to Solomon. "Me for the girl—unharmed. But first I want the truth."

All eyes go to Art Solomon, which tells me he's the one calling the shots.

Solomon shrugs in agreement.

"If that's what it takes," Buck says, which tells me he's the one giving the orders to Thomas and Roach.

"I know you promised Jacobsen a role in return for killing Josh," I say. "What I can't figure out is why. Why the hell do it in the first place?"

"Because Josh was toxic," Solomon says. "The drink, the drugs, the scandals. He was hurting the franchise."

"So drop him, don't kill him," I say.

"The kid was on a three-movie extension. Watertight," Buck says. "This was a chance to start over. Reboot."

"You're talking about a life, here," I say.

"That's funny coming from you," Roach says.

"You know how hard it is to do good box office these days?" Solomon says. "New World are over the road with their fucking multiverse, breaking the billion mark with every picture. Meanwhile, the Nightburner universe is one flop away from going under."

"So you get a guy desperate for a break to kill the kid," I say. "And Thomas and Roach make sure the death is written off as accidental."

"In the meantime, the first three Nightburners get a shot in the arm," Buck says, seeming almost pleased with his own plan.

"And we had one hell of an insurance policy on the kid," Solomon says, blowing a ring of smoke into the air.

"So that's why it had to look like an accident," I say. "Looks like you're gonna forfeit that now."

Solomon shrugs. "It was a nice bonus. We can do without it."

I shake my head. The balls on these guys.

"You knew the kid, Charlie," Buck says. "He was a firecracker. He would have burned himself out before too long. They always do."

"Actually, he was getting better," I say to Buck. "And the funny thing . . . the night you had him killed, he was on his way to your place to tell you he was quitting the franchise."

Buck looks at Solomon.

Solomon at Buck.

"That's right," I say. "You killed him for nothing."

Solomon puffs on his cigar. "We did what we had to do."

"Yeah, to line your pockets," I say.

"You know how many people work at this studio?" Solomon says. "Decent, hard-working people? Professionals, with families?"

"Hollywood isn't black and white," Buck says.

"Just like the LAPD," I say, turning to Thomas and Roach.

"That's it Mary Poppins," Roach says, drawing his new duty pistol. "Conversation's over."

"Alright," I say, hands raised. "But before we do this, what's your involvement? What do you get out of this? Your own cop show?"

"Introductions for our new security business," Thomas says. "And start up cash for when we retire."

"Which'll be straight after we bring in Joshua Speed's killer," Roach says, smiling for once in his life.

"Let me guess, you force Carlos Campuzano to intimidate A-listers like Josh. Bucky here drops your names into the conversation and in you ride on your white stallions."

"Yeah, or white Lamborghinis," Thomas says, laughing.

"Sounds like you thought of everything," I say.

"Would've been a lot simpler if you hadn't come along," Buck says with a sigh. "Josh's death could have been a lot more ... pleasant."

"Oh, so it's my fault?" I say.

"It is now," says Roach.

Buck shrugs at me. "I like you, Charlie. But what can we do?"

The fact that they're starting to brag about it means they've already decided to kill me, whether before the trial or in a prison cell. Just long enough for me to take the public rap.

With Naomi, they'll probably wait until it all dies down.

Until the discovery of her body is a small article buried towards the back of a local newspaper.

Or maybe they'll go one better like Solomon suggested. They'll pin her death all on me. Double homicide followed by a shootout or another fake suicide.

Detective Thomas brings out a pair of handcuffs.

With the doors to the sound stage left open, I hear the faint sound of sirens blaring. Nothing too unusual about that, except that this is an upscale part of town and they seem to be getting closer.

Solomon laughs to himself. Takes another puff on that cigar. "Here they are now, Charlie. I hope you like prison food."

60

Buck seems confused. He looks at Solomon. "Did you call 'em?"

"No," Solomon says.

"Well I didn't call 'em," Buck says.

Solomon's face drops. He and Buck turn their attention to Thomas and Roach.

"Don't look at us," Thomas says as the sirens continue to grow louder, closer, greater in number.

"I thought we were gonna whack the pair of 'em," Roach says, looking at Thomas.

"Me too," Thomas says.

I look up into the darkness and give the signal—a hand waved across my throat.

"And cut!" an English voice yells through a loudhailer.

Everyone looks around for the voice. The ceiling lights above shunt on. Christopher Lipton appears on a gantry with a cameraman and a young guy holding a sound boom high above our heads.

"Thanks everyone," Lipton says. "I think that's a wrap."

As the sirens converge outside Studio Seven, Solomon

glares up at Lipton. "You got one chance to give me that film, or you'll never work again."

"You'll never walk again, either," says Buck.

"Don't worry," Thomas says. "That recording won't make it out of here."

"And neither will any of you, you motherfuckers." Roach says, looking up at the film crew.

"Who said anything about recording?" Lipton says. "It's called live stream you arseholes. Smile, you're all over social media."

"And the Chief of Police is watching you right now," I say to Solomon. "Shove that up your arse and smoke it."

As the sirens cut out, the sound stage is invaded by cops in uniform. They run towards us, a stampede of jackboots thumping off the hard studio floor.

Roach puts his pistol away. Thomas his cuffs. Buck lets go of the girl and tosses the revolver. And Solomon has one last smoke on his cigar.

As for me, well, I wasn't anywhere they said I was. The LAPD won't charge me with anything and I won't report 'em for trying to arrange my suicide out in the viaducts.

* * *

THE COPS LEAD SOLOMON, Buck, Thomas and Roach away. Naomi is still shaking a little. I take off my suit jacket and put it around her shoulders. I guide her outside into the California sun.

"It's over," I say.

She nods, smiles, sucks it up. "I'm okay," she says. "I'll be okay."

Lipton rocks up alongside me. "You know what? I think that might be the best bloody movie I've ever shot."

I shake his hand. "Thanks, Chris."

"No need to thank me, Charlie. I did it for Josh."

"Oh, uh, Chris, have you met Naomi?" I say. "Naomi Jones. She's an actress."

"And you were bloody fantastic," Lipton says to Naomi, shaking her hand. "How you stayed in character throughout all of that, I'll never know."

Naomi looks at me funny. I wink at her to play along.

"Like you said," Naomi says to Lipton. "I did it for Josh."

Lipton looks Naomi up and down. "You've got real screen presence. Anyone ever told you that?"

"Just the once," she says.

"I've been looking for an actress for a while," Lipton says. "An unknown, if you pardon the phrase. I reckon you'd be perfect. How do you feel about wearing a superhero outfit?"

"I'd love to," Naomi says, a stunned, excited smile lighting up her face.

"Great, let's talk about it over lunch," Lipton says. "If you're okay to eat?"

"Uh, well, I think I may have to go down to the precinct and give evidence."

"Ah, of course," Lipton says. "Me too." Lipton walks with Naomi towards a waiting black and white, "We can talk over a machine coffee."

Naomi stops and turns. "You coming, Charlie?"

I'm already peeling away while the cops' backs are turned, pushing Solomon and pals into separate squad cars.

"I've got something to do," I say. "I'll catch you up."

"Uh, okay," Naomi says, turning back to her conversation with Lipton.

As Lipton guides her to the squad cars, outlining his plans for the film, I backpedal around the corner of the sound stage.

I walk fast between buildings and come to a crossroads.

Something catches my eye.

Someone.

On the corner of the rooftop up to my left.

It's Josh as Nightburner. He stands on the edge looking down.

He nods at me. I nod at him.

He slips away, out of sight.

So do I.

EPILOGUE

I sit on the green fold-up camping chair I brought with me. I twiddle my thumbs and check my watch. I've brought a small red portable stereo, too. It has a CD player.

"Moods" by Neil Diamond is playing.

"Song Sung Blue" comes on.

"Oh, now this is one of my favourites," I say, humming along. I check my watch again.

It beeps midnight.

I decide it's time. Especially judging by the way the two bodies are wriggling in those big blue plastic tubs.

I get up and look around me. This warehouse is coming in really handy. First Carlos. Now these two clowns.

I found another chain with a hook too. Rigged it up so that if I pull down hard on the one chain here, both bodies rise at the same time.

Or fall, if I let go.

I put some muscle into it and pull down on the chain, one hand over the other.

The bodies rise out of the barrels. Water rushes off them and splatters over the concrete floor.

I tie the chain off around the base of the winch and walk around the front.

We've got Aaron Zweltsmann and Guy Meddles from Hornblower Productions.

They choke and spit out water. Gasp for air. Shiver right down to their bones, wet right up to the waist as they hang upside down, each over their own barrel.

I stand in front of 'em. That's dunk number three. They should be softened up by now.

"There's nothing better than a pair of sopping wet tits hanging upside down," I say. "Isn't that right, Aaron?"

Aaron doesn't speak. I'm not entirely sure that he can.

The tune on the CD player really gets going. "Oh, this is a really good bit," I say, breaking into song. "Come on lads, sing along . . ." They don't seem in the mood. "Alright, have it your way."

"What do you want?" Aaron says, voice almost a squeal.

"What I want, is for you two numpties to stop taking advantage of young women."

"We will, we will," Meddles says. "We'll stop."

"We'll make different movies," Aaron says.

"Whatever movies you want," Meddles says.

"See, that's not enough," I say. "I'm gonna have to ask you to shut down your operation. Move out of town."

"We can't just shut everything down," Aaron says. "We're filmmakers."

"Yeah and besides, what are you gonna do? Drown us?" Meddles says.

"Oh, the water was just to get us acquainted," I say. "The real fun's yet to come. But exactly how much fun we have, well that's up to you."

"We've got connections, man," Aaron says.

"Yeah," Meddles says. "You don't know who you're talking to."

"No gentlemen," I say, opening a black plastic bag by the side of the camping chair. "You don't know who *you're* talking to." I take out a pair of tools and hold both out in front of 'em. "Now, I've got Mr Hammer, here, and Mr Chisel. And they'd really rather prefer it if you did as I ask."

"Look," Aaron says, "Maybe we can come to some kind of, I dunno, financial settlement. Right, Guy?" he says checking with Meddles.

Meddles nods as fast as his head'll move.

"I mean, you seem like a reasonable guy." Aaron says.

"Reasonable, yeah," Meddles says. "Real reasonable."

I put the hammer in my right hand to my ear. "Wait, what's that Mr Hammer? I *am* a reasonable guy?" Mr Hammer nods in my hand. "Well thank you," I say to Mr Hammer. "You're very kind."

Aaron and Meddles exchange a look.

Again I put the hammer to my ear. "What was that?" I say. "But you and Mr Chisel *aren't* very reasonable? You're not very reasonable at all?"

As Aaron and Meddles twist and squirm and whimper, Mr Hammer shakes his head.

"Well okay then," I say, turning my attention to my dripping wet captives. "You lads like anal, right?"

Aaron and Meddles stare at each other, eyeballs bloodied and ready to pop.

"Then let's begin," I say.

Mr Hammer nods.

<<<<>>>>

ALSO BY ROB ASPINALL

Breaker (Charlie Cobb #1)

Death & Back (Charlie Cobb #2)

The Holdup (Charlie Cobb #3)

Walk Away (Charlie Cobb #5)

The Charlie Cobb Series Boxset

Truly Deadly (#1 YA Spy Thriller Series)

Infinite Kill (Truly Deadly #2)

World Will Fall (Truly Deadly #3)

Made of Fire (Truly Deadly #4)

Slave Nation (Truly Deadly #5)

Truly Deadly: The Complete Series Boxset

Crisis Point (Sam Driver #1 Espionage Thriller Series)

Homecoming (A Gripping Crime Thriller)

CONNECT WITH ROB

Did you enjoy the book?

Rob would love to hear what you think. Please leave an online review wherever's convenient. Your honest feedback will make a huge difference. Thanks for sharing.

Follow Rob:

Instagram: rob_aspinall
Facebook: facebook.com/robaspinallauthor
Twitter: @robaspinall
You can also find Rob on BookBub and Goodreads

robaspinall.com